THE SPECTACULARS

For my family

This edition first published in the UK in 2023 by Usborne Publishing Ltd., Usborne House, 83-85 Saffron Hill, London EC1N 8RT, England. usborne.com

Usborne Verlag, Usborne Publishing Ltd., Prüfeninger Str. 20, 93049 Regensburg, Deutschland, VK Nr. 17560

First published 2022. Text copyright © Jodie Garnish, 2022

Cover illustration, map and chapter head illustrations by Nathan Collins
© Usborne Publishing, 2022

Author photo © Michael Wharley 2018

A CIP catalogue record for this book is available from the British Library.

FMAMJJASOND/23 ISBN 9781803708102 7584/3

Printed and bound using 100% renewable electricity at CPI Group (UK) Ltd CR0 4YY.

MIX
Paper | Supporting responsible forestry
FSC
www.fsc.org
FSC® C171272

THE SPECTACULARS

JODIE GARNISH

USBORNE

A Most Daring Escape

*A*s a government-owned locomotive, the tram was *not* supposed to be careering wildly up a steep mountainside, rattling noisily along a set of rusty tram tracks and scaring the wits out of several unsuspecting sheep. Then again, it also wasn't supposed to be being driven by three runaway rebels with a backpack full of mysterious light at their feet, and zero driving experience between them.

"Can't we go any faster?" a man with long, black locs called to the two other figures inside the driver's cab. "Lahiri?"

Nadia Lahiri, a woman with dark hair and sharp eyes, scowled back at him. "In case you hadn't noticed, we're trying to drive a stolen eight-carriage tram up a rather steep mountain," she snapped. "We'll get there as fast as we can, although you're obviously welcome to go and push the wretched thing yourself."

The man, whose name was Morgan Fletcher, chewed his lip. He was a tall, broad figure, clothed in a royal blue coat and black leather boots. "We need more light," he said, first to himself, then calling across to the third figure, "Roper! We need more light!"

Georgina Roper, a short-statured woman with a mass of blonde curls, nodded and ripped open the backpack at her feet. She rifled through it, throwing out a harmonica, a singing biscuit tin and a fat book entitled *101 Uses for Stardust in Musical Theatre*, before coming up with a single, tightly sealed jar. Within the jar was a silvery light, swaying gently in long, shimmering tendrils.

"Is that all that's left?" Fletcher looked at the jar disbelievingly.

"That's it," Roper confirmed.

Behind them – far too close behind them – a sound echoed, bouncing around the mountains they were hurtling through. A klaxon. A warning.

"TRAM THIRTEEN. STAND DOWN. BY ORDER OF THE MINISTER OF THE SUNLESS PROVINCES, STAND DOWN."

Every eye in the driver's cab turned towards the window, looking back at where a stream of shiny black sledges was speeding after them, pulled by sleek hounds and gaining on them with every second.

"Fletcher," Roper said urgently, glancing towards the engine that sat before them, sending out silver sparks. "We still have the astral flare. We can use it."

"Are you joking?" Lahiri hissed. "It's far too dangerous!"

Fletcher shuddered slightly as he recalled packing the astral flare. Unlike the light shimmering gently in the jar before him, the flare had hummed and pulsed, vibrating with power. He'd had to wrap it in several layers of cloth, not to mention his woolliest jumper, just to keep it from shaking the tram carriage apart.

"We don't have a choice," insisted Roper. "It's the only thing that will get us out of this alive!"

Fletcher glanced back at the sledges again. He was the leader of the rebels who'd planned this escape. It had been his idea; it was his responsibility to keep everybody safe.

"Fletcher, don't be a fool," said Lahiri. "We should only be using approved Star-Stuff: dust and light. Astral flares are a restricted substance for a reason. We don't know what will happen!"

"Well, we *do* know what'll happen if they catch us." Roper gestured backwards towards the sledges. "I'd rather risk the flare."

Fletcher held up a hand to silence them both. He took a breath.

"Fetch the astral flare."

Roper nodded and dived back into the backpack. This time, she retrieved a jar with a label taped across it:

ASTRAL FLARE. HIGHLY EXPLOSIVE. VOLATILE. EXTREMELY DANGEROUS. ONLY USE IN CASE OF EMERGENCY. THAT MEANS YOU, McCUBBINS.

Roper carried it towards the engine.

Fletcher pressed his hands to his forehead and sent up a silent plea. *This has to work*, he thought. *Please let this work*. He leaned back against the door that separated the cab from the rest of the tram carriages and closed his eyes.

Unbeknownst to him, directly on the other side of this door were two children engrossed in an equally important conversation, whispering between themselves in a serious fashion. The girl, whose name was Harper Woolfe, bobbed her head decisively.

"Mr Grinwart. Definitely," she said.

The blue-haired boy next to her snorted. "Nah. When we took that bend earlier, he barely blinked. It's going to be Hattie Dwight; she's already looking green."

"You've forgotten one very important thing."

"What?"

"Grinwart had second helpings of beans at dinner." Harper nodded, satisfied. "That's definitely going to be coming back up." She opened the book in her lap and carefully wrote down the wager:

Harper Woolfe: Mr Grinwart. Trick Torres: Hattie Dwight.
Winner gets seven chocolate plums.

Another klaxon wailed out from behind them, and Harper looked over her shoulder. They'd been instructed to stay seated during the escape, but no one had listened to that. Instead, everyone was crowded around the windows, watching the mountains flash past and craning their necks to see the black sledges speeding after them.

"What'll happen if they catch us?" Harper whispered to Trick.

"Fletcher said we wouldn't want to know," Trick replied.

Harper twisted a lock of coppery hair between her fingers. "I don't understand. Why can't they just let us go?"

"*STAND DOWN. STAND DOWN.*" The booming voice came again.

"I think they need a cup of tea," Trick suggested. He believed very strongly in the healing powers of tea.

Harper closed her eyes and tried to pretend that she wasn't sitting in a stolen tram, being chased by the police forces of the Sunless Provinces. Instead, she pictured home: the city of the Smoke, the largest – and dirtiest – city in the Provinces. Specifically, she pictured the borough that she'd grown up in: a borough lined with grand theatres and music halls, lit up by neon lights, rich with the smell of buttered popcorn and roasted nuts. She could practically hear the sounds of the ushers as they tried to attract people into their venues…

"*Adriana Phillips – she can sing up a storm! No, literally – watch as she conjures thunder and lightning with her repertoire of tempestuous tunes! Half-price tickets for seats in the 'Splash Zone', complimentary rain ponchos provided.*"

"*The Utterly Un-Royal Theatre Troupe presents 'Lost in the Jungle', complete with immersive scenery – watch as the theatre around you transforms into a real-life jungle! Patrons enter at their own risk; compensation not offered for tiger bites.*"

"For one night, and one night only, presenting Buster Yang and his reflection – the greatest comedy duo in town! Tickets on special offer, six bob each!"

Harper's reminiscing was cut off by a huge shudder that suddenly rocked the tram. A blinding flash burst out from the driver's cab, and Harper and Trick both threw themselves away from the door as a roar of triumph rose up from the crowd gathered around the window. Harper and Trick glanced at each other, then ran towards them, elbowing their way through the mob to get a look outside.

As soon as she did, Harper felt a bit sick. The mountains were now flashing past at blinding speed. Twisting around, Harper could see the police sledges quickly disappearing out of sight, becoming no more than a line of tiny black dots, unable to keep up with the speed at which they were now moving.

"Three...two...one...YEESSSSSSS!" Trick threw his hands up as Hattie Dwight turned, ran to the corner, and was promptly sick all over the floor.

"What?" Harper yelled as Mr Grinwart carried on staring out of the window, unperturbed.

"I win!" Trick cheered. "Seven chocolate plums, please!"

Harper huffed. "Well, don't blame me when all your teeth fall out and the Tooth Raven comes and steals them for his child-chomping machine."

Trick blinked. "That isn't what the Tooth Raven does."

"That we know of," muttered Harper.

"Oi, shut up, you two!" An old man leaning by the window scowled at them. "I'm trying to hear the radio!" He turned the volume up, and a broadcaster's voice came echoing through Carriage One.

"...*Going live now to the latest in several major security breaches across the Sunless Provinces, concerning the so-called 'Spectaculars'. Categorized as beings with 'unique performance abilities', these Spectaculars have been growing in numbers ever since they first appeared at the turn of the last century, with large communities emerging all over the Sunless Provinces. The great city of the Smoke has seen a particular upsurge in these Spectaculars, converging in the Theatre Borough in the underskirts of the city. Despite our great Minister graciously allowing them to practise their abilities peacefully over the years, their powers have increased exponentially, leading the Minister to regretfully deem them a Grade Six Dangerous Species last year...*"

"'Dangerous species'!" the old man exclaimed. "As if we ain't even human!"

"Because of our 'unique performance abilities'," another muttered. "What does he think we're going to do – lead a tap-dancing revolution? *Pas de bourrée* him straight out of office?"

"That's how they turn people against each other, you see," the old man said darkly.

Harper looked down. It wasn't pleasant to remember the Minister's sudden campaign against the Spectaculars – the curfews, the restrictions, the suspicious looks from neighbours who'd always been perfectly friendly before.

"This morning, in a series of planned revolts, Spectaculars all over the Sunless Provinces hijacked multiple public transportation vehicles, from commuter trams in the Smoke, to the Minister's personal turtle-drawn submarines in the Cragg Islands. Citizens reported 'scenes of chaos' as they were 'strongly encouraged' to remove themselves from the vehicles…"

"That was funny," guffawed the old man. "Remember that woman with all the poodles? The look on her face when we told her to get off the tram!"

"She threw one of them at me!" a woman said indignantly. "Literally *threw a poodle at me.*"

"The stolen vehicles appear to be heading north, although their destination is as yet unknown. The Minister's police forces are giving chase as we speak…"

"Don't you worry, kids," said the old man, noticing Harper's anxious face. "We're not the first to have this happen to us. The Sunless Provinces have never been able to tolerate those with magic in their bones. They drove out the Witches centuries ago, the Fae-Folk, the Goblins and Kobolds. They were bound to do the same to us sooner or later. But you know where they all went." He winked. "Through the gateways, where no one could find them."

Harper felt a shiver run down her spine at the mention of the gateways. At six years of age, they hadn't been party to the rebellion plans, but she and Trick had eavesdropped on enough conversations to have picked up the gist; a series of secret gateways that led to a hidden land – a place of refuge for magical folk. A date had been set: one day for Spectaculars across the Sunless Provinces to make a break for the gateways. They'd boarded the trams with whatever possessions they could carry, dodged any flying canines, and turned their attention to the mountains. Harper didn't want to think about what would happen if they failed.

To distract herself, she turned back to the matter of Mr Grinwart. He was still standing at the window, and was starting to look a little peaky...

"Ooh. You've got your plotting face on. What are you thinking?" Trick demanded.

"Let's bet again," Harper suggested. "Double or nothing?"

Before Trick could answer, the door that separated Carriage One from the driver's cab opened, and Fletcher – their leader, and Trick's uncle – strode through.

"Everyone, I appreciate that this is an exciting and nerve-wracking time. However, we are almost at the gateway, so could I please ask all of you to return to your seats until we're safely across."

Harper groaned. Her seat was next to her parents', all the way back in Carriage Eight – the very last carriage of the tram. She'd snuck up to Carriage One to see Trick as soon as she could – after all, if you were going to see a new world for the first time, you wanted your best friend beside you.

"Do we have to?" she wheedled, trying out her most endearing expression as she looked up at Fletcher. ("What's wrong with your face? You look like you've got gas," Trick muttered next to her.)

"It's just till we're on the other side of the gateway," Fletcher assured her. "Trick – back to your seat."

Trick rolled his eyes, then jumped up. As he stood, he suddenly swayed slightly, stumbling and putting his hand against the wall for support.

"You all right?" Harper frowned.

"Just – felt dizzy." Trick blinked.

"You're not gonna throw up too, are you?" Harper asked. "*That* wasn't part of the bet."

Trick seemed to shake himself, then grinned at Harper. "I'm fine. Anyway – see you on the other side!"

Carefully avoiding the puddle of sick on the floor, Harper set off, making her way down the long aisles, until she finally got back to Carriage Eight.

Harper's dad glanced at her as she stepped into the carriage. "Betting game?"

"Yep," Harper sighed. "Trick won."

"Harper, come look at this!" Her mother gestured to Harper. She lifted Harper up so she could see out of the window, where a blue light was shining on the horizon ahead of them.

"It's the gateway! We've made it!" Her dad punched the air.

Harper's father was a Spectacular musician. He and his band played stardust-infused instruments that filled people with so much joy it literally levitated them off the ground.

Harper had seen an old lady float out of her seat at one of their concerts and dance a sprightly two-step in mid-air. Her mother, on the other hand, wasn't a Spectacular at all, but a mechanic – but had anyone suggested that she allow her husband and child to escape without her, they would have received a firm bop to the nose.

The tram gained speed as it approached the blue light. As it did, however, Harper suddenly felt something strange: a clunking beneath her feet, like something had fallen.

"What was that?" she asked.

Her mother frowned. "I don't know," she said. "Michael…"

The rest of her sentence was drowned out by a huge shudder that had them all tumbling against the wall. The whole tram tilted sideways, and Harper assumed that the first carriage must be passing through the gateway. For a moment, everything was screeching brakes and screaming, and a strange blue light that now seemed to surround them all. Then, with an almighty bang, something beneath them seemed to give way. Looking out of the window, Harper saw with horror that their carriage was still moving very fast – only now they were going *backwards*, falling away from the rest of the tram, which continued to speed through the blue light.

"What happened? What's going on?" Harper yelled. Her dad grabbed on to her and pulled her away from the window, just as one of the frames juddered and detached, glass shattering into the carriage.

"Harper, hold on!" he yelled.

There was a shrieking of metal, and Harper was vaguely aware of the sensation of a collision before she was catapulted across the room, and everything turned black.

Later that evening, Fletcher sat in the driver's seat, staring out of the window. They'd brought the tram to a halt for the night alongside a mass of gleaming trees (were their leaves *blue*, Fletcher thought, or was he just exceptionally tired?). Most of the Spectaculars were already at work, harvesting Star-Stuff to replenish their stores and making plans for the conversion of the tram.

For all intents and purposes, the day had been more successful than they could have dreamed. Fletcher had already received messages from the other hijacked vehicles – the Spectaculars of the Cragg Islands had driven the turtle-drawn submarines through a gateway behind a waterfall, while those from the southern coastal cities had commandeered an airship and passed through a gateway hidden within a storm cloud. They were all safely in the Hidden Peaks, the place that had been a refuge for so many magical folks before them.

However, Fletcher couldn't concentrate on any of this. He sat with a tumbler of honey water, slowly swilling the liquid around as one singular thought echoed around his mind. *I failed. I failed them.*

He had no idea what had happened with Carriage Eight.

If there had been any indication that the carriage was faulty, that it was coming loose... But the crossing had been so loud, so chaotic, that they were through and racing out the other side by the time anyone had realized that an entire carriage – and the four families inside it – had been lost in the process.

There was a sudden smell of smoke from a battered toaster that sat on the floor at Fletcher's feet. Fletcher looked at it expectantly, and a moment later, a piece of paper popped up. Fletcher seized the slip and scanned it, then yelled at the door.

"Lahiri!"

Lahiri popped her head into the cab. "What?"

"I've just heard from the Spraggs – they've found the gateway, they're on their way."

Lahiri sprang into action. "Right. I'll send a canoe to pick them up." She pulled out a notebook and flicked through it. "So...the McCubbins and the Ruizes are through already. With the Spraggs heading across... That just leaves the Woolfes."

Fletcher frowned. "And nobody's heard anything from them?"

Lahiri shook her head. "Nothing. And with the mother being a non-Spectacular...We're a bit worried about them, to be honest."

"Well, keep looking." Fletcher rubbed his eyes. "I should go and speak to Trick; he's good friends with the Woolfe girl..."

"He's outside," said Lahiri. "Maybe give him a bit of time. It'll be all right, chief. We'll find the Woolfes. And once we do, we can start actioning the plans for converting the tram!"

"Sounds good." Fletcher gave a huge yawn.

"Get some sleep, Fletcher," Lahiri said firmly. "It's been a hectic day."

"I might take a quick five minutes," Fletcher agreed, his eyelids already drooping. "But if there's any word from the Woolfes, wake me up straight away."

"I will." Lahiri nodded. "Straight away."

When Fletcher woke up, the Woolfes had not arrived. It was midnight, and the stars were falling.

CHAPTER ONE

The Exploding Storeroom

Five years later.

On the day that it happened, there was nothing to suggest that it was going to be anything other than an ordinary September afternoon in the Smoke. It was drizzly and cold, and a mixture of bikes, sledges and trams packed the streets, their owners apparently having competitions as to who could Shout the Loudest and Almost Kill the Most People. Rain splattered down in sheets, and tall chimneys belched out clouds of the dark purple smoke that had given the city its name.

On this very ordinary day, Harper Woolfe was hurrying down the street towards a tram stop, holding on to a red umbrella as though her life depended on it.

Seeing her tram come into view, Harper picked up speed, accidentally splashing through a puddle and earning a dirty look from a passer-by. The tram pulled up, and Harper managed to leap on board and grab a seat at the front. She dropped her backpack on the floor and began squeezing water out of her hair.

"...that's right, we'll be having dinner at ours before the parade."

Harper rolled her eyes heavily as the Carver twins and their loyal followers walked past her on their way to the back of the tram. Lawrence and Laci Carver were in Harper's year at school, and placed joint first on her list of people she *heartily* disliked.

"Father's been cooking *all* day," Lawrence declared.

Apparently, they'd also invited most of the kids in Harper's class round for dinner before the Parade of Progress tonight. Despite her dislike for the twins, Harper couldn't help feeling a slight pang at not having been included. The Carver twins lived up the hill in the Ivory Borough, in a house shaped like a wedding cake. Harper was surprised they'd deigned to get on the tram at all – they were usually picked up from school in a golden sledge pulled by two sleek white dogs.

"He's a four-star chef," Laci chimed in smugly. "He's made salmon bouillon."

This made Harper feel a little better. Bouillon, in her opinion, sounded like something that had been thrown up – and sick was still sick, even if it was four-star sick. Besides, Harper's mum had promised to take her to the parade *and* make apple crumble – a far superior choice of cuisine as far as Harper was concerned.

The tram pulled up at Harper's stop, and as Harper made her way off, she heard the mutterings of her fellow students.

"*Creepy...*"

"Those buildings..."

"Who would *ever* choose to live here?" Lawrence Carver said from the back, and this time Harper knew it was for her benefit. She supposed she couldn't blame them: the deserted streets and boarded-up buildings of the Theatre Borough looked like something out of one of the horror novels that Harper sometimes sneakily checked out of the school library.

For as long as Harper had lived here, she'd heard rumours that these streets had once teemed with life, lit up by neon lights, bustling with people that performed in the theatres. People whispered of singing voices that summoned thunder, instruments that lifted you off your feet, stages that transformed into cities or jungles or entire, glittering oceans. Only whispered, mind: open discussion of such things was strictly forbidden.

Like everyone in the city, Harper knew the story of the night when, at the turn of the last century, the citizens of the Smoke had awoken to find stardust raining down like a soft covering of snow, and starlight trickling in shining fronds that crept down chimneys and seeped through open windows. Reports had flooded in from all over the Sunless

Provinces, rumours that the Star-Stuff had come to bestow magic on their citizens.

Things had turned a tad awkward when it became clear that the Star-Stuff hadn't come to everyone: it had come to the underskirts of the cities, to the winding streets where, from the Smoke to the Cragg Islands, theatres and playhouses were hidden away from *civilized* society. It had been gifted to the people who played accordions and sang shanties and danced, who were looked upon as riff-raff by the rich and elite. With the arrival of the Star-Stuff, their abilities were lifted to a fantastical new level – and when they had children, those abilities were passed on. But those people were gone now – they'd been driven out by the Minister, leaving nothing but streets of deserted theatres and the ghosts of singing voices.

Harper hurried past Gulliver's Café, which sold the best hot chocolate in the Smoke, and drew level with Flora's Fix-It Shop. A small, sandy-coloured cat with a diamanté collar sat outside the door, glowering at everyone who walked past. Harper scowled at it.

"Oh, go away, Truffles."

Truffles belonged to one of Harper's neighbours and was her mortal enemy. She liked animals on the whole, but Truffles hissed at her whenever she walked past and, on one memorable occasion, did his business in her new pair of sandals.

Once Truffles had slunk away, Harper pulled open the

door to the shop, only to be stopped short by the unmistakable feeling of someone's eyes on her back. She glanced over her shoulder to find herself being watched intently by a woman across the street. The woman was short and pale, with tumbling blonde curls. Harper met her gaze, and something seemed to shift in the woman's eyes. Harper wasn't sure what it was, but she knew the city's rules about talking to strangers (generally a bad idea), so she tore her eyes away from the woman and stepped inside the shop.

The bell above the door dinged as Harper let the door swing shut behind her. She waved to her mother, who was dressed in her customary hot-pink boiler suit, her hair tied back with a rag. She shared her daughter's copper hair and freckled, lightly tanned skin.

"Hi, Mum."

"Hi, sweetheart."

Harper loved the shop: the smell of oil and metal, the random jumble of machinery littered about, the buzzing and whirring of tools. It was the only home she'd ever known.

Or, at least, the only one she could remember.

The first six years of her life were a whirl of confusion for Harper. If she tried very hard, she could just about remember being involved in some sort of accident ("a crash between two commuter trams", her mother always said firmly). Harper and her mother had survived, but her father had been lost. Shortly afterwards, they'd moved to a tiny flat in the almost-deserted Theatre Borough. Harper sometimes had dreams about these places – in her mind, she saw bright lights and dancing figures and the sound of thunderous applause – but her mother always brushed them off.

The boy was somewhat harder to explain.

"He had blue hair," Harper told her mother repeatedly.

"I've told you, Harper," her mother would always reply. "He must have been an imaginary friend."

Harper supposed this was possible – after all, she spent a lot of time alone – but despite her mother's protestations, she couldn't shake the feeling that the boy hadn't been imaginary. He felt too real to her: she could imagine his voice, his laugh, his eyes glinting with mischief.

The door to the shop suddenly banged open again, and a scowling man in a frankly outrageous gold fur coat strode into the shop. He slammed a pocket watch on the counter and barked, "I need this looking at. Quick as you can."

Flora glanced over with a frown, but she was already dealing with a customer. Despite the fact that the man had not said please, or even hello, Harper decided to make herself useful and picked up the pocket watch.

"The clockwork is completely fried," she said to the man after a short inspection. "You should get a new watch."

The man sneered. "Oh, that's your advice, is it?"

"Yes." Harper blinked. "That's why I just gave it to you."

"Well thanks, but I'm hardly going to trust the expertise of some little girl," the man scoffed. He yelled over to Flora. "Oi! I haven't got all day here."

Harper sighed. It was somewhat galling to have her expertise sniffed at by a man who was now attempting to fix his watch by banging it repeatedly against the counter, but she bit her lip and kept quiet. Flora finished with the other customer and made her way unhurriedly over to the counter.

"What appears to be the problem?" she asked pleasantly.

The man picked up the watch and shoved it under her nose. Flora examined it for a moment before looking up at him.

"Well, I'm afraid you've gone about this in a rather roundabout way, because my daughter had it right the first time. It's dead. Get a new watch." Flora smiled sweetly. "That'll be ten bob for the consultation."

The man glared between them both as he slapped a ten-bob note on the counter. Harper glared back fiercely and was pleased when he looked away first.

"I shouldn't have expected any better from this part of town," he jeered, before turning and storming out of the shop.

"My word," said Flora mildly. "What a strange man." She turned to Harper. "Good day at school?"

"Actually…" Harper hesitated. "I have a detention note for you to sign."

"Do you now?" Her mother raised an eyebrow. "What for?"

Harper sighed. The detention had been a *complete* overreaction. She'd already got into trouble that morning for staring out of the window in a manner that her teacher had deemed "suspiciously dreamy" – so when he saw what Harper had done to her worksheet later that afternoon, he'd practically passed out on the spot.

"What in all the Provinces is that?" he'd asked, his eyes bulging.

"Oh…" Harper had looked down at the sheet. They were meant to have been labelling a diagram of some boring, beige contraption designed to suck dirt from the floor (and, presumably, the joy from your life). Harper hadn't taken to it, so she'd turned her page over and started designing something a bit different.

"It's a dragon," she said. "A mechanical dragon."

"A – a mechanical dragon?" Mr Gorgon spluttered. "Why would you want a mechanical dragon?"

"Um…" Harper had struggled to come up with an answer to this that wasn't simply, "Why *wouldn't* you want a mechanical dragon?"

"I just imagined it. For fun," she'd said eventually.

Mr Gorgon looked like she'd just told him that she ate puppies for breakfast. "You imagined it? For fun?"

"Yep. I think I could make it fly."

"Harper," Mr Gorgon had sighed. "You need to be concentrating on your lessons. You children are the future of the Sunless Provinces, the future of our progress!"

"Really?" Harper had wrinkled her nose. "All of us?"

"Yes."

"What about Gavin Grundell?"

"What about him?"

"Yesterday I saw him put a caterpillar up his nose," Harper informed her teacher. "I'm not being funny but if he's the future of the Provinces, I think we might be in trouble."

That's when Mr Gorgon had given her detention.

Harper's mother laughed as Harper relayed the story. "When's your detention?"

"Tomorrow after school. It would've been tonight if it wasn't for the parade."

Flora's expression turned guilty. "Harper – I'm so sorry, we've had an order for a new batch of submarine engines from the Minister himself. He wants them ready for tomorrow, so I'm not going to be able to take you to the parade after all."

Harper's heart sank. *Everyone* went to the Parade of Progress. It wasn't an especially fun event, but it was about as good as life got in the Smoke. Still, she knew her mum couldn't ignore a new order, especially if it had come straight from the Minister.

"All right," she sighed, swallowing her disappointment. "I have a lot of homework anyway. At least there's apple crumble."

Flora twisted her hands together. "About that…"

"*Mum.*"

"I was going to make it in my lunch break, but it got so busy that I didn't end up having one! I'm sorry."

"Don't worry," Harper sighed. "I'll fix something else to eat."

"Next week, I promise," Flora said firmly. "There'll be so much apple crumble you'll be eating it for breakfast!" She kissed Harper on the forehead, then hurried off to greet another customer. Harper took herself off to the back of the shop, where she'd made herself a little reading nook, complete with a nest of blankets and a *big* pile of books.

"Hello," she greeted them. "Have you all had good days?"

The books didn't reply. Harper sighed. Books were nearly a substitute for people, but they never talked back. Harper ignored the first book on the pile – a tale about a dashing Sir Something-Or-Other slaying a dragon, something that always made her slightly sad, as she tended to prefer dragons to knights in shining armour – and opted instead for a pleasingly terrifying novel about a group of zombies attacking the local knitting circle and being fought off by a group of old biddies. Settling down into her nook, she opened the book and began to read.

Miles away, across mountains and valleys and through a magical gateway, a woman was running down a corridor, out of breath. She burst into a cluttered office, rather surprising the man who was bent over some papers at an oak desk.

"We've found her," Lahiri panted. "The missing Woolfe child, we've finally found her!"

In the corner of the office, a blue-haired boy who was sat by the window, sketching, looked up sharply.

Morgan Fletcher stood up. "Where?"

"She's down in the Smoke," Lahiri informed him. "I just had a toast post message from Roper. She saw her."

Fletcher frowned. Over the years, they'd sent out multiple search parties to look for the missing Woolfes and combed every inch of the mountains surrounding the gateway, with no results. He'd been reluctant to dispatch a party down to the Smoke, sure that the Minister's police would be lying in wait for any who dared to show their faces again – but with Intake Night rapidly approaching, he'd allowed a small, stealthy group to infiltrate the city.

"Fletcher, she – from what Roper overheard – she doesn't appear to know anything about us," said Lahiri hesitantly. "Apparently she attends an ordinary school, and as far as we can tell, she seems to have little or no memory of all of this." She gestured around them.

"But – why wouldn't Flora tell her about us?" Fletcher frowned. "She knows that Harper will need to come to us to train."

"I don't know." Lahiri shrugged.

Fletcher thought for a moment. "Prepare the canoe."

"Fletcher – Roper's there already; she can do the pick-up…"

Fletcher shook his head. "I don't want them staying there any longer than they need to. Besides, the girl will be confused – I think it's best I explain everything to her."

"All right." Lahiri nodded. "Which canoe do you want?"

"Whichever is the fastest. I'm leaving. Now."

In the corner, Trick grinned widely, his brown eyes glinting.

It was time.

Harper had been reading in her nook for an hour or so when she noticed the first unordinary thing happening. A low humming sound began to fill the air around her, growing steadily louder by the second. Harper looked towards the source, only to find herself staring at the door to the storeroom.

The storeroom, as far as Harper knew, had not been opened since they'd moved in. When they'd first arrived, Flora had carried in a box containing the few of her dad's possessions that they'd salvaged from the crash, closed the door and padlocked it.

Not once in all the time since, however, had the room *hummed*.

"Do you mind?" Harper asked the room. "I'm trying to read."

At this, the humming grew louder.

Harper closed her book. Rising from her nook, she edged across the room until she stood in front of the storeroom door. Hesitating only briefly, she raised her hand and placed it against the wood.

There was a pause; then the door promptly exploded.

More specifically, it felt like something *inside* the storage room exploded, and the force jolted the door from within. Harper was propelled backwards, falling gracelessly into a wooden chessboard. The pieces clattered around her as she hit the floor, skidding several feet. She looked up to find sparks bursting out of the storeroom keyhole like fireworks.

"Harper?" Flora came running from the front of the shop to find her daughter wild-eyed and surrounded by pawns. "What happened?"

"I – I –" Harper spluttered. She pointed towards the door, but the sparks had disappeared. The humming noise faded back to a low drone, like a distant tram.

"You're not hurt, are you?" Flora pulled Harper to her feet, checking her over quickly.

"No," Harper managed to reply. "But there was – something in that room. It…"

"What?" Her mother peered down at her. Harper bit her lip, trying to think of how to say "the storeroom exploded" in a way that wouldn't immediately convince her mother that she was dangerously ill and needed confining to her room for the rest of the night.

"Nothing," Harper said eventually. "Just…tripped."

Flora ruffled her daughter's hair affectionately. "Why don't you head upstairs?"

She steered Harper firmly towards the steps that led up to the flat. Harper peeked over her shoulder to where the storeroom door stood looking perfectly innocent, as though it would never dream of doing something so undignified as exploding.

As she climbed the stairs and let herself in to the flat, Harper couldn't help mulling over the explosion in her mind. There was something about the silver sparks and the low humming noise; something that seemed familiar somehow, although she couldn't quite put her finger on why.

CHAPTER TWO

Parade of Progress

Harper padded through the flat to the kitchen, hitching herself up onto the draining board before clambering out of the window onto the metal fire escape attached to the side of the building. Outside it was still drizzling half-heartedly, but Harper was prepared – during a particularly rainy spell one winter she'd rigged up a series of brightly-coloured umbrellas to hang above the fire escape like a great rainbow canopy. It'd earned them some suspicious stares from their neighbours, but Harper didn't care too much. She settled cross-legged under the umbrellas and peered down at the crowd gathering below her.

At six o'clock sharp, the drummers came into view. The Smoke wasn't generally a city of music: no buskers playing for silver Smacker coins in the street, or music tinkling in elegant cafés the way Harper had read about in books. The Parade of Progress was the exception, but even then, it was nothing but the monotonous beating of drums. Harper wished that one of the drummers would break off into a jaunty solo, just to see how the others would react, but there was no such luck. They all stayed perfectly in line, marching along to the rigid beat.

After the drummers came the parade floats: moving, mechanicalized displays of the Smoke's prowess as a city of industry.

"...And here we have a display of the latest tram technology, commissioned by the Minister himself..." A couple of commentators were sat in a large booth above the crowd, describing all the floats that went past.

"The housing float, always a good one – here we have models of the next generation of housing! Features include security airships, private casinos and state-of-the-art racing tracks."

Harper snorted. She doubted they'd be seeing any of these "next-generation houses" in the Theatre Borough. The Carver twins and their like would get the racing tracks and the airships, and Harper and the rest of her neighbours would continue to live in the same small, poky flats as they always had.

As the parade continued, Harper noticed with interest that every single one of the people on the floats averted their eyes as they passed through the Theatre Borough, looking determinedly straight ahead. No one appeared to want a reminder of what had once been here – or rather, *who* had once been here.

The second-to-last float was a display of the Minister's "Personal Aviary". Harper felt sick as it came into view. A giant birdcage sat in the centre, displaying a selection of beautiful songbirds, parrots and peacocks – the Minister specialized in "collecting" rare and endangered animals. Harper imagined jumping down onto the float below and wrenching open the cage so that the birds inside could stream out like a handful of confetti thrown to the wind.

The parade ended with a giant, mechanical figure of the Minister himself, complete with absurdly big muscles and a self-satisfied grin. Harper could see several sweating workers puppeteering his arms, making him wave at the crowds surrounding him. People cheered as the figure went past, and just in case they were being too subtle about it all, the parade staff let off fireworks above the Minister's head.

After the fireworks, the parade moved on, heading up the hill towards the Ivory Borough, where no doubt the Carver twins and their friends would be waiting. The crowd below milled around, and Harper watched as families shared steaming buns from the food stands, and groups of friends played tag up and down the street.

Two figures hanging about in the street directly below caught Harper's eye: a tall man with long, black locs and dark-brown skin, and a boy with an angular frame, a tawny complexion and a woollen hat pulled low over his head.

Harper couldn't figure out why, but the figures intrigued her. They were dressed in the same drab clothing as most of the citizens in the Smoke, but there was something about them that seemed…*brighter,* somehow, although she couldn't explain why.

Harper slid off the ledge of the fire escape and slowly descended the metal steps, zigzagging down the side of the building until she was just a few feet above the two figures. Crouching down, she heard snippets of their conversation float up towards her.

"…How many times do I have to tell you that a plum cake does not constitute a healthy, balanced dinner?"

"How about two plum cakes?" The boy grinned cheekily.

"Right. I'm buying a basket of oranges from the next vendor we see, and Muses help me, you will eat at least three of them, lest your parents strike me down from beyond the grave…"

Harper couldn't help but smile at the easy, joking manner in which they spoke to each other. She watched as the man surveyed the street, probably searching for somewhere that sold fruit.

"Don't you just hate what they've done with the place?" the man sighed. "All these boarded-up theatres, completely devoid of magic. Such a *waste.*"

Harper's eyes widened, and she flashed an anxious look around. If the subject of the Theatre Borough was a forbidden topic, then magic was the ultimate taboo. Stories and rumours were one thing, but to utter it aloud as casually as the man had…

The boy reached up to readjust his hat, and as he did so a few strands of hair fell loose.

Harper heard her own sharp intake of breath.

His hair was blue!

The figures began to move off, turning into a narrow alley between two buildings. Harper leaped to her feet, racing down the last few flights of steps and rushing into the street. She had to catch up with those figures – she had to get a look at that boy…

Harper skidded to a halt at the top of the alleyway they'd turned down. It was a dead end, blocked off by a chain-link fence – and yet somehow, the figures were nowhere to be seen. Harper looked up, visions spinning wildly through her head of the two figures crawling, insect-like, up the side of a building, but the walls were bare. They were gone.

Dejected, Harper trailed back to the fire escape and climbed up to the balcony. She climbed back in through the window and padded into her own room. Sitting on the bed, Harper propped a book open on her knees, but she couldn't get the sight of the figures out of her mind. Could it be a coincidence? Blue hair was hardly the fashion among boys here…but how could her imaginary friend be walking around the Smoke, real and breathing and talking about plum cakes?

With no answers to be found, Harper snapped her book shut and gazed around the silent flat. To ward off the sense of emptiness around her, she listened to the sounds of the voices that floated through from the surrounding flats: families laughing and arguing, cooking together and talking about their days. If she closed her eyes, it was almost like they were in the room with her.

Hmmm…

Harper, sitting up in bed, glanced sharply towards the door. She'd been working on her mechanical dragon design, making adjustments here and there, but now she stopped and listened hard.

Hmmm…

She sat up straighter. The humming was back.

Harper shoved her design into her dressing-gown pocket and crept out of her room. According to the hallway clock, it was half past eight. She could hear her mum pattering around the kitchen, and she tiptoed past to avoid being caught. When she reached the door that opened onto the stairs, Harper cracked it opened and listened. After a moment or two, her eyes widened.

She could hear voices down there.

They were quiet, the words blurring into one long murmuring sound, but Harper could hear them; and as she stepped onto the landing, she heard footsteps below her as well.

Harper hovered for a moment, unsure of the best course of action. If it was burglars, she knew she should alert her mother. But Harper had a gut feeling that it *wasn't* burglars, just as she had a sneaking suspicion that, given how faint they sounded, the voices were coming from the storeroom.

She made up her mind and reached back into the flat, groping for the place where her mother usually hung her keys. She gently unhooked them from the wall, clutching them in her fist, before stepping outside and pulling the door closed. She stole down the stairs, carefully avoiding the parts that she knew were creaky. As she reached the shop and turned to the storeroom, her suspicions were confirmed: from within, Harper could hear the humming noise, and the voices layering on top of each other.

"...*sure* we're in the right place?"

"...look at the writing on the boxes, that's definitely Michael's..."

Harper's head snapped up. Burglars or not, these people knew her dad! She shifted, trying to edge closer to the storeroom.

Unfortunately, she didn't see the gramophone behind her.

Her heel bumped against it with a soft thudding sound. The conversation in the storeroom halted. Harper froze, her heart thudding loudly.

"...upstairs, maybe..."

"...we're running out of time..."

The conversation continued; they hadn't heard her. Harper breathed a sigh of relief.

Then the record started.

"Oooooh, baby…"

The voices stopped dead.

"Let's go dancing underneath the summer moon…"

A hammering sound joined the song as Harper smacked the side of the gramophone with her fist.

"Shut up, you stupid piece of junk!" she hissed. But no sooner had she managed to silence the crooning voice, than she heard the sound of footsteps pounding in the storeroom, heading away from her, towards the rusted back door that led out to the alleyway behind the shop.

"No no no…" Harper darted towards the storeroom. She shoved her mother's key into the lock and wrenched once, twice, three times before it clicked open. Harper burst into the room, but it was too late: the figures had disappeared, the slightly ajar back door the only sign they'd been there in the first place.

Harper dashed to the back door and ran out into the street, looking desperately up and down for any sign of the figures who'd spoken about her dad.

Then, without warning, a pair of arms grabbed her from behind.

"What the…" Panicking, Harper began to struggle, kicking behind her as best she could, but whoever had grabbed her wasn't letting go. She was shunted along the cobbles and around the corner into an adjoining alleyway. Harper's mouth dropped open in disbelief as she saw a giant wooden canoe just ahead of them.

A canoe that was floating in mid-air.

Onboard were two more figures, but Harper couldn't quite see them in the dim light. She began to kick harder, looking around desperately, and a blur of light fur caught her eye. She whipped her head around to see Truffles the cat crouched behind a bin, watching her.

"Truffles! Go and get help! Get my mum!" Harper called desperately.

Truffles tilted his head, seeming to consider this, before turning around and starting to lick his bum.

I hate that cat, was Harper's last grim thought before hands pushed her up and over the side of the canoe. She hit the floor heavily, her yell echoing around the alleyway. She jumped up straight away, poised for a fight if it came to that.

"Now really, is that any way to— Oi, you, I thought you were supposed to be helping!" her captor grumbled. Harper turned to see who they were talking to and froze.

"You."

A boy around her age stepped forwards. He was grinning at her in a familiar way, and his hair was blue.

CHAPTER THREE

Exit in a Flying Canoe

Harper was momentarily stunned, staring at the blue-haired boy. When she found her voice again, she took a breath and yelled:

"WHAT in the Provinces is going on?"

"Funny. I was about to ask the same question," another voice said. Harper raised her eyes to see the tall man she'd noticed in the street earlier. He looked Harper over, then turned back to the figure who'd just dragged her down the alley.

"What exactly am I looking at here?" he asked.

The other figure reached up and pulled back their hood. Underneath was – well, Harper wasn't entirely sure what it was. Its face was human, or humanish, but it had wrinkly, leathery skin and glittering black eyes.

"It's the girl," the creature said.

The man closed his eyes briefly. "Yes, Helja, I'm aware that she's a girl. What I'm *not* aware of is why she's been thrown unceremoniously over the top of my canoe with apparently no idea as to what's going on."

"Well, excuse me!" the creature complained. "Just because you two bolted at the first sign of movement. I was told we were collecting a girl, so I collected a girl."

"Be that as it may, Helja," the man said patiently. "Could you not have thought of a *slightly* gentler way of carrying out your instructions? Perhaps a way that didn't involve seizing her in the street, dragging her down an alley and dumping her in a strange vehicle?"

Helja's eyes narrowed. There was a short silence, then suddenly she disappeared in a puff of smoke and an extremely grumpy-looking mop sat in her place.

"Oh, for Muses' sake," the man sighed. "Can we not do this now, Helja?"

The mop stared stubbornly back at him.

Harper looked at the boy incredulously. He shrugged. "She's offended," he said, as though turning into a mop was a perfectly normal thing to do when one was offended.

"Helja, please," the man was saying now. "Why don't we talk about this back at the Wondria – along with a discussion about your pay rise?"

This clearly meant something to the mop because it straightened up slightly, then began to shuffle off towards the far end of the canoe. As the Helja-mop passed Harper, she shook her mop-head in a stern manner and made a low, grumbling sound.

Harper huffed a laugh that was tinged with hysteria. "Did I just get told off by a mop?"

"Don't worry, it's happened to the best of us," the boy replied. "Helja's a Kobold – household spirit and shapeshifter. You don't really need to worry unless she turns into a mangle, 'cos that means you've properly ticked her off."

Harper stared at him, wide-eyed. She considered the idea that perhaps she was dreaming, or else the strangeness of the day was causing her to hallucinate.

But I remember him, she thought, looking at the boy.

The tall man sighed and looked at Harper. "Well, Miss Woolfe, I do apologize for the rather abrupt beginning to the evening." He held out his hand. "My name is Morgan Orion Fletcher. Elected Chief Spectacular, Showrunner of the Wondria, Hidden Peaks Council member. Trained barista, as it happens, but no one ever asks about that."

Fletcher. Something in the back of Harper's mind registered a dim recognition. She shook his hand. "Nice to meet you," she said. "Now please tell me what's going on, or I'm going to have to jump out of this canoe and start screaming."

Fletcher motioned for her to sit. Harper hesitated, then did so: these figures had mentioned her dad, so surely they wouldn't mean her any harm?

"Do you have any idea who we are?" Fletcher asked.

Harper swallowed, looking between them. She remembered their conversation about magic at the parade, the way they'd talked about the old theatres. "You're – the people from the old Theatre Borough…" she said haltingly.

Fletcher nodded. "Indeed. We – and by *we*, I mean yourself and your dear old dad, as well as me and Trick over there…"

Trick. The name was like a lantern flickering into life. For a split second, flashes of memory filled Harper's mind – pealing laughter, a mischievous smile, a book of childish handwriting. She blinked rapidly, trying to keep hold of them as Fletcher continued.

"…are people known as Spectaculars. We are performers – singers, dancers, actors, and so on – who were gifted special powers from the stars. Your dad was a cracking musician; he played a starlight-infused trumpet that could levitate you right out of your seat."

At the mention of her dad, Harper felt another memory spark in her mind, distant and vague, but still there. Jazz music. Four figures, playing together. An old lady dancing a two-step.

But…Harper shook her head as the logical part of her brain caught up with the image. Starlight trumpets? Levitating grannies? It all seemed fantastical, impossible – but Fletcher carried on in a perfectly serious manner.

"Now, your Minister, who isn't so keen on people who

are different, decided to deem us 'dangerous' and turn all his citizens against us. So, we commandeered a few of his prize vehicles and escaped through a gateway into the Hidden Peaks – a realm which has been a refuge for magical people for centuries now. However –" Fletcher looked down, his voice softening – "on the way there was an accident. The last carriage came loose and didn't make the crossing."

Harper let out a soft *oof* as this particular piece of the puzzle slotted into place. So, the accident *hadn't* been between "two ordinary commuter trams", as her mother had claimed. It had been a tram filled with these...*Spectaculars* – a tram that was supposed to be taking them to a new life. Except not all of them had made it.

"My dad...he died in that crash," Harper said quietly.

Fletcher bowed his head. "We heard. I'm so sorry. I can only imagine that your mother couldn't find the gateway, or didn't know how to cross...so she brought you back down here. We only just found out that this was where you've been all these years. We arrived down here earlier to collect you, but I think we accidentally set off some of your dad's stuff – *someone*" – he looked pointedly at Trick – "decided to have a go on his trumpet, but the Star-Stuff inside it hadn't been used in so long that it got a bit overexcited and exploded. We thought we'd better come back after the shop was shut. It's lucky we found you tonight – just in time!"

"Just in time for *what*?" Ever since Fletcher had mentioned her dad, a tiny seed of excitement had planted itself in

Harper's chest, ready to bloom and sprout and grow into a full-blown excitement tree. However, the fear of being wrong had her grabbing that feeling by the roots and stuffing it back down again. "What has all this got to do with me?"

"An excellent question," Fletcher agreed. "And one I think we should discuss in the presence of your mother. If I remember Flora correctly, she may have a few things to contribute."

Harper was somewhat surprised by this, but she nodded: she certainly wasn't going to object to having her mother around.

Fletcher went over to a silver engine that was perched on the side of the canoe. He turned up a dial on the side, and the canoe rose higher into the air. Harper's stomach swooped as the ground dropped away – she'd never flown in *anything* before, let alone a giant levitating canoe.

"Which one is your window?" Fletcher asked.

Harper looked along the row. "There!" she said, pointing at the familiar floral curtains. Fletcher somehow shifted the canoe sideways until they were bobbing just outside the window. Harper leaned over the side and knocked on the glass.

After a moment, Flora appeared in her fluffy dressing gown. To her credit, she didn't faint or start screaming at the sight of the levitating canoe. Instead, her eyes flickered over Fletcher and Trick, then fluttered closed for the briefest of moments. When she opened them again, she took a deep breath.

"Would anyone like a cup of tea?"

Fletcher smiled widely. "Peppermint, if you've got it."

Flora busied herself making the tea while Fletcher, Trick and Harper climbed carefully through the window and seated themselves on the sofa (Fletcher stated loudly that Helja was also invited, but the mop made no movement to join them).

"Nice cushions, Flora," remarked Fletcher as Harper's mother returned bearing mugs of tea.

"Enough with the small talk, Fletcher," Flora replied. "You didn't come here to chat about my cushions."

"No. Of course not." Fletcher looked a little flustered. "We're here to discuss the future educational prospects – that is, the potential tutelage and training opportunities, which, on the presumption that Harper accepts our proposition…"

Harper thought he might have rambled on for a long time, but Flora cut him off. "You're here to take my daughter away."

Harper spluttered. Trick leaned over and thumped her on the back as Harper stared at Fletcher. Her heart was thudding loudly – but was it in excitement or fear?

"That would be Harper's decision," Fletcher said seriously. "As the daughter of a Spectacular, Harper is eligible – and indeed, advised – to join an apprenticeship scheme." He looked at Harper now. "Our theatre – the Grand Wondria

Music Hall and Theatre, converted from the very tram that we used to escape the Smoke – tours all over the Hidden Peaks, putting on shows almost every evening. We also train the next generation of Spectaculars. From the age of eleven, you are entitled to a place on an apprenticeship with us – and the Intake Night for this year's batch of apprentices is tonight."

Harper blinked several times. Part of her was still half expecting the Carver twins to pop up at any moment, pointing and shouting, "Got you!"

"This apprenticeship," said Flora. "What would it involve?"

"Studying under great Spectacular talents," Fletcher replied. "Learning the arts of Mechanics and Theatrics. Travelling to every corner of the Hidden Peaks."

"And tasting some *excellent* cake, because Helja is the best baker in the Hidden Peaks," Trick added. Harper glanced over at the mop in the canoe, which seemed to straighten up with pride.

"How long?" Flora asked.

"Three years as a junior apprentice, then a further two as a senior," Fletcher replied.

"Well. That seems like an offer she can't possibly refuse." Flora looked at Harper properly for the first time. "Don't you think?"

"Mum…" Harper stared at her mother, a million questions flying through her head. She went with the most obvious one. "Why didn't you *tell* me?"

"I always meant to," her mother replied, clutching onto her mug. "But after the accident…I'd lost your dad, I had no idea where the gateway was, I didn't know what to do other than to bring you back here. I sent out letters, I tried to speak to people who'd known the Spectaculars, but no one would talk about them. I thought the best thing to do would be to settle here, keep our heads down, and hope that one day, they'd find us."

"And now we have," said Fletcher.

"Yes," Flora laughed tightly. "I thought I'd be ready, when it happened."

"I'm not sure one is ever ready to say goodbye to a child." Fletcher gave a half-glance at Trick. "But as I said – it's Harper's decision."

Harper sensed the weight of everyone's eyes settling on her. She suddenly felt terribly embarrassed, and wished she had something to do with her hands.

"There's also a pool," Trick added, glancing at Fletcher. "Did you tell her about the pool?"

"There is, as my nephew states, a pool," Fletcher said seriously.

Harper found herself unable to speak. One part of her brain – the part where the excitement seed had exploded into a towering canopy complete with a treehouse and a jaunty rope swing – was screaming words like "starlight" and "travelling theatre", demanding that she get back into that canoe *right away, young lady*. But another part – a smaller, but no less insistent part – knew first-hand how lonely the flat could be.

"I don't want to leave you here alone," Harper said to Flora.

"I won't be alone," Flora said determinedly. "I've got the shop, haven't I – and maybe I'll take some apple crumble over to the new neighbours, they seem like a friendly bunch."

"You can write from the Hidden Peaks," Fletcher added. "And we may be able to arrange visits at some point…"

"It's not my world Harper, but it is yours, and you need to take this opportunity," said Flora. "And if you're still unsure…" Her mother disappeared for a moment, then came back clutching a backpack.

"I packed this last month, when you turned eleven," Flora said gently. "I had a feeling that they might be coming for you soon."

Harper took the bag from her mother and peered inside. Nestled within was a jumper, some clean underwear, a toothbrush, a purse, a packet of biscuits and…

"What's this?" Harper reached in and touched the little silver bow tie that sat neatly on the top of the other contents.

"It was your dad's," her mother said with a small smile. "He used to wear it when he played with his band."

Harper felt her breath catch as she looked down at it. She was slightly concerned that she was about to burst into tears in front of everyone.

"I should warn you, this life is not always the easiest,"

Fletcher piped up. "We travel. We work hard. The Council haven't processed our insurance forms against Dragons-Taller-Than-Seven-Feet, and we can't protect against the occasional starlight explosion, although we do offer cashback for any toes or fingers lost. However, at the end of the day, we're all a family – a big, weird, colourful family, with too many opinions and slightly too few toes."

Of all of the things Fletcher had spoken about – Star-Stuff and theatres and hidden worlds – this was the thing that made Harper's heart contract with longing. No more sitting alone on trams, no more dinners-for-one with nothing but the radio for company. She'd have a whole extended family – and not only that, they'd be *her* people. People who created and performed, and would presumably never tell her off for drawing a mechanical dragon. In that moment, she knew that she *had* to go.

"Of course you have to go," said Flora, seeming to read her daughter's mind. She set down the mug of tea she'd been clutching and hugged Harper, hard. Harper squeezed her back, breathing in the scent of perfume and engine oil.

"I love you," she muttered.

"I love you, too," her mother said. They stayed like that for a moment longer, before Flora pulled back. "Right. I believe you have a canoe to catch."

They all made their way over to the window. Fletcher went first, hopping into the canoe with surprising grace given his large stature. Trick went next, and Harper placed her hands on either side of the window, ready to hoist herself up and follow them. She took a last look at the flat, then swung herself up and over the sill, into the waiting canoe. Fletcher twisted the silver dial once more and the canoe began to lift, slowly gaining height until the city was an open book below them. Flora blew a kiss up, and Harper waved, then watched as she faded to a tiny spot below. Her heart gave a squeeze of sadness, but she couldn't help her eyes straying towards the horizon, and what might lie beyond.

CHAPTER FOUR

Through the Gateway

When Harper looked back around, Fletcher was making his way to the far end of the canoe – presumably to try to continue reasoning with the mop – but Trick was still there. He grinned. "I suppose we should get properly reacquainted. I'm Trick. I'm not offended if you don't remember me, though," he added quickly. "Traumatic crash, scrambled memory…it's understandable."

"I do remember you," Harper told him. "Sort of. My mum told me you were an imaginary friend."

Trick looked offended. "Imaginary?"

"She wasn't very convincing."

"I should hope not." He ruffled his blue hair until it stuck up like peacock feathers. "I'm *extremely* memorable."

Harper blinked – then, suddenly, she was laughing.

Really, properly laughing, holding on to her stomach as she doubled over. After a beat, Trick began to chuckle as well. After the shock of the previous half-hour, it was a relief to laugh – and better than that, it felt natural, like they'd laughed together a hundred times before.

Trick arranged his face into a serious expression. "We have a very important First Order of Business to sort out."

"Oh," Harper faltered. "What's that?"

"I'm afraid you owe me two chocolate plums."

This wasn't what Harper had expected to hear. "Sorry?"

Trick took a book out of his pocket and tapped a page. "Our last bet, on the day of the crossing, was the Great Puking Bet, during which I won seven chocolate plums. However, , taking off the three I owed you for the Bannister-Sliding Wager, plus the two that I ought to pay as a forfeit for plunging head first into your birthday cake *during* said wager, overall, you still owe me two."

He rattled all this off at an impressive speed. Harper grinned. "Okay. I'll put it on my list – right after *get kidnapped by strangers in a flying canoe,* and *casually find out that magic exists in a hidden realm somewhere in the mountains.*"

The canoe rotated in the air until it pointed north, then began to skim above the smog that engulfed the city, leaving the towering factories and belching chimneys in its wake. Trick leaned down and picked up a package from the bottom of the canoe. "Do you want a drink? Fletcher always says there's no shock on Earth that can't be fixed with the appropriate amount of tea."

Inside the package was an array of flasks and a tin of biscuits. There was also a radio, which Trick set on a seat and switched on, turning the dial on the side until it reached a station playing cheerful banjo music.

"We're technically not allowed to bring Food, Drink or Life Forms What Breathe back through the gateway," Trick informed her. "But we thought we'd try to smuggle some across while we're here. Nowhere in the Hidden Peaks sells Foggytime Tea *or* Shortbread Stars. It's *devastating*." He sighed and held out one of the flasks.

"No thanks," said Harper with a shudder. "Tea tastes like soggy mud."

Trick gasped and clutched at the flask. "She didn't mean it. Don't listen to the nasty girl."

As they sipped their drinks (Harper from a flask of hot chocolate, which was pleasingly rich and did *not* taste of soggy mud), Harper asked Trick if he was going to be starting the apprenticeship this year as well.

"Yep," Trick said. "Honestly, it's been *torture* growing up at the Wondria and not being able to do any of the fun stuff. They have special family quarters for the kids of performers, but we weren't allowed near the backstage departments or the workshops – all because of this one incident with a tutu and a starlight blowtorch, which was *not* my fault and did *not* require that much of an overreaction..."

They carried on sailing above the clouds for about an hour more, during which time Trick gave Harper an overview of the Spectaculars. He told her about the dancers who could waltz with their own shadows, the actors who could change their appearance in order to play multiple characters and the singers whose voices could make anyone in the vicinity become convinced that they were the best dancer in the world (a skill that apparently once caused *quite* the political embarrassment, involving the current mayor of a major city and an extremely ill-advised chicken dance). Harper tried to take it all in, but she wasn't sure she could quite believe it until she saw it.

A sudden blast of wind informed Harper that they'd picked up speed. When she looked ahead, she saw Fletcher turning the silver dial as the canoe approached a strange blue light that shone from a narrow gap between two sheer rock faces.

"This is the gateway," Fletcher called to them. Harper's stomach twisted as she realized that this was where the accident had occurred – the accident that had taken her dad from her, that had changed the course of her life for *years* to come. She found herself staring fixedly at the floor of the canoe, unwilling to look around in case anything triggered a memory – the kind she *didn't* want to remember.

Fletcher twisted the dial again, and the canoe surged forwards. They were almost fully through when…

BOOM.

They shot backwards, as though the rock face was spitting them out. For a split second, Harper worried that the Hidden Peaks was rejecting her – after all, the gateway had denied her entrance once before – but then a small creature that looked like Helja (another Kobold, Harper presumed) appeared from an alcove in the mountain and fixed Fletcher with a stern gaze.

"Anything to declare, Fletcher?"

"Declare? Let's see…" Fletcher tapped his chin, adopting a slightly-too-casual expression. "Three Spectaculars, two pre-teen, one…"

"Old," Trick said helpfully.

"Mature," Fletcher corrected, jabbing Trick in the ribs. "What else…one Kobold, extremely grumpy. Flying Canoe, standard size…and a packet of Shortbread Stars and three flasks of Foggytime Tea."

He said this last bit very fast, as though he were hoping that the Kobold wouldn't hear. It didn't work.

"Hand them over."

"Oh, come on!" Fletcher wheedled. "What harm could possibly come from shortbread?"

"They're contraband," the Kobold said firmly. "Hand it over!"

Reluctantly, Fletcher surrendered the food package to the Kobold. Trick stroked the tea flask mournfully as he passed it over the canoe, as though he were saying goodbye to a beloved pet. The Kobold examined the package shrewdly, then waved them on. The canoe creaked back into motion, and they carried on towards the blue light.

"They never used to be this strict," said Fletcher mulishly. "But there was an incident a couple of years ago with some ostrich-smugglers and some contraband radishes…honestly, some people just spoil it for everyone, don't they?"

They passed through the gateway without incident this time and shot out the other side into a vast landscape that nearly knocked Harper's breath clear out of her. They were surrounded by towering mountains dotted with sparkling waterfalls and dense pine forests. The sky seemed to stretch on for ever. Harper blinked – she couldn't remember the last time she'd seen a sky so clear. In the Smoke it was permanently hidden from view by smog, but here, it felt as if someone had laid a great blue blanket across the sky. In the distance, bright lights lit up the horizon – blue and purple, pink and white, dancing around as though the sky was throwing a party.

For a moment, Harper simply stared out of the canoe, utterly in awe. Then, she gradually became aware that the music on the radio had stopped, and a news announcer was talking instead.

"…*welcome to* The Spectacular Daily Show. *I'm your host, Ace Malone. An overview of our top stories this evening: Yolanda Fierce and Tornio Nocturne top* The Spectacular Times's *list of Most Influential People for the third year in a row… The Opulence Theatre has completed its one-million-bob refurbishment, and now boasts fifteen crystal chandeliers and a solid gold stage… And the cast of new musical* One for the Money *respond to reviewers who called the production 'punishingly cheerful'…"*

Fletcher snickered as he switched the radio off. "We'll be landing soon. Trick – best send a message ahead to Captain Roper, let her know we'll be back sharpish. Harper, far be it for me to make any judgements on your fashion choices, but you might be more comfortable in these." He held up a pair of tough leather boots and a thick coat. Harper blushed slightly as she looked down at her dressing gown and slippers. She pulled them off quickly and took the boots from Fletcher. They were heavy but soft on the inside, and when Harper took the coat, she saw that it, too, had a thick, fleecy lining.

"Who's Captain Roper?" Harper asked as she laced the boots onto her feet. "A pirate?"

"Oh – no, but…" Fletcher rolled his eyes. "When we first opened the Teaching Wing of the Wondria, we thought 'Mr' and 'Ms' felt a bit stuffy, so we let the staff choose their own titles. Bit of a mistake, really – we've got Dames, Generals, a couple of Right Honourables… Don't worry, it's only taken me five years to remember them all. People mostly go by surnames anyway."

During this exchange, Trick was scribbling a letter and folding it carefully into quarters. Then, to Harper's bemusement, he rummaged around the bottom of the canoe and came up with a battered old toaster. He popped the folded-up piece of paper into the toaster and pressed the lever down. The note slid down into the toaster and disappeared.

Fletcher guided the canoe downwards, towards a ledge that jutted out from the side of a mountain. They landed smoothly, greeting the stone beneath them with nothing more than a gentle bump.

"We're going this way," called Trick, pointing to a pair of rusty iron tram tracks that seemed half-buried in the mountainside, as though the mountain had become hungry one day and begun to eat them as a snack.

They climbed steadily up the tracks for a while – Fletcher at the front, Helja (back in her Kobold form) bringing up the rear. As they walked, Harper heard signs of life from around a corner up ahead of them – cheers and shouts, and the occasional roar of laughter. Her heart leaped – this was it. There was a whole new life waiting for her around that corner. Fletcher grinned at her as they rounded the bend and stepped into a clearing,

"Welcome home."

CHAPTER FIVE

The Teapot Trait Initiation Ceremony

Harper blinked as she looked around the clearing. Everything was a blur of colour and noise. Blazing paper lanterns lined the perimeter, while brightly-coloured bunting had been strung between the trees. A crowd of people – maybe two hundred or more – milled about, shouting and laughing and singing snatches of songs. Just behind the crowd, through a clump of pine trees, Harper could see a line of tram carriages, sleek and crimson-coloured. She felt a lightning bolt of excitement as she gazed at the scene around her.

One of the figures from the crowd suddenly came flying towards them with impressive speed.

"Trick! You're back!"

The figure turned out to be a petite girl, with long, black hair, warm brown skin and excited eyes. She hugged Trick, then turned to Harper and grabbed her hand, shaking it vigorously. "Hi! Are you a first-year apprentice too? My name's Anvi Patel, I'm eleven, well, my birthday was literally yesterday so I *just* scraped in to start training this year isn't that *wild*, what's your name?"

She barely drew a breath throughout this entire speech. Trick raised his eyebrows.

"Anvi. Slow down."

"Oh – right, yeah." Anvi took a breath and looked back at Harper, now with a deadly serious expression on her face. "Hello. My name's Anvi Patel, and I'm just about to begin apprentice training. How do you do?"

Harper had a terrible feeling she was going to giggle at the girl's sudden change of demeanour. "Nice to meet you. I'm Harper, and I'm starting too, I suppose – I only found out about all this Spectacular stuff about an hour ago, so I'm still catching up."

"Really?" Anvi's eyes grew wide, enthusiasm creeping back into her voice. "That's amazing! Well don't you worry, we'll get you caught up faster than you can say…" She trailed off with a gasp, looking behind them. "Muses – are those Cinnamon Mice? They're my favourites, I'm going to have *five*! Got to keep my strength up for the Initiation!" And she was off, running through the crowd, dodging past groups of Spectaculars who laughed or tutted as she sped past.

"Anvi's – enthusiastic," Trick chuckled. "We grew up at the Wondria together."

Harper wasn't listening. She stood very still, suddenly gripped with an overwhelming fear.

Initiation.

"Trick," she said slowly, turning to face him. "What was she talking about? What initiation?"

Trick held up his hands. "Don't panic."

Harper was most definitely panicking. "No one said anything about an initiation!" What would happen if she failed? Would she be banished before she'd even had a chance to begin? This seemed unusually cruel – to have this life dangled before her and then snatched away at the last minute.

"You barely have to do anything, I promise. Stop worrying," said Trick.

Harper opened her mouth to inform him that she most certainly would *not* stop worrying, not until she knew exactly what the premise of the initiation was, but Trick pointed over her shoulder.

"Look, Fletcher's about to start it all off!"

A wave of cheers and whistles went up from the crowd as Fletcher climbed a ladder onto a makeshift podium in the middle of the clearing. He coughed before looking around at them all.

"Good evening, everyone! I hope you've all been having a merry time so far…"

An answering roar came from a group of Spectaculars who were drinking heavily from wooden tankards.

"And welcome to the Teapot Trait Initiation for this year's apprentices!"

This time the whole crowd cheered, not just the ones with the tankards. Harper looked around wildly. Was she going to have to fight a *teapot*?

"To all the young Spectaculars who are beginning training this year, we wish you the best of luck. Your years as an apprentice will be some of the most rewarding years of your life. So, without further ado-ing or adon't-ing, let's begin the initiation!"

Fletcher gestured over to one side of the clearing, where a round table had suddenly appeared. At the centre of the table was a large willow-patterned teapot, with teacups and saucers arranged in rings around it.

The new apprentices – thirty or forty, as far as Harper could see – began hurrying towards the table. Trick grabbed Harper's arm and pulled her forwards as well. Apprentices were milling about in front of the teapot, swiping for the biggest teacups or the ones with the brightest patterns. Once they each had a teacup in hand, they lined up, single file, before the teapot.

Harper followed suit, selecting a crimson teacup and clutching on to it as she joined the queue. Visions swam wildly in her head of a boxing glove protruding, jack-in-the-box-like, from the spout of the teapot and punching each of them on the nose. She shook her head and tried to calm her breathing.

The teapot sat silent and still for a moment, before starting to whistle. The apprentice at the front – a fair-skinned girl with a plum-purple bob – stepped closer and held her teacup up to the spout, and the teapot leaned forwards and poured a stream of burgundy liquid into her cup.

The colour of the tea was unusual, but it wouldn't have been entirely extraordinary if the next apprentice to proffer their teacup – which happened to be Anvi Patel – hadn't received a thick peach liquid from the very same pot.

This went on down the line. Each apprentice had their cup filled with a different type of liquid: a syrupy marigold brew, a watery stream of jet black, a gooey violet substance. As Harper got closer, she also noticed that once each teacup was full, a little tag appeared on the handle of the cup, with squiggly writing that she couldn't quite read.

When Trick's turn came, he ran forwards and stood in front of the table, looking unconcerned. A few moments passed before the teapot started to whistle, and as Trick held his cup up, it poured out a pale-green liquid. A tag appeared on Trick's cup, and he held it out for Harper to read too:

Honey-pineapple and spearmint: flair and cool-headedness.

"What does it mean?" Harper whispered.

"The teapot assesses each new apprentice: their ambitions and fears, their intelligence and passion, their talents and shortcomings. Then it picks out the two core personality traits that it thinks will help them in their training. Your

Teapot Traits, we call them," Trick explained. "I've wanted to know what mine would be for *years*."

"Why a teapot?"

"It's a tradition – before every show the performers always gather in the green room for a cup of tea. The teapot's passed through so many hands at this point that they decided it was probably the best qualified to assess a person." He looked down at his tag and frowned. "Flair…here, are they trying to suggest I'm *dramatic* or something?" He feigned outrage, and Harper couldn't help but secretly agree with the teapot.

Harper was next in line. She padded forwards nervously; never in her life had she been so concerned about what a teapot would think of her.

After a beat, the pot began to sing. Harper quickly proffered up her teacup and held her breath as a smoky orange stream came pouring out of the spout and into her cup. A tag appeared, and Harper quickly bent forwards to read it:

Chilli pepper and sea salt: bold and practical.

"Those are good ones!" Trick said from over her shoulder.

Harper considered them. "Bold" was good, she supposed. Who didn't want to be bold? And "practical"…Harper grinned. Well, she was her mother's daughter, after all.

"So…is that it?" Harper asked, turning around with her teacup. "We just get our Teapot Traits, and that's the initiation?"

"Not quite," Trick said. "We've still got to perform the Spectacular Oath."

"*Perform?*" This time, Harper felt like her heart really might stop. "But… I don't know the Spectacular Oath!"

"No one knows it!" Trick replied cheerfully. "It changes every year. Just watch."

All at once, every new apprentice raised their cup as if toasting the night, then drank down their tea. Harper copied them, choking slightly as she did (chilli-pepper-flavoured tea was *not* designed to be downed).

As she fanned her mouth, Harper suddenly had the strangest feeling: words were floating into her head, as though she were remembering song lyrics she'd long since forgotten. They gathered in her mouth like a swarm of bees, then pushed their way out into the world.

"May we always Bring the House Down,
And sometimes Steal the Light
We'll Chew the Stage
And hope and pray
For Broken Bones on Opening Night
We know that there are No Small Parts
Our Belief we will Suspend
Till 'Happy Trails'
Sets us sail
Upon our story's end."

There was a beat of silence as the oath finished. Harper blinked; as far as she was concerned, she'd just uttered a load of nonsense. But then the crowd burst into rapturous applause.

"It gets more beautiful every year," said one of the tankard-wielding Spectaculars, wiping tears from his eyes.

"That concludes the Intake Night Initiation!" Fletcher called over the crowd. "New apprentices – welcome!"

Suddenly, all throughout the crowd, people were shouting "Welcome!" and "Happy Intake Night!" People whom Harper had never met were grinning at her and clapping her on the back, as though she really was one of them. A warm feeling, like sinking into a hot bath, spread through Harper, and she found herself grinning back at the people around her.

"You are now all free to set up your camping equipment for the night," Fletcher announced. "If you're using a tent, we do request that you keep it to two storeys or below, and anyone caught not sharing their marshmallows will be subject to a most grievous punishment."

"That means you, McCubbins!" someone in the crowd yelled, followed by a wave of laughter.

There was a flurry of movement, and suddenly benches and tables were being speedily packed away as people rolled out squashy sleeping bags and assembled camp beds.

"It's tradition for everyone to camp on Intake Night," Trick said, gesturing over to a line of cosy-looking yurts. "Do you mind? From tomorrow we'll be in the apprentice quarters of the Wondria."

"Not at all!" Harper beamed. She couldn't imagine minding anything, particularly; she was too relieved. The initiation was over, she'd survived, and no one had packed her off back to the Smoke. She'd have slept on a bed of hedgehogs at this point.

She and Trick began making their way over to the yurts. Some of the Spectaculars had gathered around a bonfire, chatting quietly and toasting marshmallows. Harper watched them curiously – they were so different to the people of the Smoke it was hard to imagine that they'd once lived there.

"So – is this all of you?" she asked Trick. "All the Spectaculars?"

To her surprise, Trick laughed. "Muses, no. There are tons of other Spectacular theatres. And there are Spectaculars who work freelance. Or just go and perform in the woods for the squirrels."

"Right." Harper snorted. "So – are your parents Spectaculars?" she asked Trick.

"They were," Trick replied. "But now...Fletcher's all I've got left. He's my mum's cousin twice removed or something – but I just call him my uncle."

He didn't elaborate on how he'd lost his parents, and Harper didn't want to pry. Instead, she turned the conversation back to the Teapot Traits and what they meant. ("Fletcher always said that his Traits were *ridiculously handsome* and *just the cleverest person to ever walk the Earth*," Trick told Harper. "But I think he was joking.")

Harper could feel sleepiness overcoming her, and she yawned widely. Trick pointed her to one of the yurts, and as she pulled back the flap, she found a cosy little camp bed within.

"'Night." Trick grinned and headed to the next yurt. "See you tomorrow!"

"Goodnight!" Harper beamed.

She took off her boots and climbed into bed. She closed her eyes, listening to the chatter of the Spectaculars outside as they laughed and joked. She smiled to herself as she realized that this time, she wasn't listening to voices through a brick wall – these voices were right next to her, and belonged to people who might soon be her closest friends. With this thought warming her from the inside out, Harper turned over and dropped off into the deepest sleep she'd had for years.

CHAPTER SIX

Studies in Stardust

The next morning, Harper emerged from her yurt to the delicious smell of sausages. Outside, the sleeping bags and camp beds were swiftly being replaced with striped deckchairs and copper kettles whistling cheerfully over the fire. Spectaculars and apprentices alike were frying sausages and pouring steaming mugs of tea.

"Morning!" Trick called from a nearby deckchair.

"Morning," Harper replied with an excited grin. Grabbing another chair, she dragged it towards the fire until it was next to Trick's.

"Fletcher just came by. All new apprentices need to gather on the stage of the main Auditorium in an hour for our first-day briefing," Trick said, handing her a plate.

A mixture of anticipation and apprehension rose up

inside Harper. Part of her couldn't wait to get started, while a more anxious part was remembering the time she'd tried to learn to play the recorder – a brief hobby which had ended with Harper's neighbours forming the Union Against Wind Instruments and formally voting to have said recorder removed from the premises.

Shaking off her worries, Harper quickly began filling a plate with food, while Trick poured her a mug of—

"Sorry, *what* is that?" Harper wrinkled her nose at the forest-green liquid.

"Pine tea," he replied. "Try it. It's great, honest."

Harper did try it, expecting it to be sludgy and mossy; but it turned out pine tea had a fresh, sweet taste like sugar-frosted mint. Trick added six spoonfuls of sugar to his cup. Harper declined to copy him.

As she ate and drank, she stole glances at the other apprentices who were gathered around the fire. Anvi Patel was there, chattering eagerly about what the coming day would bring. The girl with the plum bob who'd gone first in the initiation was sat with a mirror, painting black stars at the corners of her eyes with the kind of easy style that Harper knew she could never pull off herself. She could scarcely believe that normally at this time she'd be setting off through the smoke-drenched streets for a day of rigid lessons and sneering teachers. As she reached for a hash brown, she wondered if her mum would try and make up some excuse for her absence, or whether she'd simply tell them the truth and watch them all faint away in horror.

"Excuse me. That's mine, I think you'll find."

Harper turned to see a girl with a pale, pinched face and slicked-back hair. The girl was scowling fiercely at Harper.

"Sorry?" Harper asked.

"I want that hash brown. So, hand it over."

Harper frowned, disliking the girl's tone. "Who are you, the warden of breakfast?"

There were a couple of gasps from the other apprentices. The girl bent down so that her face was level with Harper's.

"Maybe I should clarify," she said sweetly. "My name is Althea Reed. My mum is Demeter Reed of the Spectacular Orchestral Society, and my dad is Wallace Reed, Governor of the Spectacular Board of Theatrics."

"Right," Harper replied. "Um…good for your dad?"

Althea's eyes narrowed. "My parents are important people. Which means" – her voice hardened – "that I get what I want. And I want that hash brown."

There was a dead silence around them as Harper and Althea glared at each other. Then Harper raised the hash brown to her mouth and took a giant, deliberate bite.

"Mm. Delicious."

Trick tensed beside her, as though he were getting ready to jump up. Anvi whimpered slightly. Althea, however, smiled.

"You're that girl they just dragged up from the Smoke, aren't you? I suppose I should say welcome – but I expect you'll be gone soon enough. It's not like you're ever really going to be one of us." With a final glare, the girl turned and swept away.

Harper looked at Trick. "Who was *that*?"

"Althea Reed," Trick replied. "Her whole family are an unpleasant lot. Ignore her. Anyway – let's go, it should be starting soon!"

Harper cleared away her plate and followed Trick as he wove through the crowd, stopping in front of the tram she'd seen last night. Fletcher and a group of Spectaculars were walking up and down the vehicle, inspecting the carriages and shouting instructions to each other. Harper blinked. She remembered Fletcher saying that the Wondria had been converted from the tram that they'd escaped the Smoke in; but how could a tram become a theatre?

Fletcher did one final check-over, then nodded. He walked forwards and pulled a lever on the back of the last tram carriage.

As one, the carriages began to move and expand. They slid inwards, turning vertically and slotting on top of each other like pieces of an immense, three-dimensional puzzle. Seams melted flawlessly together, wheels retracted in a shower of sparks, and after mere moments Harper found herself looking at an enormous, grand building. It had a two-tiered domed roof, and two arched towers flanking it on either side. Fancy letters above the main entrance spelled out: *The Grand Wondria Music Hall and Theatre*. Harper felt a thrill of excitement run through her as she read the words. This was the place where she was going to be living and studying for the next five years, the place that was somehow going to transform her from ordinary Harper Woolfe into a *Spectacular*. At least, she hoped so: she was all too aware that she'd never displayed an ounce of magic in her life, unless you counted her excellent apple-crumble-making skills.

The new intake of apprentices started streaming towards the entrance, and Harper and Trick were pulled along with them, through the doors and into the Wondria itself. The lobby had a marble floor and a painted ceiling depicting clouds and cherubs. A pair of large golden doors stood beneath a sign reading *Auditorium*, while two sets of red-carpeted staircases at either end of the lobby led to the *Teaching Wing* and the *Living Wing* respectively. Trick led the way up the right-hand set of stairs, before pausing outside a blue door with a sign that read: *Apprentice Quarters*.

"Do the adults have different quarters?" Harper asked.

"Yeah, up there." Trick nodded to another staircase. "There are staff quarters and family quarters – that's where I lived with Fletcher. They were okay, although Fletcher snored like a tram engine. Beyond there, there's only the Sky Vaults."

"The *Sky Vaults*?"

"They're not in the sky – obviously. They just call them that because they're inside the domes, at the highest point of the Wondria. It's where they store all the old sets and costumes that they haven't managed to get rid of yet. No one ever goes up there."

The blue door led through to a series of rooms. The first was large and cheerful, dotted with beanbags, hammocks and cosy sofas. An archway led to a mess room, which hosted a long wooden table lined by an array of mismatching chairs, and beyond this were a pair of glass doors that opened out to a large balcony hung with fairy lights and glass lanterns.

"We've got half an hour till we have to be in the Auditorium," said Trick. "Do you want to see your room?"

"Definitely." Harper nodded. She was quite keenly aware that underneath the coat Fletcher had given her, she was still wearing her pyjamas.

They ducked under another archway which led to row upon row of doors, stacked all the way up the wall. A series of ladders – some leading up, some leading across, some rolling on wheels this way and that – had been leaned against them. Harper scanned the doors, her eyes alighting on one with her name written across it. She scrambled up the nearest ladder (a difficult task, as it seemed to have a sense of humour and kept rolling away from her door handle) and eventually stepped through into a small but cosy bedroom. There was a little bed piled with blankets, a writing desk, and a carved oak wardrobe. Investigating the wardrobe, she found a neat blue shirt and black trousers, with a note attached that read *Apprentice Uniform*. Harper donned them both, then reached into her backpack and took out the little bow tie her mum had given her, fastening it around her neck. She looked at herself in the mirror with a swell of pride, wishing that both her parents could be here to see this.

She met back up with Trick in the mess room, and together they made their way down to the lobby and through the gold doors into the Auditorium. This was a cavernous space, with four levels of plush chairs, a huge stage framed by heavy red curtains and a glittering chandelier dripping with crystals. Harper gaped in awe as they filed up on to the stage, where Fletcher was stood, beaming. He was accompanied by a boy in his late teens, with fair, freckled skin and a mop of brown hair. Harper looked around at the assembled apprentices. This was it: the big, extended family that Fletcher had promised. Would they be welcoming, as Fletcher had implied? Or would they all sneer at her, as Althea had?

"Hello, new apprentices!" Fletcher called when they were all assembled. "Welcome to your first day at the Wondria! As you know, my name is Fletcher; I'm the Showrunner of the Wondria. That means that I organize the shows, arrange tour schedules, oversee the teaching, and only occasionally scream into a paper bag. This here –" he gestured to the young man behind him – "is Lori Montgomery, my assistant. We'll be sorting you into three different groups, which will remain the same throughout your years as Junior Apprentices. When I call your names, please step forwards."

"Group One: Trick Torres, Rosie Wrenright, Harper Woolfe…"

Harper and Trick grinned at each other and took a step, along with the girl with the plum bob and the black stars on her face.

"Anvi Patel, Bernie Maddon, Althea Reed…"

Harper wasn't sure who groaned the loudest – her, Trick or Althea herself. Althea shot a disgusted look at Harper before gliding forwards and joining their group.

Fletcher read off several more names, bringing their group number up to ten, then pointed them towards a wooden door that led off the stage. "Group One, your leader will be Chancellor Lahiri. She'll meet you up in Practice Room One."

The ten apprentices of Group One walked towards the door at the side of the stage, which Rosie Wrenright pulled open to reveal a rickety staircase that spiralled upwards. They climbed the stairs, emerging onto a narrow corridor lined with practice rooms. Practice Room One was a bright, airy room, set out with a line of chairs. Chancellor Lahiri was already there, stood behind a low wooden table. She cut a very impressive figure: thick black hair coiled atop her head, deep brown skin and sharp amber eyes. Lahiri motioned for them to sit on the chairs, and Harper sat down on the front row between Trick and Rosie Wrenright, who gave Harper a friendly smile.

"Welcome," Lahiri announced. "Today, you begin your training as Spectaculars. It is a complex business – intricate, dangerous and occasionally prone to unexpected explosions."

"*Explosions*?" Althea piped up.

"If opposite types of Star-Stuff interact, they can cause explosions. You'll need to learn which types not to mix – which is precisely what we'll be starting with."

"Can't we start with something easy?" Althea demanded. "My father – Wallace Reed – would not be happy if I came home with my eyebrows singed off or something. He could have you *fired*."

Lahiri rounded on her. "Easy, you want, is it? Well, it wasn't easy to graduate top of my class back in the Smoke. It wasn't easy to become the youngest-ever Artistic Director of the Prodigious Players. It wasn't easy to complete my teacher training, plan my wedding to my wife and teach myself to cook all in one year, but you know what? I'm here, I'm married and I'm a dab hand at a shepherd's pie. If you're looking for easy, you know where the door is."

Althea turned her head away, but the tips of her ears turned red. Harper grinned delightedly up at Lahiri, who had rapidly become her new hero.

"Right. If you're all ready to begin, you can get collected by your aprons," Lahiri continued, sweeping her arm towards a row of patterned aprons hanging on pegs. As Harper and the others walked up and down inspecting them curiously, Harper suddenly found one with a scarlet check draping itself over her head, the fabric huddling against her like an enthusiastic puppy.

"It likes you!" Trick grinned.

Harper noticed with no small amount of glee that none of the aprons seemed to want to pair themselves with Althea. She strode along, scowling at all of them until eventually, one apron seemed to elbow another, and a rather uninspired grey stripe flopped itself half-heartedly over Althea's head.

"Now, I think we should start with the basics, to make sure that everyone is up to speed," Lahiri began. Harper felt sure that this was for her benefit, but she was grateful to Lahiri for not singling her out.

"As Spectaculars, we work with Star-Stuff: starlight and stardust, specifically," Lahiri explained. "There are two different branches of Spectacular magic: Mechanics and Theatrics. You will be learning the basics of both of these today."

Lahiri bent down towards a bag at her feet. "The first method of using Star-Stuff is to work it through a material. You can apply Star-Stuff to anything – metal, fabric, wood – and it will give that material Spectacular properties. For example…" She reached into the bag and pulled out a square of black silk in one hand, and shimmering silver thread in the other. If Harper squinted at the thread, she could see that it was thrumming gently, as if awaiting instruction. Lahiri's hands started to move. In quick, deft strokes, she pulled the thread through the material, gathering edges and stitching ends, until she'd sewn it into the rough shape of a pair of wings. She held them briefly, then tossed them into the air. In a beating of wings, the silk became a crow, which flew upwards and perched on her shoulder.

"See?" Lahiri said as the apprentices muttered appreciatively. "First, you must set your intention: you must know what it is you want the Star-Stuff to do for you, or you'll just confuse it. Then you apply the Star-Stuff to a material, giving it a channel – in this case, the silk – and thus, you create a Spectacular object. This is how our costumes, lights and sets are made, and we call it the branch of Mechanics. Your Mechanics training will take place around the Wondria with a variety of teachers – Captain Roper in the Costume Department, Dame Juma in Lumineering, Master Tulsia in the Scenery Workshop, and so on."

Harper felt a great rush of relief. Mechanics, at least, sounded familiar to her, so perhaps she wouldn't be completely out of her depth.

"Now, the most important thing when it comes to Mechanics is to be confident handling Star-Stuff. So…"

Lahiri bent down and retrieved a battered leather suitcase from under the table. She clicked it open and turned it around to face them.

Harper uttered a soft "Oh" of awe. Strapped to the underside of the suitcase lid was a line of glass jars. Some of them held bright, shining lights, swirling gently around like tiny galaxies. Others contained a fine, silvery dust, as delicate as powdered snow.

There was a small crush to get to the suitcase, and then the jars were being passed around. Trick chucked Harper a jar of stardust, and she unscrewed the lid immediately, gazing down at the shimmering substance inside.

"How do you collect it?" Harper asked, running her hand gently through the dust.

"We have collection stations built at the highest points of the Hidden Peaks," Lahiri explained. "They have all sorts of methods for Star-Stuff retrieval – nets and suction devices, and Kobolds who transform themselves into giant brooms and sweep up the Star-Stuff in the air around them."

"My mum said there's been a shortage of Star-Stuff since the Falling," Anvi piped up. "Is that true?"

"Not at all," replied Lahiri. "There is still plenty of Star-Stuff."

"Sorry," Harper chimed in. "The Falling?"

"Of stars!" Anvi exclaimed. "It happened the night we arrived here, five years ago – thirteen actual stars fell out of the sky, all at once!"

"Thirteen?" Althea Reed snorted. "More like fifty!"

"My gran said she only counted three," said Rosie from Harper's other side.

"It was thirteen." Lahiri quickly headed off the debate. "That was verified by the Council. There are thirteen Fallen Sites across the Hidden Peaks, where the stars landed."

Harper frowned. "How did it happen?"

"There was some sort of – magical disturbance," said Lahiri. "Who knows – perhaps the impact of us breaching the gateways all at once sent shock waves through the sky."

"And – what happened to the stars?" Harper asked.

"Once they reached Earth?"

"No one knows," Lahiri replied. "It's the strangest thing – we all saw them fall, all saw them reach Earth, but since then no one's ever seen one. It's like they disappeared."

Harper felt a thrill at her words. Thirteen *actual* stars, somehow out there in the world? She wondered what they'd look like, what they'd *feel* like if you got close to one.

For the rest of the morning, Lahiri took them through a lesson on how to handle Star-Stuff and combine it in a way that wouldn't cause explosions. (Harper was a *little* disappointed by this – she'd been rather hoping to see Althea Reed with her eyebrows singed off.) When the bell rang for lunch, they returned to the apprentice quarters. Lunch had been provided by Helja – and sour-tempered though the Kobold might be, she was an *excellent* cook. Harper was soon full to bursting with hot bacon rolls and buttered biscuits.

She was glad she'd fortified her stomach, because the afternoon was a *lot* harder.

"The second branch of Spectacular magic is called Theatrics," Lahiri explained. "Theatrics involves manipulating the Star-Stuff in the air around us."

"In the *air around us*?" Anvi squinted comically into the middle distance.

"It isn't visible," said Lahiri with a wry grin. "By the time Star-Stuff gets to ground level, it's dispersed to the point where it's invisible to the human eye. However, you should be able to *feel* it, and therefore, direct it. In this instance, the channel that you give Star-Stuff to work through is yourself – your voice, your music, your movements. This is how Spectacular singers, musicians and dancers work."

This time when Lahiri delved into the bag at her feet, she came up with a candle and a small mandolin. She set the candle on the desk, placed the mandolin on her lap and strummed the strings.

The sound that came from the mandolin was soft and clear, and Harper felt the hairs on the back of her neck stand up. But the sound wasn't the most incredible thing – as Lahiri played, a tiny flicker sparked into life on the candle. It grew steadily, until it was a fat flame dancing about cheerfully on the wick.

"You *set it on fire!*" Harper said in a hushed voice.

"Technically, Star-Stuff did," Lahiri corrected her. "I simply set the intention – to light the candle, and gave it a channel to work through – the music.

"Now, Theatrics can be trickier than Mechanics, as you need a clear, calm mind in order to influence Star-Stuff. Because of that, your Theatrics training will take place with one specialized teacher – namely, me. For today, we're going to focus on being able to tune into the presence of Star-Stuff around us."

Harper knew immediately that she was going to have trouble with this. Her mind didn't err towards calm: it chattered and whispered, and rarely shut up. Still, she followed suit when she saw the other apprentices closing their eyes.

Okay, she thought. *Clear mind.*

It was devilishly tricky. Every time Harper thought she'd managed to clear her mind, unpleasant images would suddenly appear: her mother sat alone in an empty flat, Althea's smirking face, Fletcher waving her onto a canoe and banishing her back to the Smoke...

Harper took a breath and brought her hand up to rest against her dad's bow tie. Feeling the silk against her fingers calmed her somewhat. Keeping her hand where it was, Harper closed her eyes and tried again.

And – *there.* Harper felt a strange sensation against her skin. It felt cool and sharp, like freezing water, or a biting wind, or a bolt of lightning. Harper gasped, her eyes flying open, and at once, the sensation disappeared.

"Interesting, isn't it?" Lahiri nodded to her. "I always think it feels like stepping into a cold shower – invigorating, but not altogether pleasant."

It *wasn't* altogether pleasant, Harper agreed. There was something wild about the energy that she'd felt: Harper couldn't imagine trying to *control* it.

By the end of the afternoon, Harper was exhausted. As the final bell rang and they tramped back to the apprentice quarters, all she could think about was a vat of hot chocolate and a bath with a frankly ridiculous level of bubbles.

Trick, however, had other ideas for their evening.

"All right, people." Trick clapped his hands at Harper, Anvi and Rosie, who had converged by the fire. "We have one hour to change, eat and get down to the lobby before it gets overrun with patrons. Go, go, go!"

"Wait," said Harper as the other two dashed for their rooms. "I mean – don't we have homework to do?"

"Harper," said Trick. "It's opening night of the new season. Trust me – you *don't* want to miss this."

Harper thought about Trick's descriptions of the Spectaculars' powers and decided that he was right: she most definitely did *not* want to miss that.

"All right." She grinned at Trick. "One hour."

CHAPTER SEVEN

Opening Night

Harper stood in her dressing gown, arms folded, staring into the contents of her wardrobe.

"*Really,*" she muttered. "This is ridiculous."

Upon arriving back in her room ("Fifty-nine minutes!" Trick had called at her retreating back), she'd investigated a door that she hadn't spotted that morning, and discovered a clean, bright bathroom with her own claw-footed bathtub, a sea glass shower cubicle and a cupboard filled with interesting-looking bottles (*Chameleon Hair Formula: creates up to 107 hairstyles in one use! Singing in the shower gel: three drops will have you belting like your favourite singer for up to an hour!*). After showering and wrapping herself up in her dressing gown, Harper had padded over to the wardrobe and opened it, only to be immediately half buried in the avalanche of clothes that had come bursting out. Apparently, her wardrobe had been restocked since the morning, and whoever had filled it (she suspected Fletcher) had a very over-the-top idea of what an eleven-year-old girl needed. She managed to fight her way out of the pile of garments until she could stand and look at the wardrobe sternly.

"A diver's helmet?" she asked the wardrobe, shaking her head. "A feathered cloak? A *ball gown*? Why on Earth would I need half of this stuff?"

The wardrobe, predictably, didn't answer.

Harper sighed and prepared herself for battle. Forcing her way through the absurd outfits (at one point she discovered a row of bejewelled cowboy boots and almost gave up completely), she thankfully managed to find an array of normal clothes in some pleasingly bright shades. She changed into a scarlet jumper and a turquoise skirt before climbing back down to meet Trick, Anvi and Rosie in the mess room. She found them huddled around one of the walls, which had been plastered in posters of various sizes.

"What's all this?" she asked Trick as she approached.

"Clubs and societies," Trick said gleefully. "I didn't even know there *were* this many!"

Harper peered at the posters on the wall. She noticed with interest that they were organized in sub-groups that corresponded to different Teapot Traits. Harper looked under the *Bold, Courageous, Daring* group and found, among other things, a tightrope-walking club, a knife throwers' association and a club which did live-action role play on weekends: *You too could fight your way through a fictional apocalypse while highly realistic zombies attempt to eat your face!* Rosie was examining an *Extreme Crocheting* poster filed under *Artistic, Creative*, while Trick had found a club under *Flair* that seemed to be dedicated to discussing the best death performances of famous Spectacular actors.

"My favourite was Jackson Chen," Trick informed Harper. "He was supposed to be poisoning himself next to the body of his dead lover, but he took so long about it that she got up and walked off stage – and he still carried on! What a legend."

Dinner arrived in the form of a large trolley being pushed by Helja the Kobold. As they sat down to a steaming noodle soup with big, fluffy dumplings, Harper turned to Rosie Wrenright, who tonight had painted several neon-coloured stripes into her sleek plum hair.

"Do your parents perform here?" Harper asked.

"No. My parents travel around different theatres for their jobs," Rosie replied. "Well. Mum travels – she's a make-up artist. Dad mostly stays at home and cooks *terrible* pies that we all have to pretend to enjoy."

"My mum works here!" Anvi chimed in eagerly. "She's a song-mistress – her speciality is growing things with her voice. On my seventh birthday she made a whole field of sunflowers grow up through my bedroom floor. It was *amazing*! I hope I've inherited it…"

Rosie looked at Harper carefully. "Your parents...they're not Spectaculars?"

"My dad was," Harper replied. "But my mum isn't. She's a terrible singer – she'd be more likely to kill a flower than grow one with her voice." The others laughed, and Harper hoped fervently that she hadn't inherited her mother's singing ability.

After dinner they left the apprentice quarters and made their way down to the lobby, which was already a hive of activity. Fletcher was piling glossy programmes on top of a large merchandise stand, while in the fancy Gilded Bar, black-and-white-uniformed staff were constructing a precarious-looking pyramid of champagne flutes. Performers in various stages of costume and make-up were milling around, fetching last-minute jugs of water and trying to peek at how many patrons were gathered outside. Two men were having a heated debate about the running order of the show, and Harper leaned in curiously to hear their argument.

"*We* want to open to the second act. We've just finished the immersive scenery for our new show; it transforms the whole Auditorium into a beach – sand, seagulls and all!"

"What, so afterwards the rest of us have to perform while trying to avoid rogue seagull poo? Not a chance. We have instruments that literally *levitate people out of their seats*, it's the perfect thing to open the second act with!"

Harper's heart stuttered slightly as she looked at the man who had just spoken. He was dressed smartly in a sapphire-blue suit and clutched in his hand was a polished trombone.

"Um – sorry," she said, causing both men to stop and stare at her. "Did you say you had instruments that made people levitate?"

The man with the trombone huffed. "Yeah."

"It's just – my dad used to be in a band like that." Harper felt oddly nervous. "Michael Woolfe?"

The man's eyes lit up. "As I live and breathe – you're never his little girl?"

Harper nodded, and a grin split across the man's face. "Harper! Little Harper! Blimey, you were no taller than my knees when I last saw you! Right little one you were, you and that blue-haired mate of yours were always nicking our instruments."

Trick pretended to be very interested in the merchandise stand. Harper laughed. "Sorry."

"Not to worry. I'm Yosef – Yosef Jones. Your dad was my best mate." He shook Harper's hand with a wide smile. "You ever need help, I've got you covered, all right? Me and the rest of the boys."

"Thanks." Harper ducked her head, her cheeks pinkening.

"Right – I best be off. Still need to tune the old trombone before the show." Yosef winked, then made for the Auditorium doors.

"Good fortune!" Harper called after him as he hurried off.

It had been a fairly innocuous thing to say as far as Harper was concerned – it was what everyone in the Smoke said before business meetings or games of cards – so she was somewhat confused by the looks of mingled amusement and horror that followed her comment. Trick and Rosie were grinning as though she'd told a great joke, but Anvi and several other nearby Spectaculars were staring at her as though she'd just let off a stink bomb in the lobby.

"Muses," Althea's voice echoed through the lobby. "Did she really just say *that*? On opening night?" She approached them with a pitying look on her face. "You really don't know *anything* about Spectaculars, do you?"

"What's wrong with saying good fortune?" Harper frowned. "It's a *nice* thing to say."

"Not on opening night it isn't," Althea replied. "Not unless you think it's *nice* to doom the entire theatre and everyone in it."

Harper blinked. "Excuse me?"

"It's only a superstition," Trick chimed in, rolling his eyes. "Some people think that saying *that* on opening night will attract great forces of ill luck to the theatre."

"Oh, excellent," Harper groaned.

"Don't worry, most people don't really believe that stuff," Rosie said.

"All superstitions are rooted in truth," Althea shot back. "You just wait."

She swept past them before Harper had a chance to reply,

pulling a programme out of the bottom of Fletcher's display and causing the rest of them to fall.

"Ignore her," said Trick. "She's just trying to freak you out."

"So, what am I *supposed* to say before a show?" Harper asked.

"You're supposed to say, 'May you be cursed with the stings of a thousand bees and may your toes be chewed off by wolves'," Trick informed her.

Harper stared. "And *that's* better to say than what I said?"

"Yup."

Harper shook her head. This was a very strange place.

As they passed through the golden doors into the Auditorium, Harper couldn't help but stare again at the plush red seats, the crimson curtains, the sheer size of the stage. She felt a pang of regret for those old theatres back in the Smoke, sitting empty and abandoned with no one to use them.

Instead of settling in any of the chairs, Trick led the way through a side door and up a set of narrow steps. It was dingy and dark, but eventually they emerged on a ledge high above the audience, where the spotlights were operated by a group of Lumineers.

"This is a way better view – you get to spy on the audience as well as the performers!" Trick whispered.

Harper quickly saw why you'd want to spy on the audience. As the doors to the Auditorium were thrown open and patrons began to flood in, it became clear that they'd all dressed up for opening night. Men and women alike sported tuxedo jackets, feathered headdresses and reams of sparkling jewellery. One man wore a tasselled suit with a velvet lampshade as a hat, while the woman on his arm had paired a ball gown with a biker helmet.

"Are they all Spectaculars?" Harper asked, scanning the crowd below.

"No – we get Witches, Fae-Folk, Kobolds and all the rest coming to the shows as well," Trick replied. He pointed to a couple wearing glittering carnival masks. "They're Fae. You can tell, 'cos it's tradition for them to wear masks in public. *She's* a Witch, though." He nodded to a woman with a waterfall of rainbow-striped hair that reached to her knees. "Witches go everywhere barefoot. Painful, if you ask me, but there you are."

Once they were all seated, Fletcher strode out onto the stage.

"Welcome, friends and patrons!" he announced. "It is my great pleasure to welcome you all to opening night of the Autumn Season here at the Grand Wondria Music Hall and Theatre! We have a truly excellent line-up of acts tonight, so without further ado – let the show begin!"

The lights went down, and Harper felt a frisson of excitement. She wondered if, back before the accident, she'd ever sat like this waiting for her dad's band to come onstage.

Up first was a woman in an elaborate gold dress, who positioned an ornate mirror on the stage and proceeded to sing a soaring duet with her own reflection. Next was a group of actors who performed a murder mystery, transforming their appearances every time they changed character (one man managed to play a rich old widow, an international spy, a dashing young sailor and, at one point, a three-headed dragon). A musician played an organ that shot green flames out of its pipes, a couple in silver body paint waltzed on a giant crescent moon, and a comedy act performed alongside a series of balloons which responded to the audience's laughter, gradually swelling with each guffaw until they popped and showered them all with glittering confetti. Harper's eyes grew wider and wider with each act, her grin almost splitting her face in two.

After a few more acts, Trick leaned over to whisper, "Shall we go and check out the rest?"

Harper raised her eyebrows. "The rest?"

The four of them crept carefully back along the ledge and down the stairs, exiting through a door that took them backstage. Here, the air smelled of hairspray and oranges, and Harper was surprised to see several patrons wandering around, peering into doors and murmuring excitedly to each other. Lori Montgomery, Fletcher's assistant, appeared at the bottom of a stairwell.

"Lady Roberta Helix and her ravishing reflection are ready to receive fans in Dressing Room One," he announced. "They will be giving autographs, but ask that you keep your bouquets and/or extravagant gifts to one per person."

Harper was about to laugh, until she noticed that there was indeed quite the queue of patrons, bearing elaborate floral arrangements and ribbon-wrapped gifts.

Unlike a traditional theatre show where people took their seats at the beginning and stayed there until the end, people at the Wondria were free to come and go from the Auditorium as they pleased, watching the acts they liked and spending the rest of the time exploring the backstage areas. Down in the Costume Department, Harper watched as guests tried on powdered wigs that enabled them to sing opera and furry cloaks that transformed them into fully-grown yetis. In the Workshop, immersive scenery was being built, allowing patrons to wander around elaborate model cities or landscapes that moved and changed around them. Once they'd explored all of these, they returned to the Front of House, where the Gilded Bar served cocktails decorated with rose petals and sparklers, and patrons buzzed around the merchandise stands buying books about the history of the Spectaculars, or little models of the Wondria.

Finally, on aching feet, they returned to the apprentice quarters. Once inside, they all sat around the fire and launched into an in-depth discussion of everything they'd seen that evening. As they did so, Harper began jotting down all the details, so that she'd remember everything when she came to write a letter to her mum.

It took longer than she expected to write about everything she'd seen. Trick went to bed first, yawning and ruffling his hair, and Anvi and Rosie followed shortly after. Harper was the last person left by the time she finished the last description. She was just stretching out her writing hand when she was distracted by a strange scuffling sound outside. Frowning, she looked towards the glass doors that led out to the balcony. For a moment there was quiet, and then she heard it: an immense clanging, a crash, and then the sound of something running away from the Wondria.

Harper darted out to the balcony. Several of the lanterns had been knocked to the ground, their glass panes smashed, metal frames twisted all out of shape. On the ground next to them was a strange mark. It was shaped like… Harper leaned closer, frowning. Like a paw print of some kind, as though a large animal had been standing there just moments before. Harper took another glance around but whatever had made the print was gone.

"What's going on out here?"

Harper whipped around to find Althea standing at the balcony doors, peering at her. She wore a pair of frilly pyjamas, and her hair was rolled up into a series of pink curlers.

"Nothing," Harper replied quickly. "I was just…"

Unfortunately, Althea had already spotted the mess.

"What happened?" she demanded, her eyebrows rising up towards her hairline. "What did you do?"

"I didn't do anything!" Harper protested. "It just… happened."

Althea turned her piercing eyes on Harper, her expression accusatory. The conversation from earlier floated into Harper's head, unpleasantly clear and sharp.

Forces of ill luck.

Althea sighed, as if she could read Harper's mind. "I suppose that's just the start," she said mournfully.

"It's not the start of anything," Harper snapped. "It was an accident. The wind probably blew them down or something…"

Suddenly, a terrible groaning sound came from their left. Harper whipped her head around to see one of the metal poles that held up the strings of fairy lights swaying slightly. To her horror, it gave another groan – then began to fall forwards, right towards them.

"Watch out!" Harper shoved Althea out of the way, jumping aside herself just seconds before the entire pole crashed to the ground, pulling the fairy lights down with it. They lay tangled among the broken lanterns, flickering on and off erratically.

"Ow!" Althea complained. "You made me stub my toe!"

Harper looked at her incredulously. "I just stopped you getting your brains smashed in by a metal pole! I think that would have been worse than stubbing your toe."

"I wouldn't have been in any danger of getting my brains smashed in the first place if you hadn't brought bad luck down on our theatre!" Althea shot back.

Harper found that she had no comeback to this. She

stared around at the mess on the balcony – the tangle of lights, the ruined lanterns, the shattered glass everywhere – and a small, traitorous part of her brain wondered if Althea was right. *Had* she caused this?

"I'll – I'll go and get Helja," Harper said, her voice wavering slightly. She turned away from Althea and climbed back into the apprentice quarters, heading for the exit. It was hardly going to improve her relations with the Kobold, turning up after midnight to say that she needed help clearing up some smashed lights, but at least it got her away from Althea's smug face.

It's just a superstition, she told herself firmly as she walked. *This was just an accident. It's just a coincidence.*

Harper thought that if she told herself enough times, she could *probably* believe it was true.

CHAPTER EIGHT

The Four Curses

Despite the fact that the Wondria was a travelling theatre, Harper soon found a sort of routine to life in the Hidden Peaks. The apprentices' weekdays were spent scattered across the theatre, in lessons which surpassed Harper's wildest imaginings. Their morning "Warm-Up" sessions were held on a cavernous subterranean floor with no fewer than *five* sunken stone swimming pools, filled with steaming, lemon-and-honey scented water ("To literally warm the voice," Lahiri told them). In the grand Music Parlour, they tried out a variety of musical instruments, which could do anything from summoning a swarm of emerald dragonflies to conjuring up the precise feeling of the first bite of a warm scone on a chilly morning. Their sessions with the Costume Mistress, Roper – who turned out to be the woman who'd recognized

Harper in the Smoke – saw them learning how to construct costumes that would enable the wearer to levitate, sprout extra limbs, or turn invisible.

The most confusing thing was the travelling: the Wondria usually moved to its next location overnight, seamlessly transforming from theatre to tram and back again, and on more than one occasion Harper went to bed in her room in the apprentice quarters, only to wake up in the middle of the night in a moving carriage.

The only real sore spot in her new life was Althea Reed, who'd still not forgiven Harper for what Trick had dubbed "The Great Hash Brown Showdown" – not to mention what had come after. She'd formed her own little clique with Bernie Maddon and a girl named Khyla Griffin, and all three of them seemed to have taken against Harper.

It didn't take long for their growing animosity to come to a head. They were – aptly – in a stage fighting class, with a Spectacular named Tyger. (He never gave a title, nor did he indicate whether Tyger was his first or last name; "Just Tyger will do," he'd said mysteriously.)

The array of Spectacular stage weapons was fascinating. There were swords which produced clouds of fog whenever they clashed, silhouetting the duellers against a dramatic backdrop of smoke; jewelled daggers that could carry on a duel by themselves as their respective fighters had a cup of tea at the side of the stage; and weapons that were built for comedy, and changed shape every time they clashed. (Tyger had given them a demonstration and had ended up fighting with a leek, then a feather duster, then a plastic flamingo.)

When Tyger announced that they'd be practising in pairs, Harper took an automatic step towards Trick, but Tyger reached for the register instead, scanning the names quickly.

"Trick with Rosie...Anvi with Khyla...Harper with Althea..."

Harper's stomach dropped and she heard Trick give a little "oof" of sympathy next to her. Grim-faced, Harper turned to Althea and indicated an empty corner of the room.

"Shall we...?"

Althea didn't reply, but stalked over to the weapons table to grab a ruby dagger. Harper hastily followed her, feeling quite strongly that she didn't want to be unarmed while Althea was brandishing a small sword (even if, according to Tyger, their weapons had been enchanted to "pop like bubbles" if they came into contact with skin). She picked up the only weapon left – a neat little mace – and turned to Althea.

"Look, Althea," she said. "I know we didn't exactly get off to the best start, but—"

She cut herself off with a yell as Althea suddenly lunged forwards with the dagger. Harper automatically brought round her mace to defend herself, and as the weapons clashed together a shower of bright blue sparks flew off them.

"What was that?" Harper hissed, her heart starting to beat a little faster.

"What? Struggling to keep up?" Althea asked, whirling her dagger round again. Harper ducked, glancing around the room. Tyger was at the opposite end, helping Anvi.

"Is this all because of breakfast that first day?" she asked. "'Cos if you're prepared to try to murder someone over a hash brown, I think that you *might have some issues*."

"Please. I don't care about *that*," Althea snorted. "But I *do* care about you bringing bad luck down on all our heads – *literally*, in some cases."

Until today, neither Harper nor Althea had told anyone about what had happened on opening night. Harper tried to tell herself that it was because it wasn't worth mentioning; but deep down, she was worried that Althea was right – that she had brought ill fortune to the theatre, and everyone would shun her if they knew. Harper had absolutely no illusions that Althea was keeping the secret for Harper's sake; she was simply holding on to it, waiting for the opportune moment to use it.

Harper tightened her grip around her mace. "That wasn't my fault! The lights falling was an *accident* – an accident that I saved you from, if I remember rightly."

"Accident, my left foot!" Althea scoffed. "It was the forces of ill luck – the ones that *you* brought here. And it'll only get worse from now on. You should *never have come here*."

She brought her dagger wheeling forwards, slamming against Harper's mace so hard that Harper dropped her weapon with another yell.

"Bit heavy-handed there, Miss Reed!" Tyger called from across the room.

"Ooh, sorry," Althea simpered. "It's just so exciting!"

Tyger clearly wasn't convinced by this as he stayed close to them for the rest of the session, to Harper's great relief. When the bell rang for lunch, she traipsed up to the apprentice quarters in a subdued manner, trying not to let Althea's taunts get to her.

"Harper, I'm telling you," Trick said once she'd filled him in. "Slugs in the bed. It never fails. We can find a few nice, big, slimy ones, sneak into her room…"

The idea of this made Harper feel slightly better. But only just.

That afternoon they had a Theatrics session with Lahiri in Practice Room One. Dumping her backpack on the floor, Harper opened it to retrieve the homework they'd been set the day before. She frowned as her hand came into contact with something damp and sticky.

"What the…!"

Harper's jaw dropped as she drew out her homework. Concealing her neatly printed notes about Star-Stuff safety procedures were the words ILL LUCK painted across her sheet in thick black ink. Harper looked around, and sure enough, saw Althea, Khyla and Bernie all looking very pleased with themselves.

"You…"

Harper stepped forwards, just about ready to fling the lot of them out of the window, but Trick grabbed her jumper and held her back. Before Harper could do or say anything else, Lahiri swept into the room.

"Homework, please."

Harper shot an agonized look at Trick. "What am I going to do?"

In response, Trick shoved his own sheet of paper at her. At the top of the page, he'd quickly erased his name and written *Harper Woolfe* instead. Harper shook her head and tried to shove it back. "Don't be silly, you'll get into trouble."

"And if you don't hand your homework in on time, you'll whinge about it for the rest of the week."

Harper frowned. "I do not *whinge*."

When Lahiri reached them, Trick pulled a surprisingly convincing remorseful face. "I haven't got my homework, sorry."

Lahiri narrowed her eyes. "Do you have a good reason for not completing homework set by me? Did your writing arm fall off?"

Trick sighed. "Would you believe me if I said my dog ate it?"

"You don't have a dog."

"That's why it was such a shock."

"Detention, Torres," Lahiri said. She turned to Harper. "Miss Woolfe, is that yours?"

"It's hers," Trick said. "It's got her name on it and everything."

Lahiri gave them an odd look, but took the page and moved away.

Harper glanced guiltily at Trick. "Thank you," she said. "I owe you one."

"Do my homework for the rest of the year?"

"Absolutely not."

"Right. No sitting around today!" Lahiri said as she dumped their sheets on her desk. "We crossed over into the Brightwood district last night, which means…educational trip!" She smiled at them all. "This afternoon, we will be paying a visit to the Obelisk."

This prompted a lot of excited murmuring among the apprentices. Harper nudged Trick and asked quietly, "What's the Obelisk?"

"The biggest library in the Hidden Peaks," Trick replied.

Directed by Lahiri, they all lined up and filed down the staircase to the lobby and out of the main exit. On their way through the town, Lahiri pointed out red-brick college buildings covered with ivy and towering assembly halls with marble doorways. Harper couldn't help but stare at them all – they were as different from the ugly factories and belching chimneys of the Smoke as it was possible to be.

"The Brightwood district is one of the most academically advanced areas of the Hidden Peaks!" Lahiri informed them as they walked. "Scholars from all around the realm come to visit the prestigious universities, museums and observatories."

They made their way to the centre of the town, before rounding a corner and coming face to face with a tall stone building. Lahiri led them up a set of steps and pulled open a heavy oak door.

"Welcome to the Obelisk!" she said, ushering them inside.

Harper was expecting a grand building filled with elaborate shelves and row upon row of books. She was quite surprised, therefore, to be confronted with nothing but a tall stone hall, impressive in its scope and size, but decidedly empty.

Trick laughed at her expression. "Look up."

Harper did, and her mouth promptly dropped open in awe. There, high above their heads, was a twisting labyrinth of jam-packed shelves, floating in mid-air.

"How do we get up there?" she whispered to Trick. He pointed to a series of glass pipes that ran up and down the considerable height of the building. Each contained an old-fashioned elevator, manned by porters sporting scarlet jackets and hats.

"Floor Two: Classical Music and Dance!" one of the porters shouted. The doors of the lift sprang open, and several people stepped out into mid-air.

Harper squeaked in horror, expecting to see them plummet to a rather gruesome death, but instead, those who had stepped out simply began walking along in the air.

Harper squinted and saw that there was a series of glass

walkways stretching between the pipes, looping around the floating library and allowing people to explore among the shelves. In the centre of these walkways was a giant glass disc, upon which sat a help desk and a smattering of tables for people to sit and read.

"Right," Lahiri said, clapping her hands together. "We've got two hours in here. You're free to go to any floor and explore any subject."

Harper and Trick glanced at each other, then ran towards one of the elevators as it trundled to the ground floor.

"Where d'you want to go?" Trick asked.

Harper scanned the list of subjects inside the lift, her eyes flickering over several options before being drawn to one in particular.

Spectacular Folklore and Superstition.

Harper thought about opening night, about Althea's taunts and the message on her homework: *ILL LUCK.*

"*Spectacular Folklore and Superstition,* please," she said. The porter pulled a lever which sent them rolling smoothly up towards the floating bookshelves. When the doors opened, Harper recoiled slightly at the transparent walkways, but she quickly shook off the wave of vertigo and stepped out smartly onto the glass.

The walkway led between two rows of shelves, both crammed with books. Harper peered at as many as she could, reading some of the titles aloud.

"*The Curse of the Troll Trot: The Dance That Brought a Theatre to Its Knees.*"

"*Mayhem, Murder and Minuets: Unsolved Mysteries of the Ballroom Dancing Scene.*"

"*The Legend of Hermes Havelock: The Man Who Could Sing You to Death.*"

Harper continued to scan the titles, keeping a sharp eye for anything that mentioned theatre rituals or etiquette. She heard a burst of giggling and turned to find a large group of students sporting Brightwood University jumpers. They were gathered around one particular collection, grinning wickedly as they flicked through the pages.

"Tornio Nocturne," Harper murmured, reading the cover of the book the students were holding. "Who's that?"

One of the students heard her and turned around to gape at Harper. "You don't know who *Tornio Nocturne* is?"

"He's a famous composer," Trick told Harper. "He wrote the opera of the Four Curses. It's based on this old kids' rhyme, about Four Curses who are said to haunt theatres and other Spectacular dwellings… How did it go…" Trick screwed up his face, then sang:

"*When Death comes, it comes on wings;*
Of misery, grief and woe it sings.
Discord thunders on cloven hooves,
Stamping out hope and destroying youth.
Malady scurries on tiny claws,
Striking in darkness till winter thaws.

Misfortune stalks its prey by night.
Beware Misfortune; beware its bite."

"Well, I'm sure that didn't give any children nightmares," Harper said drily.

"Yeah, bit miserable, isn't it?" Trick agreed. "So, Tornio Nocturne did what you do with all miserable stories – he turned it into an opera. There's murder, betrayal, gore…all the good stuff. Me and Fletcher have seen it five times."

Harper tried to run through the rhyme again. "So, the Four Curses are Death, Discord, Malady and…"

"Misfortune," a blonde student filled in for her. "A creature who causes terrible accidents everywhere he goes."

Harper felt an awful swooping sensation in her gut. *Misfortune* was about as close to *ill luck* as it was possible to get. A creature that caused accidents… Harper thought of the smashed lanterns, the paw print, the metal pole that had nearly decapitated her and Althea. Could *this* be what was happening? Had Harper drawn Misfortune to the Wondria?

"But – it's just a story, right?" she asked carefully. "The Four Curses aren't real?"

The blonde student looked slyly at her friends. "Depends who you ask…"

One of the boys rolled his eyes. "Not this again…"

"They've been seen," the blonde girl said, almost gleefully, turning back to Harper. "You remember the Winter Playhouse disaster?"

Harper answered "No" at the same time as Trick nodded: "Yes."

"The Winter Playhouse was the first theatre to get up and running after we crossed over to the Hidden Peaks." Trick filled her in.

"For the one-year anniversary of the crossing, they organized a special Winter Gala," the blonde student continued enthusiastically. "There were going to be all these cool performances and rides and stuff…but then, the Four Curses awoke. No one knows how or why, but they awoke – and Misfortune attacked the Winter Playhouse."

"My mum was there, she saw it!" another student piped up. "She said it looked like a giant cat, with huge claws and glowing eyes."

"There was pandemonium, obviously," said the blonde girl. "The crowd stampeded, the stages were destroyed, half the performers ended up running for their lives in their underwear…" She giggled, then sobered up. "It seemed like a bad omen, though – some mythical creature turning up and causing havoc on the anniversary of us coming here."

"So…has it been seen since then?" Harper asked.

"Allegedly. And not just Misfortune; the other Curses too. Malady, turning up as a giant rat in a theatre and causing a spate of illness. A sighting of an enormous black bird, followed by a death in the cast. There've been the odd few since the Winter Gala, but they've really started to snowball over the last few weeks or so – and no one knows why."

Harper's stomach twisted into an unpleasant knot. *She* knew why. After all, it'd only been a few weeks since her opening-night blunder. Was she the cause of all this? If she was, Althea Reed was going to have a field day.

"Are there any books about the Four Curses?" Harper asked.

The blonde student nodded. "Third row to the left."

Harper thanked her, then set off with Trick, turning left at the end of the row. Trick glanced at Harper. "You all right?"

"Yeah," Harper said quickly. She wanted to tell Trick about the print and the near-brain-squishing experience, but he clearly didn't think the Four Curses were real and she didn't want him to think she was being silly. She tried to shake off the anxiety pooling in her stomach, glancing back instead towards the students, who had started giggling again.

"Anyway, what's with all the giggling?" Harper asked.

"Ah. Well..." Trick grinned at the students' expressions. "Tornio Nocturne also happens to be – what does Rosie call it? 'Outrageously Good Looking'. She's got about seventeen posters of him up in her room. I *think* she sleeps with one under her pillow."

"Oh." Harper laughed, surprised. "That's – unexpected."

"Yeah. Nocturne's a recluse, though. He lives in some mansion in Raven Falls, and rarely makes public appearances – so books are as close as they'll get to seeing him."

When they reached the third row, Harper flicked through

a few titles before selecting one entitled *The Four Curses: The Stories, the Sightings, the Superstitions*. They had to return to the glass disc to check it out, where a librarian with purple, cat-eye glasses sat at a help desk. The librarian stamped the book and handed it back with a beaming smile.

"When you want to return it, just tell the book," she said. "It'll know what to do."

"Will it?" Harper glanced semi-nervously at the book in her hands. Thanking the librarian, she zipped the book into her backpack and she and Trick crossed over to an empty walkway. They began to weave their way through the shelves, but after just a few steps, Harper flung out an arm to stop Trick. "Do you hear that?"

Above the general chatter of the Obelisk, she could hear the sound of heavy, laboured breathing, as if someone had been running laps of the library. She glanced at Trick, who shrugged, and sidled closer to where the sound was coming from.

Peering around the corner, Harper saw a figure in an oversized coat crouched behind the bookshelf. He was panting slightly and checking frantically over his shoulder.

"Excuse me? Can we help you?"

The figure spun around to face them. He was an older teenage boy, with a generous quantity of gingery curls that fell forwards over his face, half concealing wide blue eyes and a rosy complexion. His feet were bare, which Harper assumed meant he was a Witch.

"Oh. Hello."

Harper glanced at Trick, who shrugged. "Um...are you all right?"

"Well, as you mention it, I've actually got a magical hunter chasing me through this very library intent on capturing me and probably chopping my head off, so you know...I've had better days."

Harper blinked. "You...what now?"

"I— Quick, get down!" The figure suddenly dived behind another bookshelf, motioning for Harper and Trick to do the same. They both ducked just as a tall, bulky figure appeared at the end of the walkway.

"Are you here, Thief?"

The second figure was one of the strangest-looking people Harper had ever seen. He wore a chequered suit which ballooned at the arms and legs, giving him the impression of having been filled with hot air. He was completely bald, but he had strange runes painted all over his head. He was smiling, but it was an unpleasant expression – the sort of smile that might invite you out for tea, then pickpocket you while you were enjoying your scones.

"Come on, Thief... If you come quietly then I'll make it nice and quick for you..." The figure paused for a moment, scanning the shelves, then turned and walked in the opposite direction. Once his footsteps had died away, Harper crawled out from behind the shelf.

"Well – I can't say I warmed to him." Trick frowned. "Although – have we seen him before somewhere?"

"I think I'd remember if we had." Harper shuddered before looking at the ginger boy. "I'm assuming that 'Thief' is you?"

"Hm – charming misnomer, isn't it?"

"So it isn't your real name?"

The boy fixed his eyes on her. "What's it to you?"

"Fine." Harper sighed. "So, why's he after you? Did you steal something from him?"

"Not technically. There was a...misunderstanding." Thief huffed. "I sold him a Witch spell, which apparently didn't work the way he wanted it to. He demanded his payment back, I refused and he got a little bit antsy about it. Apparently, he has a strict code – no snitches, no thieves, and anyone who crosses him gets their head lopped off. He's very particular about that one." He suddenly looked at Harper hopefully. "I don't suppose you have any spells on you? I'm all out. Disappearing-suddenly-in-a-puff-of-smoke? Running-faster-than-the-fastest-thing-that-ever-ran?"

"We're not witches," Trick replied. "We're Spectaculars."

"Oh." Thief looked down at their feet, both shod in boots. "Damn. Well...can't you sing me up a helpful explosion or something, to distract him?"

"We're only first-year apprentices," Harper admitted. "We can't do explosions."

"Oh. Bit useless then, aren't you?"

Harper folded her arms. "That was rude," she informed the boy before her.

"Was it?" Suddenly, Thief looked curious. "That's interesting. What was it that was rude, exactly – what I said, or the way I said it?"

"Um – well, both, I suppose?" Harper replied.

"Okay." Thief nodded. He reached into his pocket and took out a small notebook and pencil. Flipping the notebook open, he turned to a page that was titled, *Basic manners/ etiquette/how to not get punched in the face.* Very seriously, he inscribed the words *tone* and *no insults to people's faces.*

Harper didn't know what to make of this odd boy. "Okay. So without an explosion or a disappearing spell, how do we get you out of here without your friend noticing?"

"I don't think you can." Thief sighed. "Oh well. Me and my head had a good run."

Harper looked around, her mind cataloguing the layout of the library, the practicalities of the exits, and the likelihood of being caught.

"Ooh – I call this her plotting face," Trick said to Thief. "Plan incoming in three…two…one…"

Harper looked at Thief. "Can I borrow your coat?"

CHAPTER NINE

The Star-Hunter

Harper scurried along the glass walkway, Thief's grey coat flapping around her ankles. It was far too big on her, but she was counting on the hunter not taking too close a look at it. As she reached the main disc, she made sure to bring her boots down as loudly as she could – it was no mean feat to be heard above the chatter and bustle of the library.

Harper had barely stepped on the disc when she suddenly felt herself being swept upwards off her feet. Arms locked around her from behind, and an unpleasant voice hissed in her ear.

"There you are, Thief!"

Harper took a deep breath and mentally channelled everything she'd learned from watching the Spectaculars onstage. Then she opened her mouth and *screamed.*

"Help! I'm being kidnapped – HELP!!!"

The effect was instantaneous: the scholars and students seated at the surrounding tables all jumped up, running over and tackling the hunter to the ground.

"Oi!"

"What d'you think you're playing at?"

"Trying to kidnap a little girl!"

"Little girl?" The hunter looked at Harper, his eyes widening. "No – I wasn't – I was looking for someone else!"

"WHAT is going on over here?"

The librarian had ventured away from her desk and was glaring down at them.

"There was an attempted kidnapping, Mrs Baptiste!"

"Was there now?" Mrs Baptiste narrowed her eyes.

The hunter looked furious. "Let me go! Don't you know who I am?"

Mrs Baptiste waved a hand. "I don't give a hoot who you are. You can explain that to the authorities. Snoodge?" she called across the floor.

One of the porters who manned the elevators immediately stood to attention. He pulled a lever on the wall of the elevator, and the entire thing shot out from the pipe, skidding across the glass disc to arrive next to the crowd. Then he pressed a black button, and a large hole appeared in the floor of the elevator.

The porter addressed the pit politely. "The gentleman

in the chequered suit to the Brightwood Authority Station, please."

The black hole seemed to understand these instructions, and a loud suctioning noise suddenly filled the air. The hunter was lifted off his feet, limbs flailing in mid-air, before he was sucked straight into the hole.

"Yeah, in you get!" Mrs Baptiste said triumphantly. "Right, this young lady might have to go along too, no doubt the authorities will want a statement about what happened…"

But when she looked back, the girl was gone.

"That was excellent!" Thief whispered as Harper skidded back around the corner. "Amazing!" He looked between Harper and Trick. "Would a high five be appropriate for this situation? Is that still a 'thing', as it were?"

"Um…sure." Harper held up her hand for a high five.

"I feel like you could have given your character a *little* more backstory," said Trick. "I mean, sure, 'Help! Kidnapping!' gets the job done. But I personally would've gone with, 'Help, this man is the mortal enemy of my great-great-grandfather, and now he's come to exact bloodthirsty revenge upon our family!'"

"Well, you can do the acting roles in the future," Harper retorted. She looked at Thief. "So, this hunter – what spell did he try to buy off you?"

Thief pulled a face. "A tracking spell – he's hunting."

"Eugh." Harper scrunched up her nose. She remembered seeing the Minister and his buddies in the Smoke going hunting in their ridiculous outfits. "What was he hunting?"

"Stars."

Harper's eyes widened. "Sorry?"

"Fallen stars, to be precise. I assume you know about the incident, five years ago – when thirteen stars fell from the sky?"

"Yes." Harper frowned. Lahiri had said that the stars had disappeared almost as soon as they'd fallen, but Harper had never imagined that people would try to *hunt* them. "But – who'd want to hunt a fallen star?"

"I dunno. Alistair Sharpe, apparently."

Trick gasped. "Alistair Sharpe – I *knew* I recognized him!" He turned to Harper. "He was the leader of the Spectacular Society of Magicians."

"That bloke was a *Spectacular*?" Harper couldn't believe it. He was nothing like the Spectaculars she'd met so far.

"Yep. He and the rest of the Society were always experimenting with dangerous tricks: trying to use Star-Stuff to saw people in half, or make them disappear. They didn't often go well." Trick shuddered. "When we arrived in the Hidden Peaks, the Council put a blanket ban on Spectacular magicians. Alistair Sharpe and the rest of them were *not* happy about it."

"But – if he can't even work any more, why is he hunting a fallen star?"

Trick looked discomfited. "The Society of Magicians thought we should be going further with Star-Stuff. They weren't content with just dust and light; they thought we should be seeing if there's anything else we can siphon off to make Spectaculars even more powerful."

"So, he wants to find the star and use it to give himself more power?" Harper surmised.

"I guess." Trick nodded. "I should probably tell Fletcher. He'll want to know about something like that."

Thief looked over his shoulder. "I better go." He reached in the pocket of his coat and brought out a small, lavender-coloured egg. "Here."

Harper looked down at it. "Um…I've had breakfast already, thanks."

Thief snorted. "No – it's a Witch custom. It means I owe you a favour. If there's ever anything I can do for you, smash the egg against the floor and it'll let me know that I've got a message from—" He blinked suddenly. "Oh. What's your name?"

"Harper Woolfe," Harper supplied. "And this is Trick Torres."

"Nice to meet you both," Thief said, proffering the egg.

Harper took it, feeling pleased – she'd never even met a Witch before, let alone been owed a favour by one. "What if I smash it by accident?"

"Then it'd be a terrible waste of my time, so try not to do that."

With a final nod, Thief vaulted over the shelf and disappeared among the maze of books.

Later that evening, Harper stood outside Fletcher's door, clutching a letter in her hand. She'd got so swept up in these first few weeks of training that she'd forgotten to finish the letter to her mum she'd started on opening night. She felt a little guilty – her mum was no doubt dying to hear how she was – so she'd quickly scrawled a few more lines when they'd returned from the Obelisk before heading up to Fletcher's study.

"Come in," called a voice from the inside as Harper knocked on the emerald-green door. Harper gently pushed it open and stepped inside.

Fletcher's study was a circular room with large windows. The walls were covered in maps, and the bookshelf along the back wall bowed under the weight of a whole host of exotic-looking plants (the books themselves were piled haphazardly all over the floor).

"Ah, Miss Woolfe. What can I do for you?" Fletcher was sat in an upholstered chair behind a gleaming but very cluttered desk.

Harper held up her letter. "I'd like to post a letter to my mum. Are you busy?"

"Not at all. I was just going through some accounts… rejigging schedules…attempting to play Cupid among my staff... Anyway. A letter, you say! Well, the forecast said that this evening would be Cloudy With A Chance Of Bottles, so there should be some coming past any moment. Feel free to take a seat while you wait. Of course, by take, I mean sit – please don't remove any of the chairs from my study, they do get dreadfully homesick."

Harper had no idea what any of this meant, but she sat down in a squashy armchair. A series of popping noises came from one of the shelves to their right, and Harper looked around to see a whole row of iron toasters, all of which had just popped up at once with various letters and notes. The toasters themselves were all labelled with things like COUNCIL CORRESPONDENCE, WONDRIA BUSINESS and GREAT-AUNT HATTIE – IGNORE AT ALL COSTS.

Fletcher stood up and walked over to the shelf and picked up the (slightly singed) papers. "Apologies, Miss Woolfe. Just give me a moment to sort through these..."

Harper began inspecting the strange array of objects on Fletcher's desk while she waited. An antique cuckoo clock, a framed photo of him and Trick grinning on a hot-air balloon, something that looked suspiciously like a skull... Harper skipped quickly over that one.

"Blasted rumours," Fletcher muttered from the corner. "Ridiculous..."

"What rumours?" Harper asked curiously.

"Oh – it doesn't matter. Nothing to worry about," Fletcher said, waving a hand.

Harper thought about this – Fletcher wasn't the first person that day to mention rumours. "Is it…about the Four Curses?"

Fletcher looked up at her in surprise. "How did you know that?"

"We just got back from the Obelisk…" Harper relayed what the students they'd run into had said.

Fletcher rolled his eyes when she'd finished. "Yes, well. People do like to believe in these old tales – they think it makes life more interesting. I myself put absolutely no store by them, no matter how many old biddies write into the radio saying they've seen Death in the form of a giant, savage-looking butterfly."

Harper felt a little better when he said this – Fletcher obviously didn't believe in superstitions either, and he was extremely clever. But she still couldn't help asking, "Why have all these rumours started *now*? Could something – or someone – have caused the Four Curses to increase their activity?"

"I shouldn't have thought so." Fletcher shook his head. "Like I said – these are *superstitions*, Miss Woolfe. I don't know why the Council are taking it all so seriously. They're using it to try to poach my assistant now."

Harper tried to remember the name of the serious-faced boy who'd stood behind Fletcher on their first day. "Lori?"

"Exactly. They think he could help them, given that he's a skin-singer and all. Run scouting missions, do some recon…

I keep telling them that he works for me, but they're not having it."

"What's a skin-singer?" Harper asked.

Fletcher blinked at her. "Of course. Apologies – I sometimes forget that you… Anyway. Skin-singing is a special type of Spectacular gift – a rare one. It refers to someone who can sing themselves into the form of an animal."

Harper blanched. "They WHAT?"

"Yes, it's rather impressive. They sing or hum a certain tune, and that allows them to enter the skin of the animal, and travel with them for a bit, like a passenger. Once they're done, they sing themselves back out again, with no harm done to either party."

Harper let out a slow breath as she processed this. "And Lori can do it? Sing himself into any animal?"

"Just the one – the song of a skin-singer will only work with one animal," Fletcher replied. "Lori's is a hawk. It can be a useful skill, but the Council seem to think that this makes Lori some sort of twenty-four-hour watchdog available at their beck and call – an assumption that I have refuted in the strongest possible terms."

Harper felt a sudden flicker of excitement. "Can anyone learn to skin-sing?" It would be quite something to not only be a Spectacular, but one who could sing themselves into an animal.

"Unfortunately not," Fletcher replied. "Skin-singing is a gift that one must be born with. We don't know how or why –

it doesn't run in families, as far as we can tell. It's just a strange genetic quirk. It usually manifests at quite a young age – starts with dizzy spells and faintness, followed by a strange singing in the person's ears that will lead them to an animal. I've heard of it yielding disastrous results if people try it too early. I had a friend once who tried to sing himself in and out of a warthog and ended up with a permanent pig nose. I'm afraid he was always in the back of group photos after that."

Before Harper could ask any more about skin-singers or the Four Curses, Fletcher looked towards the window. "Ah! Here we are."

Harper squinted out of the window as a whole flock of silver-winged bottles came bobbing into view, glinting like a cloud of soap bubbles against the sky. Harper gaped as they floated up to Fletcher's study and paused outside, like a well-trained flock of birds.

"Address?" Fletcher asked.

"19 Carrow Road, Theatre Borough, the Smoke," Harper replied. Fletcher selected a purple ribbon from a drawer and looped it around Harper's letter, then turned to one of the bottles. He prodded the letter through the neck of the bottle, which dipped for a moment before righting itself and rejoining the flock. Harper watched the bottles flutter out of sight, hoping that it would get to her mum safely.

"Oh – did Trick tell you about the hunter in the Obelisk?" she asked, turning back to Fletcher.

"He did." Fletcher looked concerned. "The Council have

been keeping an eye on Alistair Sharpe and his cronies for years, but I must admit we hadn't got wind of this star-hunting business. I hope he's not up to anything too nefarious – I confess, I prefer to have as little to do with the Society of Magicians as possible."

Harper had more questions – about Alistair Sharpe, the Society of Magicians, the fallen stars – but at that moment, the dinner gong rang through the air.

"Excellent!" said Fletcher, perking up. "I hope Helja's made something good – once the weather gets cold it does tend to be all hearty stews and casseroles, and personally I prefer something with a bit of spice. Don't tell her I said that, though." He sighed. "Last time I gave her some gentle pointers on seasoning I was picking mop hairs out of my soup for a *week*."

After bidding Fletcher goodnight, Harper made her way back to the apprentice quarters, but she didn't join the others for dinner. Instead, she headed straight for her room, picked up the copy of *The Four Curses: The Stories, the Sightings, the Superstitions* she'd borrowed from the Obelisk, and flipped it open to the contents page. The first chapter was entitled *The Four Curses: An Overview*, which seemed as good a place to start as any. Most of the first page was taken up with a written copy of the song Trick had sung, followed by a description of each Curse:

Death: bringer of fatalities and endings; a winged creature of indeterminate size.

Discord: a horned, hoofed creature; a cause of conflict and estrangement.

Malady: bringer of illness and weakness; a small creature with sharp claws.

Misfortune: a silver-furred, feline-esque creature; where Misfortune goes, accidents must surely follow.

Harper's stomach fluttered uneasily. *Accidents must follow…* A feline-esque creature… Had the paw print she'd seen been feline-esque? It had all happened so quickly it was hard to tell. It seemed like too much of a coincidence that she and Althea had almost had a horrible accident mere moments after she'd seen the paw print.

Harper shut the book, trying to quell the panic rising in her. What would happen if she had attracted Misfortune to them? Would something terrible strike the Wondria, like it had at the Winter Playhouse?

With no immediate answers to her questions, Harper climbed into bed and lay back on her pillows. She hoped against hope that the rumours of the Four Curses would stay as rumours – but as she closed her eyes and tried to sleep, she couldn't shake the image of the paw print from her mind.

CHAPTER TEN

The Great Pumpkin Chandelier

*A*s the weeks passed, Harper began to pay special attention to the radio. If there had been any further alleged sightings of the Four Curses, they were usually the first thing to be reported on. If *The Spectacular Daily Show* started with news about a burst water pipe in a theatre, or a famous singer's latest scandal, then Harper knew that she could relax for the day. But if it started with an ominous report of a winged creature being spotted near a theatre, followed by a death of someone who worked there (*"When Death comes, it comes on wings,"* Harper's mind whispered), or the sound of scurrying feet heralding a spate of illness within a cast (*"Malady scurries on tiny claws,"* the voice reminded her), then Harper knew she was in for a day of anxiety and guilt. Trick always rolled his eyes, claiming these were mere coincidences ("If your theatre has an infestation of rats, maybe the cast are getting ill *because of the infestation of rats*"), but Harper wasn't so sure. The one thing she had to hold on to was that she hadn't seen any more paw prints or witnessed any more horrible accidents like the one that had befallen her and Althea. She could only hope that whatever was happening with the Four Curses, Misfortune wasn't going to target the Wondria.

Luckily for Harper, All Spooks' Eve was approaching, and everyone's attention had begun to turn excitedly towards that. Spectaculars, as a rule, couldn't resist a theme, and preparations for a special show had started weeks in advance. The night before All Spooks' Eve all the first-year apprentices received a mysterious summons to go to the Costume Department after training.

"What do you think it is?" Anvi asked, practically bouncing with anticipation. "A secret concert? A game? Some sort of All Spooks'-themed second initiation?"

When they entered the Costume Department, Fletcher was stood in the centre of the room, beaming. Roper, the Costume Mistress, was on one side of him, while Fletcher's assistant Lori stood calmly on the other. Harper couldn't help giving Lori an appraising look, but there was nothing in his demeanour that suggested he had the ability to sing himself into the skin of a hawk and soar through the air on wings. Harper thought that if *she* had that ability, she'd probably scream it at the top of her lungs every time she entered a room.

"Welcome, all!" Fletcher cried. "Tonight, we'll be hosting an event that's something of a tradition for first-year apprentices. I give you…the All Spooks' Costume Dash!"

There was a smattering of excited murmuring among the apprentices.

"A number of silver sacks are hidden around the Costume Department," Roper explained. "Inside each sack are pieces of costume, ranging from simple accessories to full outfits. Some are merely hidden, while others may involve a bit more…leg work."

"You have until Lori's second whistle to gather as many sacks as you can." Fletcher grinned. "And your time starts… now!"

Lori Montgomery blew on the whistle around his neck, and the apprentices were off.

Predictably, the sacks weren't anywhere that could be easily reached. Some were hidden deep in costume trunks, while others were stuffed into wigs or buried among smelly socks. Harper searched for the first ten minutes or so without having much luck. Breaking off from the pack, she rounded a corner, and groaned.

"Really?"

A mannequin had been suspended from the ceiling, arms out as though it were flying. Dangling from one of its hands was a silver sack.

"*Leg work*," Harper muttered mutinously.

It was no mean feat getting to the sack. First Harper had

to clamber up onto a stack of trunks, then haul herself on top of a wardrobe, *then* half dangle from a light fitting as she swiped at the sack, edging it off the mannequin's arm. She gave a final swing, and watched triumphantly as the sack fell from the mannequin...

Straight into Althea Reed's waiting arms.

"Oi!" Harper yelled indignantly. "That's mine! I earned it fair and square."

"Yes," Althea said. "And I stood and let you do the work, then took it for myself."

"That's cheating!"

"No, it's not. It's strategy." Althea smirked at Harper's empty hands. "Oh dear. I don't think *you're* going to be winning the competition." With that, she raced away.

Harper was fuming as she climbed back down to the floor. She'd wasted precious minutes getting that sack, only to have it snatched away. She turned despondently on her heel and began walking back to the centre of the room. As she did, she noticed Lori Montgomery observing Althea with a troubled frown.

"Only one sack left!" Fletcher called. "Your last chance to win the contest!"

Harper gave a half-hearted search through a rack of brocade coats, but her heart wasn't really in it. She was considering whether Trick would share his sacks if she bribed him with sweets when she saw a flash of silver out of the corner of her eye. Her heart leaped – there, half hidden among a heap of sequinned dresses, was the last sack.

No one else had spotted it yet. Harper began to edge towards the heap, trying to look nonchalant. She was still a fair distance away, but if she could get there before anyone noticed what she was doing…

She had no such luck. Althea Reed was squinting at her from across the room. Her eyes drew a line from Harper to the pile of dresses, and her face lit up.

Abandoning her original plan, Harper broke into a flat-out run. Out of the corner of her eye she saw Althea do the same. *Come on, come on!* she urged her limbs, but a quick glance told her that it was useless. Althea was closer to the pile than she was; there was no chance Harper would get to it before she did…

"Wha— Agghh!"

Suddenly, Althea was pitching forwards through the air. She fell, arms flapping like a wild turkey, and toppled head first into a pile of unwashed costumes. After a moment her head popped up, a dirty sock stuck to her cheek and a mutinous expression on her face.

Harper blinked. Althea hadn't seemed like she'd been about to fall… She looked at the place where Althea had tripped, to see Lori's foot rapidly retreating back to a normal standing position. His face was perfectly innocent, but Harper thought that she may have caught the faintest of smiles as she ran past.

"Yes!" Harper scooped up the last sack and held it aloft.

Lori blew his whistle, and the apprentices gathered back in the centre of the room.

"Right. Now comes the fun bit!" Fletcher beamed. "You've each got to create an individual spooky character based on whatever you find in your sacks."

"What?" Althea looked outraged. "But – I got the most sacks! I won!"

"The winner isn't the person who gathered the most sacks." Fletcher shook his head as though this were a ridiculous suggestion. "Spectaculars will often find themselves in a position where they need to throw things together at the last moment. Maybe a shipment of costumes hasn't arrived, or a piece of set has broken or an actor is skiving off – I mean, has unfortunately been taken ill." He winked. "So, being able to think on your feet is something you should get accustomed to. Whoever creates the best character wins!"

"Well, then it's not a costume competition, is it?" Althea said. "It's a character competition."

"Oh, my dear Miss Reed, no one likes a pedant," Fletcher said breezily.

Biting down a laugh, Harper opened her own sack and started hurriedly pulling out the contents. She had a floor-length black veil, a vial of fake blood and an excellent set of stick-on warts.

"Oooooh," Trick groaned from her other side, and Harper spluttered as she looked at him. Somehow, he'd already donned every single costume piece he'd got, including a long purple cape and a pair of plastic fangs.

"I am the Lord of Nightmares!" he cried, waving his arms. "I am the King of the Shadows! I am the Master of All That Haunts Your Dreams at Night…"

"You've got chocolate on your face," Harper informed him.

Once they'd all assembled their costumes, they lined up before Fletcher and Roper, going down the line and introducing the characters they'd created. Rosie managed to look effortlessly cool as a murderous spirit in a long white gown and black wig. Trick did his Lord of Nightmares routine, hissing and spitting before demanding that they all kneel before him and pledge eternal allegiance to the Kingdom of Shadows.

"Harper?" Roper looked at her expectantly.

Harper took a breath. "My name is Ada Hemlock. I was burned at the stake for dark magic, but now I've crawled out of my grave to seek revenge on those who wronged me. I will tear out their spleens and eat them with horseradish sauce!" She opened her mouth wide and allowed the fake blood, which she'd been holding somewhat uncomfortably in her cheek, to run down her chin. Althea recoiled with a shriek, but Fletcher looked delighted.

"Excellent!" he enthused. "A backstory *and* a character objective, all in one speech! Very good work, Miss Woolfe."

Harper felt a warm glow of pride in her chest. Trick gave

her a double thumbs-up, which would have been less intimidating if he hadn't still been sporting a set of talons.

Fletcher, Roper and Lori conferred for a moment before turning back to face them.

"I am pleased to say that the winner of this year's All Spooks' Costume Dash is...Harper Woolfe!"

Trick, Rosie and Anvi all cheered loudly. Althea looked as though someone had forced her to drink spoiled milk.

Harper stepped forwards to receive her prize: a giant, frilly, orange-and-black rosette that declared her the "All Spooks' Champion". It looked ridiculous, but Harper couldn't help beaming with pride as Fletcher pinned it onto her jumper. Even if it was just a fun competition, she felt like she'd proven herself in some small way tonight.

Walking back to the apprentice quarters, Harper began to feel more optimistic than she had in weeks. Perhaps whatever ill luck she'd awakened had begun and ended on opening night. After all, if she had Misfortune trailing her, surely she wouldn't have won the costume dash? Harper beamed down at her rosette, remembering Althea's face when her name had been announced. Now *that* was worth any number of smashed lanterns.

The next evening brought the All Spooks' Eve show, and patrons had already begun arriving as Harper and Trick walked back from a session in the Music Parlour. The

Wondria had had quite the makeover for All Spooks' Eve: giant cobwebs hung in the bar where guests were being served Black Cat Cosmos and Green Slime Gimlets, the curtains that framed the stage had been changed from red to black, and to top it all off, the chandelier had been stripped of its glittering crystals, and was lit instead by hundreds of tiny pumpkins, all with individually-carved faces.

Just before the show began, Harper, Trick, Rosie and Anvi climbed the narrow staircase and took their usual seats next to the spotlights. Once the curtains rose, the acts came thick and fast. One of the Bedazzling Blues Brothers played a double bass made of bones, topped with a skull that sang along in a deep, booming voice. Min Kyung, the Wondria's lead dancer, performed a rumba which saw mechanical bats swooping out from the rippling folds of her onyx skirt as she spun around. Harper's favourite was an actor who recited a monologue about a doctor who was being taken over by a devilish alter ego. As he performed, his skin slowly turned grey and mouldy, twisted horns grew from his head and his eyes turned fiery red until he ended the last line with an evil cackle and disappeared through a hole in the stage. Harper marvelled at how easily he must be able to control Star-Stuff to change his appearance so thoroughly.

After the interval, they ventured down to the Costume Department, where Roper was demonstrating a box of All Spooks' products. There were Blood Pills, which gave the illusion that you were bleeding horribly from some part of your body, and giant temporary tattoos of spiders or snakes which came to life to crawl or slither down your arm. Trick and Rosie immediately joined the queue, debating which to have done. Harper felt absolutely no desire to have a large insect crawling across her limbs, so she and Anvi headed to the Gilded Bar, where they were serving mugs of green hot chocolate topped with blood-red cream. Harper and Anvi managed five mugs between them while Anvi recounted all the acts she'd enjoyed most during the show.

"I think the skull-bass was my favourite. Ooh, and those dancers who did the vampire tango...ooh, and the song-mistress who turned herself into a ghost! How did she *do* that..."

Harper was just contemplating a sixth hot chocolate when she heard a strange sound that had her frowning at the ceiling. It came from directly above them – a faint creaking, as though someone was walking on old floorboards.

"Anvi – can you hear that?" Harper frowned.

The creaking sound came from above their heads again – but it sounded as though it was *moving*. Harper motioned to Anvi, and they hurried out of the bar. The lobby was almost completely deserted. After a moment, Harper heard it again – the creaking, this time coming from behind her. She turned around, and her blood ran cold.

There, on the floor of the lobby, was a set of paw prints. They were slightly smudged, and they led directly into the Auditorium.

CHAPTER ELEVEN

Misfortune

Harper's heart thudded unpleasantly. She knew, deep in her gut, that this was the same creature she'd seen on opening night – only tonight, it'd somehow got *inside* the Wondria. The words of the Four Curses rhyme echoed in her head as she gestured to Anvi and opened one of the Auditorium doors, slipping quietly inside.

The crowd inside were rapt, watching as Lady Roberta Helix duetted with her reflection, backed by a choir of scarecrows with jack-o'-lantern heads. Harper could hear the creaking sound louder than ever – and she could see a few patrons turning their heads too, their eyes scanning the Auditorium for the source of the noise.

"Um…Harper…" Anvi said faintly. She pointed upwards. Harper followed her gaze to the pumpkin chandelier above their heads. With a sickening twist in her stomach, she saw that it was gradually coming loose from the ceiling.

Harper wasn't sure which of the patrons noticed it first, but suddenly there was pandemonium. Audience members were jumping out of their seats, pointing to the chandelier as they vaulted over armrests and dashed for the exits.

"Finnius! Finnius, not too fast, I can't run in this dress!"

"I told you not to wear that blasted dress!"

"Well one of us had to look good, darling, and it wasn't going to be you…"

Harper dived out of the way as the crowd stampeded towards the doors. "Anvi, get back to the lobby!" she yelled. Lady Roberta Helix gathered up her mirror and scuttled off into the wings, passing Fletcher, who was running out onto the stage, holding his arms out.

"Friends and patrons, if you could please try and make your way to an exit in an orderly fashion…"

The chandelier chose this moment to creak even louder, sending a shower of tiny pumpkins raining down upon the audience below. Some patrons screamed and dived out of the way, while others seized their umbrellas to shield their heads from the sudden onslaught of pumpkin pulp.

Knowing that there was no point in fighting the crowds now swarming up the aisles, Harper ducked into an empty row and started climbing across the seats. She scanned the ground for more paw prints, determined to see what it was this time.

"Harper! What are you doing?" Anvi yelled, the crowd forcing her back towards the Auditorium doors.

"I'm just…" Harper trailed off as she came face to face with a paw print on the wall, at her eye level. Heart thumping, she craned her neck up and saw that there were several more, leading vertically upwards.

Slowly, Harper rotated on the spot, keeping her head up. As her eyes landed on it, the chandelier snapped entirely on one side. It swung sideways, sending more pumpkins hurtling downwards – and as it did, Harper saw exactly what she'd been looking for.

An enormous, panther-like creature was perched on top of the chandelier. It had silver fur and glowing eyes, and its paws were the size of Harper's head.

"I don't believe it!" a voice shrieked from the back of the Auditorium. "Finnius, look!"

"I know, I can see it!"

"It's one of the Four Curses!" The woman turned and screamed out into the crowd, "IT'S MISFORTUNE! MISFORTUNE IS HERE, IN THE WONDRIA!"

Fletcher leaped off the stage, trying to herd the crowd through the doors. Harper stayed where she was, frozen in horror.

"Harper, look out!"

She heard Fletcher shout just as the final bolt slipped. There was a terrible shrieking of metal, and the chandelier came hurtling downwards. Harper threw herself out of the way, seconds before the chandelier smashed against the ground. The intricate metal bent and twisted on impact, the remaining pumpkins reduced to liquid on the ground. The last of the crowd gasped and screamed as they fought their way through the doors out into the lobby.

Looking up, Harper saw that the creature had leaped from the chandelier into one of the theatre boxes at the side of the stage. Now, it was crawling over the edge and down the wall, directly towards her.

Harper felt rooted to the spot. It was all she could do to keep breathing as the creature advanced, its dagger-like claws glinting. As it approached her, Harper saw something flash across its eyes. Something that looked like – recognition?

"Back! Get back!"

Suddenly, Fletcher was in front of her, wielding a mahogany walking stick from the Props Department. He jabbed one end towards the creature, forcing it backwards.

"This is my theatre," he cried. "And you, Sir, are barred!"

He jabbed again, hitting the creature square between its eyes. The creature leaped backwards with a hiss, its giant paw swiping through the air inches from Fletcher's face. Crouching briefly, it sprang from the stalls all the way up to the Grand Circle and darted towards the door that led to the roof.

"Oh no you don't…" Fletcher ran for the exit, passing Lahiri on the way.

"Ah, Lahiri, perfect – can you please make sure Miss

Woolfe here gets safely back to the apprentice quarters? I have to go and chase a cat."

Lahiri nodded, looking somewhat bewildered, and Fletcher ran out of the Auditorium, walking stick held aloft like a spear.

"Right. Come on, Harper."

"But—" Harper looked around. They were the only ones left in the Auditorium. "Anvi – and Trick and Rosie…"

"We are ensuring that everyone is safe." Lahiri placed a firm hand on Harper's shoulder and steered her through the lobby, towards the stairs that led up to the Living Wing.

When they reached the apprentice quarters, it was eerily silent. Lahiri pointed Harper towards the wall of doors.

"You're to stay in your rooms until we've sorted this out." Her tone was not to be argued with.

Harper climbed the ladder to her room and tumbled on top of the bed. Her thoughts whirled round and round in her head, like the world's least-fun carousel.

There could be no denying it now. Any hopes she'd entertained of the opening night accident being a one-off, or having nothing to do with Misfortune, were dashed. She'd seen it with her own two eyes: seen the silvery fur, the giant feline shape, just as her book had described. And more than that, it had *looked* at her, had crawled right towards her, as if it knew somehow that *she* was the one who had brought it here.

Harper burrowed down under her duvet, miserable and scared. It was going to be a long night.

Harper awoke early the next morning – so early that the mess room was completely empty, and the table that was usually heaving with breakfast food courtesy of Helja stood bare. Still shaken from the events of the night before, Harper made her way over to the glass doors and stepped out onto the balcony. She took a deep breath and looked over their surroundings, trying to shake off the images of glowing eyes and enormous claws that had haunted her dreams. The Wondria had moved overnight: they'd travelled further into the Free Winds district and were now overlooking a series of winding canals that formed a large, meandering city. The canals were lined with boats that formed little floating neighbourhoods. Some of the boats were several storeys high, and boasted rustic signs declaring themselves to be restaurants, hotels, and *The Hidden Peaks' only glass-bottomed bowling alley!* Early-morning commuters were making their way to work by rowing boat, or bicycles that skimmed the top of the water. A large sign just to the left of where they sat announced:

Welcome to Richton-on-the-Water
The proud home of the Underwater Cabaret Club,
featuring the Mega Mermaid Ukulele Band!
A Hidden Peaks Council Grade Five
Listed Municipality.
Please do not feed the swans.

Just below this a smaller wooden sign had been somewhat haphazardly tacked on. This one read:

The Old Town Ruins in the East End of the city have now been certified as a Fallen Site. Please proceed with caution.

Harper frowned slightly. *Fallen Site...* Somewhere, beneath all the fear and worry, she recognized that phrase. She took a deep breath, ignoring the slightly fishy smell, and tried not to think about just how many *more* dangers there were out there.

"Harper?"

Harper was immediately distracted from her thoughts by the arrival of her friends. A feeling of intense relief washed over her as she saw Trick, Anvi and Rosie all stepping out onto the balcony, and she fought down the urge to rush over and hug them all.

"Hey!" She couldn't help eyeing them all anxiously. "Are you all okay?"

"Not really," Trick said with a grimace. "It's *morning.*"

"We're fine." Rosie elbowed him. "Are *you* all right? Anvi said you were almost squashed to death by falling pumpkins."

"Something like that," Harper said with a shaky laugh. "But I'm okay."

Rosie reached into her satchel and pulled out a radio,

which she settled on the ledge of the balcony. "There's supposed to be a special on *The Spectacular Daily Show* about what happened last night…" She turned a knob, flipping through a few stations before they heard a voice crackling through the static.

"*…I'm Ace Malone. Welcome to* The Spectacular Daily Show. *Our top story today: scenes of horror at the Grand Wondria Music Hall and Theatre last night, as patrons enjoying an All Spooks' Eve show fled the premises in terror after the appearance of an unknown creature… We have two eyewitnesses from the scene to give their description of what happened.*

"*'Is it on me? Should I talk now? All right – well, I tell you what, it was terrifying, really terrifying—'*

"*'They want to hear about the creature, Finnius. Tell them about the creature!'*

"*'Right, yeah – so it was sort of cat-like, except it was probably the size of a smallish horse…'*

"*'A smallish horse? Rubbish, it was the size of an elephant! Here – give me that microphone… I'll tell you something else, it wasn't an "unknown creature", it was Misfortune – it was one of the Four Curses.'*

"*'That's quite a bold claim…'*

"*'Rubbish. You know the rhyme – "Misfortune stalks its prey by night." And in the opera, it's a sort of cat-thingy, isn't it?'*

"*'I always thought it was a raccoon…'*"

Rosie leaned forwards and switched the radio off. "What rubbish."

"It's not rubbish!" Anvi said, looking outraged. "It *was* Misfortune – I saw it!"

"You saw a creature – one that was probably *not* the size of an elephant, mind. But that doesn't mean you saw one of the Four Curses. You can't have – *because they don't exist.*"

Harper glanced at Rosie. She seemed adamant…but then, she hadn't been there.

"They do exist!" Anvi argued. "What else would that thing be?"

"I don't know – a creature from the forest? Something that crawled over from the Southern Mountains?"

"Right, because we see giant panthers all the time in the Southern Mountains…"

"All right!" Trick interrupted, waving his hand between them like a white flag. "There's no point arguing about it. Whatever it was, you said that Fletcher sent it packing, right? So hopefully it won't be back again."

Anvi huffed and Rosie rolled her eyes, but they dropped the subject. They both headed inside as Helja appeared with the breakfast trolley, and Trick made to follow. Harper motioned for him to hang back, then lowered her voice. "It's my fault."

Trick frowned. "What?"

Harper took a breath and told him about opening night – the print, the lanterns, the almost-accident with the pole. She told him about what Althea had said, and how when

Misfortune had looked at her the night before, it had seemed to recognize her.

"There's no other explanation," she finished. "It turned up because I summoned it here by saying 'good for—'…by saying *that* on opening night. Now it's visited twice, and it's caused accidents both times, just like my book said it would!" She hung her head. "Maybe Althea's right – maybe I should never have come here if I'm already causing so many problems…"

"Harper," Trick said seriously. "The Four Curses are just figments of superstitious imagination – they aren't real! Just like chewing gum in a theatre won't actually cause all your teeth to fall out, and saying 'the bloody king' into a dressing-room mirror won't actually summon a bloodthirsty monarch." He sighed. "I know, 'cos I've tried."

"What else could it have been?" Harper demanded.

"There are all kinds of weird creatures in the Hidden Peaks." Trick shrugged. "There are goblins that have wheels for feet. There are spirits that exclusively haunt roller discos. Fletcher swears that he once saw a dragon made out of *mint humbugs*. That creature could have been *anything*."

He sounded so sure of himself that Harper felt the knot in her stomach loosen ever so slightly.

"Oi – are you two coming in for breakfast?" Rosie interrupted them, sticking her head back out onto the balcony.

"Absolutely," Trick replied quickly. "It *stinks* out here."

"That'll be the fish market," said Rosie with a smirk.

"It's the biggest one in the Hidden Peaks. I lived there for a bit when I was seven," she added as an explanation, seeing Harper's confused expression. "My mum was a make-up artist at the Underwater Cabaret."

Harper decided not to delve into the practicalities of how exactly one went about applying make-up underwater. Instead, she asked, "Did you live on one of the boats?"

"Yep," Rosie replied. "We had to wear wellies to bed in case of floods. And once we got an infestation of starfish. But it was still a pretty nice place to live."

Harper looked back at the city, and her eyes fell on the sign she'd noticed earlier.

"Hey – what's a Fallen Site?"

"One of the places where the stars landed when they fell out of the sky," Rosie explained. "There are thirteen of them, scattered around the Hidden Peaks – one for each of the thirteen stars."

Harper nodded, remembering Lahiri telling them about the Fallen Sites in their very first lesson. She glanced at the words on the sign. "But – it's not still in there, surely? I thought the stars had disappeared."

"Some people think it is," Rosie replied. "They say that if you get close enough, you can hear the star crying, calling out to be let back into the sky."

"Oh." Harper frowned. "That's – horrible."

"It is, isn't it?" Rosie said. "I mean, I never heard anything. But then again, we lived on the street just above the club – it's hard to hear anything when the Mega Mermaid Ukulele Band are causing such a racket all the time. The ukulele is a surprisingly aggressive instrument in the hands of a Mermaid."

Harper had a dozen more questions about the stars and the Fallen Sites (not to mention the ukulele-playing Mermaids), but at that moment Helja's voice came floating out from the mess room.

"Don't mind me. I'll just lug all this food over to the table by myself," she called over to them. "I just *love* carrying heavy baskets on my own – it must be my lucky day…"

Rosie huffed, and they all made their way back into the mess room, where Helja was pointedly balancing about a dozen food baskets all at once. Harper couldn't resist having one more peek over her shoulder at the watery city. She couldn't rid her mind of the idea that somewhere, deep in the city, was a drifting, glowing presence, restlessly searching the Earth, trying to find its way home.

Chapter Twelve

Fallen

*A*lthea Reed, predictably, savoured the news of Misfortune's appearance like a particularly delectable boiled sweet. For the next week, as soon as Harper walked into a room, she'd begin talking loudly about the Four Curses.

"It all seems to have got so much worse in recent weeks... It just makes you wonder what – or *who* – could possibly have caused this..." She'd look over at Harper with a pointed glance, smirking if she detected any trace of guilt.

Harper *did* feel guilty. Despite Trick's assurances that this wasn't her fault, she couldn't shake off the fact that Althea was right. She'd become an avid radio-listener, and it seemed clear to her that sightings were increasing rapidly. In desperation, she read *The Four Curses: The Stories, the Sightings, the Superstitions* from cover to cover, but she could find no hint as to how to make them go away.

"You know what I'm worried about?" Althea sighed theatrically one mid-November morning. "That this is going to spoil our Muse of Stars Ceremony. I do love it so much..."

Trick scowled. "Do you think she'd shut up if I accidentally dumped a plate of scrambled eggs on her head?"

"*Is* it going to ruin the Ceremony?" Harper asked anxiously.

"Of course not," Rosie assured her. "She's talking rubbish."

Harper was excited to partake in her first Muse Ceremony. The Muses, she'd learned, were like the Spectacular patron saints – individuals who possessed a series of special powers that went above and beyond what any ordinary Spectacular could do. Ceremonies for each of them were held throughout the year, the first of which was for the Muse of Stars.

"Can anyone be a Muse?" she asked Trick as they walked to training that morning.

"Anyone can stand for a Museship, but there are a series of trials you have to go through first," Trick replied. "Apparently Tornio Nocturne once tried out for it, but he didn't get it – and he's from one of the most talented families in Spectacular history."

When they arrived in the Costume Department for the morning's session, Harper was surprised to see Lahiri there, standing next to Roper at the head of the room.

"Apprentice presentations!" she said, surveying them all. "I am pleased to tell you that on the evening of the Muse of Stars Ceremony, you will be giving a group performance to the rest of the Wondria, to demonstrate the skills you've learned so far."

Harper felt a flush of what could have been excitement or nerves.

"The Muse of Stars ceremony will take place on the evening of the Scholar moon," Lahiri informed them. "Which means you only have three weeks to prepare your presentation."

Harper smiled slightly. The full moon happened during the first week of each month, and each had a unique name – the Scholar moon, the Lioness moon, the Silver moon, and so on. Important events and occasions were often planned to coincide with them.

"You'll be working with Roper here in the Costume Department for this particular task. Now, you are the first group this year to be giving a performance, so make it count." Lahiri arched a brow as she looked around at them all. "No pressure, but if you make me look bad, I'm not above giving you all detention for the rest of the year."

With this thinly veiled threat, Lahiri marched out of the room. Roper smiled at them encouragingly, ruffling her curls.

"Don't worry – during my first apprentice performance I fell head first into a tuba. It can't get much worse than that."

Preparing for their first apprentice presentation was a tense affair. Harper loved the Costume Department, with its elaborate gowns and cloaks, and shoes that were occasionally inclined to break into enthusiastic tap-dancing; however, being stuck in a room with Althea and her cronies for hours on end was enough to test anyone's patience. Althea had taken to reading out the latest Curse sightings from *The Spectacular Times* in a dramatic manner each morning, sighing and wondering aloud what could possibly be done to stop all this. (Harper had a feeling that Althea's solution would involve Harper's swift removal from the Wondria.) Harper tried to keep her head down and focus on the presentation, but it was hard to keep her temper from boiling over every day. The work itself, at least, was fun – and gave Harper something else to focus on instead of worrying about Misfortune all the time. Harper spent days on end sawing, shaping and gluing, feeling like she was in her element. She didn't miss the surprised glances she got from several of her fellow apprentices, who apparently hadn't expected her to be good at anything.

The next three weeks sped by, and soon the evening of the Muse of Stars Ceremony arrived. As soon as training was over, Harper, Trick and the others joined the crowd of Spectaculars who were streaming out of the main entrance towards Lake Gallant, which the Wondria had settled alongside that morning. The Spectaculars, of course, had dressed – or in some cases, overdressed – for the occasion. Yosef from the Bedazzling Blues Brothers had donned a suit patterned all over with flashing constellations, while Lady Roberta Helix wore a giant eight-pointed star above her head, so big that it took three of her friends to help hold it up. Her group were talking loudly about the Muse of Stars, and the various reported sightings of him.

"I think I saw him once, on Merrimas Eve – he was flying on a giant bird…"

"Oh, that's nothing, darling. Did I tell you that he actually took me on a date once?"

"He never!"

"He did. Took me to a restaurant in the sky. We ate moon oysters and listened to celestial jazz. He had terribly bad breath, though."

Harper snorted, then turned to Trick. "So do the Muses just…walk around like normal people?" she asked.

"Not usually," Trick replied. "They have their own secret city, and they come and go as they please. But everyone's got a story about them, true or not – that the Muse of Shadows is a master gambler and plays poker among normal people in disguise; that the Muse of Hearts rides around on a white horse and leaves roses on the doorsteps of unrequited lovers; that the Muse of Death will grant you an extra year of life if you beat her at chess."

"I'm not sure I like the idea of there being a Muse of Death." Harper shuddered.

"She's fine, apparently," Trick said. "She leaves a trail of white roses wherever she goes and sings people across the border into the next world."

"Oh." Harper considered this. "That doesn't sound so bad."

While they talked, Fletcher had been walking around with a basket of little glass orbs, handing them out to everyone as they gathered at the edge of the lake. Trick collected two and tossed one to Harper. "Here. We'll need these."

As soon as the orbs touched their hands, they flared into life, glowing with a soft silver light that pulsed steadily like a heartbeat.

Harper glanced at Trick. "Now what?"

Trick grinned. "Now this!"

He pulled his hand back and flung his orb into the air. Seeing everyone around her do the same, Harper tossed hers upwards as well, although her mind protested that this was all going to end very badly. (*"Local Muse of Stars Ceremony ruined by multiple grievous injuries induced by plummeting orbs!"*) The orbs, however, did not fall; instead, they drifted out across the lake, their reflections bobbing along below them like a cloud of fireflies. When they reached the centre of the lake, they began to spiral upwards, whirling higher and higher until they were no more than tiny pinpricks of light bobbing towards the full Scholar moon.

"It's our way of giving thanks to the Muse of Stars," Trick said, staring at the lights. "For watching over the stars and keeping them safe."

There was a sudden scuffle to the right of them, and the crowd began to cheer. Harper looked round to see two Spectaculars hoisting a dignified but resigned-looking Fletcher up onto their shoulders and carrying him towards the lake.

"Go on, Fletcher!"

"Get in, my son!"

"This is my favourite bit," Trick said gleefully. The two Spectaculars reached the edge of the lake, and the crowd began counting down.

"Three...two...one..."

Harper gave a shout of laughter as Fletcher was pitched into the water. The two Spectaculars who'd been carrying him high-fived, then jumped in after him. Suddenly, everyone on the bank was whooping and leaping, fully clothed, into the lake.

"Trick..." Harper said, turning to him.

"Sorry, didn't I mention?" said Trick with a wicked grin. "There's a reason we always do this Ceremony by a lake. It's not over until everyone's gone in."

Before Harper could protest, he grabbed her hand and jumped, pulling her in after him. On their other side, Rosie and Anvi shrieked as they followed suit.

"Are you people MAD?" Harper spluttered when she came up for air. "It's WINTER! It's FREEZING!" She spat out a mouthful of water. "How does *this* give thanks to the Muses?"

"Oh, it doesn't," Trick replied cheerfully. "This is just for fun."

"Your idea of fun is deeply disturbing," Harper grumbled, splashing to the edge of the lake. She hauled herself out, shivering as the cool evening air hit her soaked skin. Trick laughed at her grim expression, then dived under the surface like a dolphin.

"I'm with you." Roper walked over to Harper and handed her a fluffy white towel. "Of all the ceremonies, this is my least favourite. But Helja usually whips up a few hot cocoas to help us all get the feeling in our toes back."

Harper wriggled her own toes, checking that they were all still there. She turned back to watch the last few balls of light disappear into the sky, only for her gaze to land on a figure who was standing, half shadowed, on the opposite side of the lake.

Harper heard her own gasp echo as she took in the figure. It looked horribly familiar – tall and bulky, with a completely shaved head. Harper's stomach dropped as she squinted through the dim light. Could it be the star-hunter from the Obelisk, Alistair Sharpe?

"Harper? Are you all right?" Roper asked.

Harper blinked, and in the next moment the figure spun around sharply and slunk back into the trees that surrounded the lake. Harper peered into the gloom, but there was no further sign of the man. Her heart thudded unevenly. *Had* it been Sharpe? Or was she mistaken?

"I just – I thought I saw someone," she replied eventually. Why would the hunter come *here*? Was he searching for Thief? Or the stars? Or – her stomach twisted unpleasantly – had he found out who *she* was, and decided to seek revenge for her stunt in the Obelisk?

Harper glanced up at the lights, glowing against the darkness like tiny night lights.

"Roper…" she asked hesitantly. "You know the fallen stars?"

Roper blinked, a surprised look crossing her face. "Yes."

"What do you think would happen if someone found one?" Harper met her eye. "Would they do something bad?"

"Well…" Roper mused. "I suppose it would depend on the person. There are people out there who would certainly see it as a chance to try and gain more power."

"Like the Spectacular Society of Magicians?"

"I suppose so." Roper frowned. "But the Society of Magicians have been defunct for years. Besides, they'd actually have to *find* a fallen star, which no one's managed to do yet. I mean, one fell less than a mile from us on our first night in the Hidden Peaks, and no one ever saw it."

Harper's eyebrows flew up. "Wait, really?"

"Yep." Roper nodded. "Once we made it through the gateway – well, *almost* all of us made it –" she threw a guilty glance at Harper – "we set up camp next to a jungle. Then, all of a sudden, there was this blinding light. We ran outside, and we saw one of the stars heading straight for us. It landed

162

among the trees somewhere. A few people went out looking for it – out of curiosity, more than anything – but no one ever found it."

Harper considered this. Perhaps Sharpe would never succeed in his search if the stars were so hard to find. She fervently hoped not – someone like *that* certainly didn't need any more power.

"What do you think they look like?" she asked. "The stars?"

"Your guess is as good as mine," Roper replied. "There have been stories, of course – my grandma used to say that if you look closely enough, every star has a true form at its centre. No one's been able to verify it, but she could be right. Then again, my grandma also used to say that eating cabbage would make me shoot laser beams out of my eyes, so I'm not sure if she can be trusted on these things."

"Who's shooting laser beams out of their eyes?" Trick asked, clambering up out of the lake. He came and stood within an inch of Harper, then shook his head at her. Harper yelled as droplets of freezing cold water hit her in the face.

"You just wait," Harper threatened. "I'm going to put extra-hot chilli pepper in your morning tea."

Trick gasped. "You wouldn't. Not the *tea*."

"Just try me," Harper said grimly.

CHAPTER THIRTEEN

The First Muses

Once the Ceremony was over, Harper and Trick dried off in the Costume Department, in a giant drying pod which blasted them with hot air from all sides. Then, they collected their projects and ascended the stairs to the lobby. As they wove their way towards the Auditorium, Harper noticed with a jolt of nerves that most of the Spectaculars who had attended the Ceremony were now gathered, waiting to watch their presentation.

"I remember my first apprentice presentation," a woman said dreamily. "We had to choreograph a dance that would make it snow inside the Auditorium. It was terribly elegant."

"We had to build a mechanical elephant that was supposed to parade through the stalls," a man next to her groaned. "But it stampeded and took out the Royal Box instead."

Harper's nerves intensified. Snow dances? Mechanical elephants? She could only hope that their creations would be *half* as impressive.

They hurried through the Auditorium and climbed the steps to the stage, slipping into the wings. Trick had been almost unanimously voted to host their presentation, meaning he'd be the first on and last off the stage, but he sauntered straight to the Sound Department and started rummaging through their biscuit tin, looking supremely unconcerned. Anvi, on the other hand, started running laps backstage, trying to "burn off excess energy".

Rosie – who, after a dip in the lake, had somehow managed to fully repaint her face and stick petals along her eyelashes – blew out a breath and looked at Harper. "Nervous?"

"Yep," Harper huffed. It wasn't so much performing in front of the Spectaculars – it was the scrutiny from the rest of her group that was *really* bothering her. It'd be enough that she'd grown up in the Smoke, away from all this, but since her opening night blunder, and Misfortune's subsequent appearances, she felt like she couldn't afford to make any more mistakes.

"You'll be fine," Rosie assured her.

"You don't know that," Harper whispered. "I might fall over. Or forget how to talk. Or have a sneezing fit during one of the important bits."

Rosie laughed. "Well, if any of that happens, I'll set fire to my hair and dance a High Peaks jig," she offered. "Then no one will be talking about you."

Harper snorted. "You'd never set fire to your hair."

Rosie ran a hand over her bob and sighed. "You're right. It *is* my crowning glory."

Harper peered out from the wings and stole a glance at the audience. Lahiri was sitting to one side with a clipboard and pen, looking serious. Fletcher, on the other hand, was sitting cross-legged in one of the chairs, throwing popcorn into the air and catching it in his mouth. The house lights went down, and the audience settled into a silence.

"May you be cursed with the stings of a thousand bees," Trick said, walking past.

"And may your toes be chewed off by wolves," Harper replied, rolling her eyes.

A single spotlight illuminated Trick as he walked onto the stage. He looked very small in the enormous Auditorium, but his face was calm and confident as he raised his head.

"Light and dark," Trick said in a clear voice, "earth and sky, air and water, life and death. All these things used to exist in complete balance. That was, until humans came along and kind of messed it all up."

Rosie snickered. "Not subtle, is he?"

"As the Sunless Provinces became a place of industry and business, the world grew increasingly out of balance: the stars were blocked from the sky, and the air grew thick with smog. This imbalance awoke a series of special powers – powers that contained the songs of the world, and with them, the ability to shape and control things," Trick continued. "Then, one day, a group of Spectaculars discovered these powers – Spectaculars who were to become the first Muses."

This was their cue. Harper hefted the objects she was holding: a mask formed of delicate metal, covered in swirling patterns of suns and flames, and a long coat made of a gauzy orange material. Harper tied the mask around her head and slipped the coat over her shoulders.

A wind whipped up around her, causing the coat to lift and swirl – and when she turned and looked into the mirror that leaned against the wall, it wasn't Harper looking back at her. Her reflection was now of a woman several feet taller than Harper, with sunburst-coloured skirts and shining waves of orange hair. Her face was painted with the same suns-and-flames pattern as the mask had been, and a wide-brimmed hat sat atop her head. Harper moved her arm and the woman's arm moved too.

She was the Muse of Light.

Group One had decided unanimously that they wanted to do a project based on the Muses. They'd created the script for the presentation, and Roper had helped them with the costumes. Harper had been fascinated when Roper had explained the idea to them.

"So – the costumes will transform us into Muses?" she'd asked.

"Not quite," Roper explained. "Rather than transform *you*, the costumes and masks will shape themselves *around* you, creating the model of a Muse – like those giant carnival puppets that are controlled from the inside."

Harper had grimaced slightly, remembering the looming mechanical puppet in the Parade of Progress. But these were entirely different. The mask and coat had grown around Harper like a chrysalis around a caterpillar, leaving her to puppeteer from inside. It had been intricate work, but Harper was hopeful that she'd done a good job. Taking a deep breath, she stepped out on to the stage.

There were nine of them in total: nine giant Muses-models, each with an apprentice at its centre. Harper saw the Muse of Air, a woman with a pearly coat and great curls of cloud-like hair, with Anvi at her centre looking like she was having the time of her life. The Muse of Shadows wore a soft velvet cape and sunglasses made of smoke – a far cry from little blonde-haired Bernie Maddon. They assembled together, towering above the audience.

"The ancient powers gave the Muses the ability to hear the music of the world, and bend it to their will," said Trick. "They could influence the wind, the stars, the darkness."

This was the bit Harper had really been looking forward to. Roper had helped them add an extra vein of starlight to the costumes, which, when activated, would allow them to mimic the Muses' powers.

Anvi – the best singer in their group – stepped forwards first. She began to sing quietly as she held out her hands.

A swirling silver breeze appeared in the air around her, rippling out towards the audience, ruffling their hair and filling their noses with a crisp autumnal scent. One by one, the other giant Muse-models stepped forwards, and the apprentices' voices joined the song. Khyla, as the Muse of Hearts, sent pink rose petals swirling through the Auditorium, causing people to sigh and sway dreamily, while Rosie's Muse of Water made streams of silver flow down the aisles and around the seats, until the stalls were a floating island in the middle of a lake. They all sang slightly different words, to correspond to the powers they were creating, but their voices overlapped and blended nonetheless. When Harper's turn came, she inhaled shakily, then joined in the singing. As she did so, she felt Star-Stuff stirring around her. She lifted her hat and ribbons of light shot out from underneath, arching and looping in mid-air.

"The First Muses lived long lives, and when they died, they passed their powers down through the generations, each new Muse tasked with the responsibility of continuing to maintain the balance of the world."

There was a beat after Trick's final words, filled only by the soft humming of the apprentices, the trickle of water around the seats, and the soft rustling of rose petals. It was beautiful.

Until it wasn't.

Afterwards, Harper wasn't sure what exactly had gone wrong. It started with a crackling: a strange, spitting sound, like the final dying flames of a fire. In the few seconds before the chaos, Harper remembered looking around, trying to find the source of the noise.

Then the stage exploded.

Harper was lifted off her feet and hurled forwards. She soared off the edge of the stage, landing in the lap of an unsuspecting woman in the first row. She heard, rather than saw, several of her fellow apprentices do the same.

"My goodness – is this supposed to be happening?"

"This is most unorthodox!"

"Oooh, perhaps it's *immersive*."

Harper heard various mutterings all around her as she struggled to her feet, apologizing profusely to the woman she'd landed on. She turned back to the stage, her mouth falling open in horror. A huge hole had been blown into the stage, jagged and smoking. The few apprentices who had escaped the blast were cowering at its edges, coughing and spluttering. A thick black smog began to creep towards the audience, threatening to engulf them…

"Is everyone all right?" Fletcher hurried onto the stage, peering around at the scattered apprentices as they tore off their masks and costumes. Once he'd satisfied himself that no one had been blown up along with the stage, he turned to the audience. "If you could all please exit the Auditorium while we sort this – um – incident out…"

The audience began to file out, muttering to each other and casting concerned glances back towards the hole in the stage. When the Auditorium had cleared, Fletcher and Lahiri turned to the apprentices, looking grave.

"Did I not warn you on your first day – your *very first day* – about Star-Stuff explosions?" Lahiri asked furiously. "About being aware of which types of light and dust *not* to mix?"

"Roper checked all of our costumes, they were safe!" Rosie protested.

"Then how, exactly, did this happen?"

"It was *her*."

Harper felt a sickening lurch of dread the moment she heard Althea's voice. She *knew* this moment had been coming.

"It's Harper's fault!" Althea said. "She said the forbidden words on opening night and awoke the forces of ill luck! Tell them." She rounded on Harper. "Tell them about how Misfortune turned up that night, and almost killed us both!"

Several apprentices gasped at this. Rosie and Anvi both looked at Harper in surprise. "Is that true?" Anvi asked.

"Well...there was a paw print..." Harper stumbled over her words. "And..."

"And we both nearly had our brains bashed in by a falling pole!" Althea snarled. "It turned up again on All Spooks' Eve – and went right for *her*, no less – and now look! More accidents, more bad luck!"

"Miss Reed, I'm not sure this is helpful..." Fletcher tried to chime in.

"The legend says that where Misfortune goes, accidents

follow," Althea said stubbornly. "It came here – after *she* awakened it – and now accidents are happening!"

"Rubbish," countered Trick. "Accidents happen all the time. *By accident*. Or did you intentionally fall flat on your behind during our last stage fighting class?"

"All right!" Fletcher said sternly. "Miss Reed – despite what the rumour mill says, we have no reason to believe what happened tonight was anything other than an unfortunate accident. Now, all of you, please hand your costumes back to Roper and return to the apprentice quarters while we clear up this mess."

Althea glared at Harper before stomping off towards the wings. Harper was left on stage with the rest of Group One. She looked around at them all, unsure of what to say.

"Come on," Trick said, stepping up next to her. "Let's go."

Harper gathered her costume in her arms and followed Trick off the stage. However, as she went, she wasn't impervious to the suspicious glances being thrown her way, or the mutters that followed her into the wings.

Harper felt shaken to her core as she dragged her feet back to the apprentice quarters. Logically, she knew that Trick was right – accidents did happen, and this could have just been an unfortunate error. But then...Roper *had* checked all their costumes. There was no reason for any of them to have blown up in that way. No reason...other than sheer bad luck.

Where Misfortune goes, accidents must surely follow. Was this what was going to happen from now on? Were they doomed to repeat disasters such as these? And what if next time, someone got hurt – or worse?

Harper *really* didn't want to think about that.

CHAPTER FOURTEEN

The Spectacular Board
of Theatrics

Two days after their disastrous presentation, the first-year apprentices were greeted with an enormous sign that had been slapped up on the wall of the mess room:

ATTENTION:
ALL JUNIOR APPRENTICES!
TODAY THE WONDRIA WILL BE RECEIVING
AN INSPECTION FROM THE SPECTACULAR
BOARD OF THEATRICS. PLEASE ENSURE THAT
YOU ARRIVE AT YOUR CLASSES ON TIME,
IN A PRESENTABLE MANNER. NO UNIFORM
ADDITIONS, JAUNTY SOCKS OR HAIR
ACCESSORIES OF ANY KIND WILL
BE PERMITTED.

Harper sighed and took off her dad's bow tie, shoving it in her pocket. She'd found it comforting having a piece of her dad with her at all times, and this was the first time she'd been pulled up on it.

"Who are the Spectacular Board of Theatrics?" she asked Trick, who was slumped on her left side, pouring sugar into his tea directly from the bowl.

"They keep an eye on the general running of the Spectacular theatres," Trick yawned. "Fletcher says it's all a bunch of bureaucratic nonsense, but the Wondria has to be inspected once a year to be allowed to stay open."

"This isn't just a formality," Anvi said as she arrived with Rosie and sat down on Harper's other side. "We were already inspected earlier this year. This is because of Misfortune."

Harper's heart sank. "Really?"

"Apparently, they've got wind of all this – what happened to you and Althea on opening night, the All Spooks' attack, our apprentice presentation…" Anvi glanced at Harper. "So, they've decided they need to come and make sure that we're fit to be open."

Harper put down her piece of toast, suddenly finding herself without an appetite. The events of their presentation were still raw in her mind. In the last two days alone, Harper had found herself pushed out from the rest of the group – everyone except Trick, Rosie and Anvi seemed to have taken Althea at her word that the accident was all Harper's fault. It wasn't a pleasant feeling – she'd gone from looking forward to the big, extended family that Fletcher had spoken of, to simply hoping that she could get through the day without too many resentful glares and barely-concealed insults. She highly doubted the appearance of the Board of Theatrics would improve things.

"Would they really close us down?" she asked quietly.

"No," Trick said bracingly. "Fletcher would never let that happen. They'll come, poke around a bit, eat all our biscuits and go home – job done."

As they left the apprentice quarters and made their way downstairs, Harper noticed that everyone seemed more than a little tense. Fletcher was striding around the lobby with a pink feather duster in his hand, polishing the menu that stood on the bar while simultaneously trying to rearrange all the portraits on the wall.

Only one person was as quiet and composed as ever in the face of the inspection. Lori Montgomery walked calmly alongside Fletcher, helping him with the general sprucing-up of the Wondria and balancing out Fletcher's fizzing energy.

"Does he ever talk to people?" Harper asked curiously.

"Lori? Not much," Trick said. Harper noticed with interest that Trick barely glanced at Lori when he said this.

"Why aren't you looking at him?" Harper turned around. Now she thought of it, everyone seemed to be giving Lori a wide berth. "Why doesn't anyone want to look at him?"

"What? Don't be stupid, I am looking at him," Trick said, staring down at the floor.

Harper snorted. "Rubbish. Seriously – what's going on?"

Trick was silent for a moment. "Lori's – well, no one really knows much about him. He's pretty reserved. But about year or so after we arrived in the Hidden Peaks, he disappeared for a while. When he came back, there were all sorts of rumours about where he'd been."

"What sort of rumours?"

"Depends who you ask." Trick shifted in his seat. "Some say he trained as an assassin with a Witch-clan. Some say he captained a submarine with a crew of sharks. Some say he came second in a secret version of *Dancing with Yetis*."

Harper stared at him with dawning realization. "Hang on…are you *scared* of him?"

"Not scared!" Trick said hotly. "I just have a…healthy respect for him. A deference that I would rather practise from several feet away."

Harper thought that Lori Montgomery looked about as frightening as a guinea pig, but just as she was about to voice this sentiment, several portraits came crashing down from the wall and landed on Fletcher's foot, causing him to emit an impressive string of swear words.

"My, Fletcher," said a smooth voice from the doorway. "Your vocabulary never fails to astound me."

A man in a long black coat was striding into the lobby. He had slicked-back hair and a familiar-looking smirk on his face.

"Ah. Wallace Reed." Fletcher walked over and shook the man's hand. "Welcome."

Harper turned to Trick, as a horrified realization dawned on her. "Wait. Reed? As in…?"

"Good morning, Daddy!" Althea's voice came bouncing across the lobby, followed by the girl herself, flanked by Bernie and Khyla.

"Good morning, my pumpkin-spiced Princess!" the man simpered back.

Trick pretended to throw up violently on the floor.

The Spectacular Board of Theatrics followed them around all day. As the apprentices of Group One filed into the Scenery Workshop for their final session, Harper saw Master Tulsia bristle from his toes to his moustache at the Board members who followed them in, standing at the back with clipboards poised. Harper couldn't help but feel nervous as she looked around at them all.

"Right," Master Tulsia announced. "I've got a few repairs to do today, so I thought it might be useful for you lot to know what to do when Spectacular-made creations go wrong."

"Do things go wrong around here very often?" Wallace Reed piped up.

"Only when people are particularly careless," Tulsia replied matter-of-factly.

"Well, you can't blame us for being concerned, given, ah – recent events…" Wallace Reed gave a half-glance at Harper.

"Anyway, if you'd like to gather over here…" Tulsia spoke as though he hadn't even heard Wallace Reed, which Harper greatly appreciated. Tulsia led the apprentices to a corner of the Workshop, where a copper bathtub stood on four clawed feet.

"Now, this here is a One-Bath-Band."

Harper was sure she hadn't heard that right. "Sorry?"

The corners of Tulsia's mouth twitched up. "See these taps?" He pointed to the two bronze taps perched atop the bath. "It's not water that comes out of them, but bubbles. Each bubble is colour-coded to a musical instrument, and if the bubble is popped, that instrument will appear and begin playing. Yolanda Fierce often performs with one at her concerts."

This prompted some excited murmuring among the apprentices.

"However, this one appears to be broken," Tulsia said. "So, I'm going to open it up and give it a tinker, and hopefully it'll be right as rain for the show tonight. So – if one of you wants to fetch me my starlight blowtorch…ah, Anvi, thank you…" Tulsia snapped on a pair of safety goggles. "Now – can anyone tell me where I need to be fixing?"

Harper pointed to the join between two pipes, which was looking worn. "There."

"Exactly," said Master Tulsia. "The piping's wearing thin, which means the bubbles aren't getting the infusion of starlight that they need to work correctly." He looked at

Harper approvingly. "Remind me again of your Teapot Traits?"

"Bold and practical," Harper replied.

Master Tulsia grinned. "You'll do well down here."

Harper felt pride swell inside her. She shot a triumphant look at Althea, who glared in return.

"Right – who wants a go with this, then?" Tulsia asked when Anvi returned with the blowtorch. Several hands went up, but Harper's was the fastest. She snapped on a pair of goggles, and gingerly took the blowtorch from Tulsia. When she switched it on, it produced a thin flame of concentrated starlight, bright and blazing.

"Stand back, everyone," Althea stage-whispered. "There might be another explosion."

Harper stopped suddenly, the blowtorch flickering off in her hands. She'd been so keen to have a go, it hadn't even crossed her mind that it might be a reckless decision. If she was the one who'd summoned Misfortune, was she likely to cause more accidents, like at the presentation?

"Harper?" prompted Tulsia.

Harper shook herself. She couldn't very well refuse to touch anything involving Star-Stuff for the rest of her apprentice training. Steeling herself, she flicked the blowtorch back on and applied it carefully to the piping. She watched in delight as the silver tubes began to meld together under her ministrations. In some ways, it was just like being back home in the Fix-It shop – only, instead of tram engines, it was a bathtub that was apparently going to produce a live band.

When they'd all had a turn with the blowtorch, Tulsia stepped back and grinned at the apprentices. "Right – let's see if we've got it working!"

He turned on the taps and instantly a stream of bubbles began pouring out of it. Harper set her sights on a big magenta one and popped it. A saxophone appeared in the air and began to play a jazzy solo that echoed around the room. She popped another bubble of the same colour, and a second saxophone joined it, harmonizing with the first.

The whole of Group One began chasing bubbles around the Workshop, and before long a string quartet, a full drum kit and a grand piano had joined the saxophones. Tulsia tapped his foot along to the music, while Trick and Rosie started doing the Willow Weave (a dance that Harper hadn't *quite* mastered yet). Wallace Reed and his cronies looked on with expressions varying from disapproval to utmost disdain.

"All right, that's enough of that," Tulsia said, turning the taps off. The bubbles and instruments disappeared instantly, leaving the Workshop looking quite normal again. However, the music and bubbles had lifted Harper's mood considerably. She'd wielded a starlight blowtorch, and nothing had gone wrong. There'd been no accidents, no explosions. Let Wallace Reed and the Board put *that* in their report.

The Board hung around all day and well into the evening, lurking in the corners of classes and observing the show from the back row.

"Honestly," Rosie muttered that evening as she painted Harper's face. "If they're going to linger like a bad smell, they could at least look happy about it."

The Costume Department was fairly quiet: a group of singers from the Wondria were performing a late-night Yolanda Fierce tribute act, and almost everyone was down in the Auditorium, fighting for space. Harper was keen to join them, but Rosie had begged Harper to come along to her stage make-up club to act as her model – which is how Harper found herself in the Costume Department mezzanine, sitting on a stool while Rosie daubed coloured pastes onto her face.

"There you go! What do you think?" Rosie held up a mirror. Harper did a double-take as she looked at her reflection – Rosie had been painting her face to look like a tiger, and somehow along the way Harper had also grown a pair of striped ears and a full set of whiskers.

"Nice!" Harper said, twitching her ears.

"Good work, Rosie." Roper, who ran the club, walked over to their station. "You've got a good eye."

"My mum's a make-up artist. She's at the Lunas Bay Opera House right now," Rosie said proudly.

"Rowena Wrenright!" Roper said delightedly. "I saw her production of *The Duchess and the Decapitator* – *incredibly* realistic decapitations—"

"Um – can I wash this off now?" Harper interrupted. Her fierce yellow eyes were starting to unnerve her.

"Oh – of course. Sorry, Harper!" said Roper. She tossed a facecloth to Harper and started packing up the paints.

"What are you developing this stuff for?" Rosie asked curiously.

Roper looked like she was trying very hard not to roll her eyes. "Yosef's decided to write an original musical about cats. Cats, of all things!" Roper flung her hands up in frustration.

Harper frowned. "But cats can't sing."

"Tell *him* that. I'd say he's lost the plot if he wasn't my fiancé," Roper muttered, then tilted her head and thought for a second. "Actually, scrap that, I'll say it anyway. But he reckons if Tornio Nocturne can write an opera about singing animals, he can as well. Although, obviously, in the current climate, perhaps that's not the best source of inspiration."

Harper stiffened at the mention of the Four Curses opera.

"My mum said they've gone wild about all this Curse stuff at the Opera House," Rosie said. "They think they've been visited by Conflict – something about hearing weird clopping noises at night – and now half the staff have walked out!"

"Yosef believes in it all," Roper nodded. "He's started wearing a giant crystal for protection; he looks ridiculous."

"Really?" Harper's stomach lurched. She wondered whether Yosef had heard those fateful words she'd said to him on opening night. She couldn't bear the thought that her dad's best friend might blame her for all this.

When the club ended, most of the apprentices raced out to get to the Auditorium. Roper looked at Harper and Rosie. "Are you two going to the concert?"

"Absolutely," Rosie said excitedly. "Anvi's saving us a place. Well – as long as she hasn't forgotten. Or given it to someone else. Or been distracted by Cinnamon Mice…"

"Why don't you go ahead and make sure we've got a place?" Harper suggested. "I'll follow once I've washed all this off."

Rosie didn't take too much persuading: she hurried after Roper, chatting excitedly about the concert.

Harper scrubbed the rest of the stage make-up off, both relieved and a little sad when the last remnants of the tiger disappeared, and she was just herself again. As she dried her face, she wandered around the mezzanine, looking curiously at all the pictures on the wall. They mostly showed Spectaculars in costume for some production or other: in one Harper recognized Lady Roberta Helix wearing a dress made entirely out of cameras, while, in another, a line of chorus girls grinned cheekily at the camera, wearing glittering pineapples on their heads.

Harper was still trying to guess what sort of production would require a kickline of dancing pineapples when the next picture brought her up short.

Harper hadn't seen many pictures of her dad; only one or two had survived the crash. Here, though, he stood with

Yosef and two other sharply-suited men. Her dad was holding his trumpet and grinning widely at the camera – and when Harper looked a little closer, she noticed with a pang that he was wearing the bow tie her mother had given her.

Harper couldn't have moved if she'd tried. Her eyes roved hungrily across the image of her father, searching for her face in his. Did her eyes crinkle like that at the sides? Was her smile a little crooked, like his? As she glanced at Yosef next to him, she wondered what her dad would have made of everything that was happening now. Would he have believed in the Four Curses? Or would he have treated it as a silly superstition?

Harper stood in front of the picture for a long time, memorizing the image. She was only startled out of her reverie by a tramping of feet a little way down the corridor.

"My microphone went out just before 'It's Not My Fault I'm Better Than You', and one of my stilettos is broken… Muses, this is a disaster…"

"Let's open the second act with 'If You Break My Heart, I'll Steal All Your Shoes' – that's always a crowd-pleaser…"

Harper realized with a start that she'd missed the entire first act of the tribute band. She felt a pang of guilt – her friends must be wondering what had happened to her. She took a last look at the picture of her dad and was about to leave when she heard a noise behind her: a rumbling, followed by a colossal smashing sound, like a dozen panes of glass shattering all at once.

Harper spun around. All along the mezzanine, the oak-and-glass cupboards were falling, hitting each other like a row of dominoes. The products inside were pitching to the ground, large bottles of Chameleon Hair Formula and Silkington's Skin Sensation smashing against the floor. Harper yelled and pulled her jumper up over her head to protect her face from the wave of broken glass. A shadow flashed in the corner of her eye, and she looked up, heart thumping, to find a massive figure looming above her.

It was Misfortune.

The huge bulk of the creature was perched at the window, its massive paws balanced almost delicately on the sill. Its head was turned away from Harper, observing the mess of glass below.

Harper risked a tiny glance backwards. The spiral staircase that led down to the main floor of the Costume Department was a fair way off. If she could get as close to it as possible without the creature seeing, then make a break for it…

Screwing up all her courage, she took a tiny step back. The creature didn't appear to notice. Holding her breath, Harper slid another foot back, then another…

"Wha— Ahhhh!"

Harper cried out as her heel hit a stray paintbrush on the floor, which rolled under her foot and sent her crashing backwards.

From her position, she saw Misfortune look straight at her. The creature drew back, eyes fixed on her, and leaped.

Harper watched it land on the floor of the mezzanine, its huge paws shaking the floor.

"No, no, no..." Harper hauled herself to her feet and began half running, half skidding across the floor, making for the staircase. She heard paws thumping behind her and heard a growl that sent needles of fear straight into her heart. Just in front of her, a huge glass cabinet fell heavily to the floor, smashing in a pile of glass and splintered wood.

Harper didn't bother checking over her shoulder: she could feel Misfortune gaining on her. She leaped desperately, vaulting off a piece of cracked wood and propelling herself over the wreckage of the cabinet. When she landed on the other side, she darted for the stairs.

"Help!" Harper yelled. "If anyone's out there, help!"

She looked behind her. Misfortune had cleared the broken cabinet and was stalking towards her. Harper took a step back.

Unfortunately, she didn't see the spiral staircase behind her.

Her foot met thin air, and her body lurched backwards into nothingness. As she teetered on the edge of the mezzanine, she became dimly aware of another sound joining the cacophony of thumping paws and smashing glass: a gentle rustling, almost a flapping. She just had time to wonder what it was before gravity took hold of her body, knocking the breath out of her, as she tumbled down and down and down...

CHAPTER FIFTEEN

Merrimas

When Harper opened her eyes, the first thing she saw was light. Her limbs felt heavy and there was something soft and comfortable below her.

"Oh, dear. Did I die?" she sighed.

"No: but you made an admirable attempt," said a wry voice from beside her. Harper turned her head to see Fletcher standing over her, grim-faced. Glancing around, Harper saw that she was in a small, plain room, lying on a futon in a corner. Light was gently trickling in from one of the windows. She propped herself up, wincing slightly as pain shot through her knee. She frowned, trying to remember what had happened. There had been broken glass, and the feeling of falling... Why had she been falling?

"Misfortune!" She sat bolt upright. "Is it still here? Did you find it?"

Fletcher shook his head gravely. "No. Lori caught a glimpse of it as he flew in, but it disappeared almost straight away."

He nodded over to the corner, and Harper realized they weren't alone: Lori Montgomery was sat cross-legged in a chair on her other side. He looked even paler than usual, and he gave a brief nod to Harper as she looked at him.

"When you flew..." Harper's eyes widened, remembering the flapping sound she'd heard as she'd fallen. "You were skin-singing!"

Lori nodded. "I was in the corridor when I heard the smashing coming from the Costume Department. I flew in through the door and saw you fall, but the creature vanished before I'd even sung myself back into my own skin."

"Lori alerted the rest of us to the accident, and Helja helped us to bring you here to the medical room," Fletcher added. "She sat with you all night."

Harper looked around the room again. There were boxes sporting bandages and plasters, a cabinet filled with medicine bottles, and a slightly disturbing poster of a giant teddy bear saying, GET WELL SOON!

"So...Misfortune got away?" Harper slumped down. "Again."

"Harper." Fletcher was frowning at her. "Do you really believe that that creature is one of the Four Curses?"

Harper looked down. "I don't know how else to explain it..." She took a breath and found it all spilling out – what she'd said on opening night, the almost-accident with Althea, the way Misfortune had seemed to recognize her at the All Spooks' attack… Once she'd finished with her account of the night before, Harper closed her eyes and said the thing she'd been dreading to say:

"Do you want me to leave?"

"Leave?" Fletcher looked surprised.

"If I brought Misfortune here…maybe it'll leave you alone if I'm gone."

She desperately didn't want to leave, but she felt like they were running out of options. She'd read the book from the Obelisk more times than she could count, but there was still no information about how to get rid of Misfortune. Perhaps, then, the only option was to get rid of *her*.

"Harper." Fletcher kneeled down so he was at eye level with her. "Whatever this thing is, you did *not* bring it here. There's a new superstition every day about what brings good or bad luck to a theatre. I myself once smashed a mirror onstage – curses you with ugliness, apparently, but I assure you, I am as handsome as ever. This is *not your fault*, and you are not going anywhere." He sighed. "But I do wish I knew why this thing keeps showing up. Not to mention *how* it's getting into my theatre. We have staff manning every door, and none of them remember taking the ticket of a large silver panther. And you'd think a creature like that would make *quite* the entrance if it was getting in from somewhere else."

Harper didn't have an answer for this – she was just as stumped as to how Misfortune had managed to get into the

Costume Department without anyone noticing.

"Well, rest assured that I will be tightening security measures from now on," Fletcher said firmly. "I *will* find out what's going on here."

He sounded so determined that Harper couldn't help but feel slightly assured. She stretched out her leg. It twinged again, but she thought that she could probably stand on it.

"What time is it?" she asked anxiously, glancing at the sun outside the window.

"Almost midday. But don't worry about your classes," Fletcher said firmly as Harper spluttered. "I've spoken to Lahiri, and we agreed that you need to rest. But, Harper – if anything else like this happens, I want you to come and tell me straight away, all right?"

Harper nodded. "I will."

"Good. Now…" Fletcher frowned down at her. "Can you walk on that leg? I'd accompany you to the apprentice quarters, but I'm waiting on an important message from the Council…"

"I'll take her," came a voice from the corner. Lori stood and padded over, offering Harper his arm.

"Oh – thanks," Harper replied, surprised. She took his arm and leaned against him slightly as they left the medical room and turned down the corridor.

"Are you okay?"

Harper almost jumped at the question. Given Lori's customary taciturn disposition, she'd been expecting an awkward silence all the way to the apprentice quarters. But here he was, actually asking her a question.

"Um – yeah, I think so," she said. "Thank you – you know, for finding me."

Lori shrugged. "It was just lucky that I was there."

Despite still feeling shaken, Harper couldn't help but glance at Lori curiously. "So…have you always been a skin-singer?"

Lori nodded. "Since I was five. I started getting these terrible dizzy spells. My mum took me to all sorts of specialist doctors, and then one day she came downstairs to find a hawk sitting on her ironing board. It's a tricky skill – I had all sorts of trouble with it at first."

"Is that why you disappeared?" Harper blurted out. "Did you go away to – I dunno, a skin-singer school, or something?"

Lori blinked, surprised. "I – no." He looked at her. "Why do you ask?"

"There are a lot of stories about you," Harper admitted sheepishly. "Trained assassin, submarine captain, champion of Yeti ballroom dancing… Which one is true?"

The ghost of a smile played around Lori's face. "Which one do you think is true?"

"I'm not sure," Harper said honestly. "None of them seem very likely so far."

"Fair enough." Lori shrugged. "Well – maybe when you hear the truth, you could let me know what it is?"

As they reached the downstairs landing and crossed into

the lobby, Harper found herself on the receiving end of several curious stares. Muttered conversations floated through the air towards her.

"...Misfortune, apparently."

"In the Costume Department..."

"...Wallace Reed is having a field day..."

Harper bit her lip. If Wallace Reed had been sceptical about the Wondria before, her accident certainly wasn't going to help matters. She was surprised – and unsettled – to see that even the senior apprentices were hanging around Jthe lobby, muttering to each other. They usually kept to themselves. ("Doing their secret projects with their secret knowledge and basking in each other's secretiveness," was how Trick had summed it up grumpily.)

"Harper!"

Her name was accompanied by running footsteps, and in the next moment Harper found herself surrounded by Trick, Rosie and Anvi.

"Are you all right?"

"What happened?"

"They said Misfortune knocked you down a flight of stairs!"

"Um – I should get back to the office," said Lori. "Will you be okay from here?"

"I think so," Harper replied. "Thanks again."

Lori nodded, then melted away so quickly it was as if he'd disappeared into thin air.

"So, is it true?" Anvi persisted. "Was it Misfortune again?"

"Um – yeah," Harper said, swallowing hard. "It showed up in the Costume Department and…" She trailed off, finding herself suddenly unwilling to talk about the previous night's terror.

"We can talk about it later," Trick cut in. "Do you need help getting upstairs?"

"Shouldn't you be in training?" Harper asked.

"We're on lunch," Rosie chimed in. "We can help you."

Trick picked up Harper's backpack, while Anvi and Rosie looped Harper's arms around their shoulders to help her walk.

"Thanks," Harper said gratefully as the four of them turned towards the Living Wing. She felt a lot better with her friends next to her – so much so that she could almost ignore the stares and mutters that followed her all the way out of the lobby.

As they drew deeper into December, the first snowfalls of the season arrived. The Wondria was soon covered in a thick blanket of white, like an elegant old lady donning her winter cloak. Apprentices began showing up to training in layers and layers of scarves, clutching hot-water bottles, and one morning, Harper awoke to find her bedroom absolutely covered in decorations.

There were jaunty streamers hung from every inch of the

ceiling, holly garlands strung between all four bedposts and, somewhat terrifyingly, an enormous blow-up penguin staring at her from a corner. It looked like a decorations factory had moved into her room, set up a thriving business, then promptly exploded.

Harper briefly wondered if this was Trick's idea of a prank, before remembering that today marked the first day of Merrimas – a seven-day-long festival, culminating in the Merrimas Feast on the twenty-fifth. Each day leading up to the feast had a different theme; today was the Day of Decorations.

Donning her dressing gown and climbing down to the mess room, Harper saw that the entire Wondria had been festooned in decorations, with Merrimas trees, apple wreaths and even more giant blow-up penguins. (Harper wasn't fond of these: their eyes seemed to follow her wherever she went. Trick, on the other hand, loved them, and gave them a series of increasingly complicated nicknames starting with "Mr Waddles" and ending up with "Sir Flippington Paddle, first of his name, devourer of salmon and overlord of silly walks".)

Despite the creepy penguins, Harper was glad that Merrimas was here: it provided a welcome distraction from everything else that was going on. After her tumble down the stairs, the Board of Spectacular Theatrics had decided to extend their assessment period and were *still* hanging around the Wondria. The other apprentices had stopped acknowledging Harper's presence altogether. Fletcher's new security measures turned out to be a team of trolls who arrived at the Wondria before the show each night, standing at the doors in ill-fitting tuxedos and glaring at everyone who walked past. With all this, Harper *needed* something fun to stop her from descending into complete misery.

For the next week, each day was an adventure: there was the Day of Snow, which saw everyone walking around with bags of white chalk powder, pelting handfuls of it at each other at random intervals; the Day of Song, where no one was allowed to speak, but had to sing everything instead; and, somewhat strangely, the Day of Round Cheeses, which had them all up on a steep hillside bowling various cheeses in a highly competitive race. (Lahiri beat Fletcher with a wheel of Brie and was in excellent spirits for the rest of the day.)

The evening before the Merrimas Feast, the apprentices all hung nets outside of their windows to attract Our Lady of Impenetrable Winter – a jolly woman who whizzed around in a blimp, dropping presents from the sky for children to catch. They'd planned to stay up late to see if they could glimpse her, but somehow Harper found herself growing sleepier and sleepier, almost dozing off on the floor of the mess room before admitting defeat and going to bed.

The next morning Harper awoke to find a huge pile of presents caught in her net. Grinning, she hauled them into her room and began ripping them open. Inside, she found a woolly hat shaped like a wolf, a woodworking knife in a leather pouch, a postbox-red jumper, a set of *Persephone the Witch-Queen* books and a box of different flavoured hot chocolates (*Merrimas edition! Includes Peppermint, Brandy Butter and Barbecued Turkey*).

Harper donned her new jumper and hat before clambering down to the mess room. Trick was already seated at the breakfast table. He was also sporting a large, woolly hat, although his was shaped like a—

"Penguin? Really?" Harper eyed the hat mistrustfully.

"Excellent, isn't it?" Trick beamed.

As she settled next to him, Harper produced a neatly-wrapped gift.

"No pressure," she said, presenting it to Trick. "But if you don't like it, I'm going to throw your sweet stash into the engine furnace."

Harper had agonized over what to get Trick for Merrimas, poring over every magazine and catalogue that had been delivered to the Wondria in her search for the perfect present. As Trick tore into the wrapping paper, Harper decided with satisfaction that all that effort had been one hundred per cent worth it to see his face.

"Harper...this might be the greatest thing I've ever seen." Trick held the jumper up, looking beside himself with delight. It was forest green, and on the front were the words *CALM DOWN AND HAVE A CUPPA*. Below the writing was a picture of a teapot with a knitted, three-dimensional spout which sprouted out of the front of the jumper (making it look, Harper personally thought, like the wearer had been unfortunately impaled by a giant teapot).

After pulling the jumper gleefully over his head, Trick reached under his chair and brought out his own present, proffering it to Harper.

Harper unwrapped her gift to find a small, square sketch pad. She was slightly confused at first – she could draw about as well as a drunk giraffe – but then she opened the front cover and found herself at an absolute loss for words. The sketchbook was filled with memories – Trick's memories, which he'd sketched out in painstaking detail. The two of them as kids, riding their bikes through the Theatre Borough, building a snowman on the steps of a Concert Hall, scoffing popcorn on a bench next to a food vendor.

Harper swallowed around a sudden lump in her throat. She found that she could only manage a nod rather than a "thank you", but Trick seemed to understand.

The morning passed in a blur of playing games, toasting marshmallows and laughing until their stomachs ached. Then, in the early afternoon, they made their way down to the Auditorium for the Merrimas Feast. Harper couldn't help gasping as they entered. The cavernous room was lit entirely by twinkling candlelight, and a series of long tables had been set up on the stage, positively groaning with food. There were sizzling roasted meats and fluffy potatoes, bowls of curries with mounds of sticky rice, creamy seafood stews and piles of pan-fried bread rolls. There were also more desserts than Harper could name, ranging from frosted lime cakes to giant Merrimas puddings dancing with blue flames.

"Helja always outdoes herself at Merrimas," Trick said, grinning. "I suppose even grumpy Kobolds aren't immune to the season of goodwill."

The season of goodwill... Looking around, Harper wasn't sure if she could quite agree with that. Even among the delicious food and beautiful decorations, there was a fearful undercurrent to the atmosphere. Harper saw more than one party conferring in whispers to each other, and she noticed that increasing numbers of people were sporting large protective talismans – they'd obviously been a popular choice for Merrimas presents this year.

"...Daddy's persuaded the Council to agree to twice-monthly inspections of the Wondria," Althea Reed announced from a nearby table. "He says that if the Wondria has one more attack, it's finished."

Harper dropped her fork with a clatter. Was that true? Were they on their last chance? Now that Misfortune had come a third time, it seemed inevitable that another attack was on its way. Was this going to be the first and last Merrimas she ever had with the Spectaculars?

Once the food had been demolished, the feast descended into a giant party, but Harper found it hard to get back into the spirit of things. The music and dancing lasted well into the night, with even the junior apprentices staying up as late as they wanted. Roper and Lahiri organized a volleyball tournament using a Merrimas pudding as a ball, and Fletcher performed a rousing karaoke version of "The Ballad of the Polar Bear King" (all twenty-two verses), before leaping from the stage and crowd-surfing across the Auditorium.

Around eleven, Trick nudged her with a yawn. "I'm heading to bed," he said.

Harper was surprised. "Already?"

Trick hopped off the stage. "Yeah – I'm tired. See you tomorrow!" He jogged off through the stalls and slipped out of the Auditorium.

Harper watched him go, confused – it wasn't like Trick to miss a party. Then again, he *had* eaten a lot of sweets today – perhaps it was a sugar crash.

"Harper!"

Harper looked up to see Yosef crossing the stage towards her.

"I'd almost forgotten – I have something for you!"

Harper stifled a giggle as he rummaged through the pockets of his velvet jacket, pulling out a glittery party hat, a handful of ribbons and a half-eaten piece of gingerbread before eventually coming up with a little leather-bound album.

"I actually started this for your dad," he said, looking down at it. "Before we knew he was – you know. Even once we heard that he'd died, I just sort of – kept at it. I thought maybe you'd like it." He held it out to her, blinking a little.

"Oh." Harper wasn't sure how to react. "Thanks, Yosef. That means a lot."

"No problem." Yosef smiled a little sadly. "Hopefully there's some stuff in there that'll interest you."

After Yosef had left to join the volleyball game, Harper didn't open the album straight away. In fact, she waited until she'd left the party altogether and was safely tucked up in her bed.

The inside of the album was a patchwork of pictures, articles and flyers. Some were stuck straight onto the pages, while others were attached to flaps or pinned at one corner, forming several layers for Harper to sift through. One of the first articles announced the opening of the Wondria, along with a picture of Fletcher beaming outside the entrance. There were a lot of theatre openings that year, in fact, along with fancy galas and play premieres. Harper smiled, realizing what it was: a diary of the last few years, a scrapbook of all the big Spectacular events that she'd missed while down in the Smoke. On one page, an inky-blue invitation with silver swirling lettering took up almost the entire page:

You are cordially invited to the Winter Gala
Hosted by the Winter Playhouse
Acts include: Felix Rios and his choir of singing snowmen,
the Aurora Spinners dance troupe, The Enchanted
Snowflake Orchestra and many more!
Snow-bunny carriage rides available upon request
(strictly two people per carriage)
Please show this invitation at the entrance. Dress warmly

Tacked below the invitation was a press cutting depicting the Winter Gala. It was just as the invite described, from the singing snowmen down to the glittering, rabbit-drawn carriages. Beneath the picture was a caption:

Scenes from the now-infamous Winter Gala, before the appearance of a creature believed to be Misfortune, which resulted in one dead and multiple others injured.

For a moment, Harper couldn't understand why she'd suddenly turned cold all over, why her blood was suddenly thundering in her ears. She read the last line of the caption again: *one dead and multiple others injured.*

Harper's mind spun wildly back to the day at the Obelisk, to the Brightwood student who'd first told her about the Winter Gala and Misfortune's appearance. Had she mentioned a death? Harper didn't think so…

The rest of the article was folded up beneath the picture. Harper hurriedly tugged it open and read on:

After bringing chaos to the Winter Gala, Misfortune disappeared into the forest surrounding the Playhouse. A few hours later, in the early morning, a group of hikers found a trail of blood leading to a body lying in the snow.

"I thought it was just my mate Gary having a laugh at first," one of them reported. "But then we saw him on

the other side of the bank, having a wee in the bushes…
Ouch. Sorry, Gary. Would you mind not printing that
last bit?"

The other hikers declined to comment.

Harper closed the album. She felt sick and shaky. She couldn't believe that no one had told her that Misfortune had actually *killed* before. No wonder the Board of Theatrics were coming down so hard on the Wondria. It could have happened again – to her, that night in the Costume Department. It could have happened to any of them.

No. Harper's mind rejected the idea flat-out. No one was dying on her watch, and no one was closing the Wondria. She needed to figure out a plan – to stop Misfortune, so it couldn't hurt anyone or anything ever again. But how? She'd need a trap, or…

An idea hit her. She clambered out of bed, overturning the album, and went to her wardrobe. Sifting through the hanging clothes, she eventually found the coat that she'd been wearing on the day they'd gone to the Obelisk. Reaching into the pocket, she closed her hand gently around the egg that Thief had given her and pulled it out.

Harper looked down at it. Thief had told her to smash the egg against the floor to get a message to him. With only the briefest of hesitations – she really didn't want to have to clean up eggy gunk – Harper raised the egg over her head and threw it at the floor. Instead of smashing into a gloopy mess, the lavender shell split neatly in two and let loose a puff of purple powder.

"Um...Thief?" Harper ventured. "Are you there?"

For a moment, nothing happened. Then the powdery cloud began to move, slowly forming itself into a head.

"Hello?" Thief's voice came from the cloud-head.

"It's Harper. Harper Woolfe."

"Oh. What do you want?" Thief's head asked brusquely, before shaking from side to side. "Sorry – that was rude, wasn't it? I mean, what can I do for you?"

Harper took a breath and told him the story – from seeing the paw print on opening night, to discovering, just moments ago, that Misfortune had once killed someone. "I was wondering – do you have something that might help us? To trap Misfortune, or banish it?"

Thief looked thoughtful. "I could use a binding spell – it would summon the creature into a protective circle, and then trap it inside indefinitely. Would that do?"

"Yes!" Harper nodded fervently. "You can really do that?"

Thief nodded. "I'd need some ingredients, though – and I can't exactly just saunter into the local apothecary and order some."

"We can get ingredients," Harper said quickly.

"All right then, consider it a deal. When you have everything, smash the egg again to summon me. It should be good for another couple of goes." The purple cloud disappeared, leaving nothing but the eggshell on the ground, which was somewhat haphazardly joining itself together again. On the floor next to it was a small, folded piece of paper.

Harper picked it up and opened it to find a list of ingredients. A wave of determination rose in her. She was done watching over her shoulder for Misfortune. This creature wasn't going to hurt anyone else – and if Wallace Reed thought he was closing down the Wondria, he had another think coming.

CHAPTER SIXTEEN

Shopping for Breezes

Harper arrived early to the apprentice quarters the next morning. She hadn't slept well: the article about the Winter Playhouse and the body in the snow had planted a hard seed of fear inside her chest, although she'd tried to hold on to the determination that speaking to Thief had instilled in her. As the other apprentices talked eagerly about sledging outside on snowy hills, or organizing gingerbread-house-making contests ("Remember last year, when Yosef made that giant gingerbread treehouse – in an actual tree?" Anvi reminisced happily), Harper waited impatiently for Trick to arrive. As soon as he appeared, munching on a large piece of Merrimas pudding, Harper ran over and filled him in on her conversation with Thief.

"He gave me a list of ingredients, but…I think it must be

wrong," Harper confided, sliding the list out of her pocket. "I mean, it's just…nonsense."

The list had baffled Harper ever since she'd opened it the night before. According to the books she'd read, Witch spells were supposed to involve herbs and plants. The list Thief had given her, however, was somewhat different.

A three-week-old odd sock. A leftover jar of peaches. An aquamarine jumper, never worn. A dream, cherished and then dashed. Water from a tempestuous source.

Trick gave a wry smile as he read it. "Yeah. Witches are scavengers – they make their spells out of all the left-behind things, the abandoned stuff that no one else wants."

"So –" Harper blinked – "if we get all that stuff, it'll actually make a spell?"

"It will." Trick looked hesitant. "But, Harper…are you sure about this? I mean… Do we want to be getting all mixed up with Witch magic?"

"Really?" Harper rolled her eyes. "You want to give up a chance to stop Misfortune, just because Witches and Spectaculars have this weird our-magic-is-better-than-yours thing? Well, sorry, I don't care about whose magic is better. I care about saving the Wondria and everyone in it." She took the list back and scanned the items again. "What does *Water from a tempestuous source* mean?"

"Water from somewhere that's rough, or turbulent – like the sea, or a waterfall, I'd guess."

"Are we passing any of those soon?"

"I don't think so." Trick shook his head. "We're still making our way through Raven Falls. It's pretty barren out here."

Harper sighed. "Fine. We'll have to focus on getting the other ingredients first. Where shall we start?"

As the new year rolled around, the days remained dark, and a bone-deep cold settled in. Over the course of January, there were no fewer than *ten* alleged sightings of the Four Curses. From Brightwood to Fortune's Edge, reports were flooding in by the day: the Opulence Theatre reported an outbreak of the Pulsing Pox after being visited by a "nasty-looking gerbil", which they claimed was Malady, while *The Spectacular Daily Show* interviewed a hysterical actor who was convinced that Misfortune had caused him to develop an unpleasant flatulence problem. Harper found herself constantly on edge: their last attack had been in December, so it felt like another one was surely looming just around the corner.

And, of course, there were their new twice-monthly inspections from the Spectacular Board of Theatrics. Althea Reed, who continued to whisper pointedly about Harper any time there was the slightest mishap in the Wondria, looked smugger and smugger as her father and his colleagues combed the Wondria, interrogating teachers and apprentices alike, and writing copious notes. Harper didn't understand – it looked like Wallace Reed *wanted* to close the Wondria down, but why shut the theatre that his own daughter was training at? Then again, Althea had mentioned several times that she had a place reserved at some fancy conservatoire in the north, should the worst happen. ("Apparently she didn't get in the first time – set fire to the Showrunner's wig during her audition," Rosie informed Harper with relish. "But Daddy made a large donation to ensure that they'll take her if he closes the Wondria.")

Harper spent any time that she wasn't in training trying to collect the ingredients for Thief's spell. It wasn't always easy, or particularly pleasant: she spent one evening combing through several bags of smelly laundry in the Costume Department to find an odd sock, and another trying to persuade Rosie to part with one of her many unworn jumpers. ("But aquamarine might come back into fashion one day!" Rosie had wailed, before eventually relenting.) She'd had to make no fewer than three dashes down to the kitchens in order to secure an old jar of peaches, her first two attempts being thwarted by Board members who wanted to question her about the Wondria's syllabus, its safety measures, or its structural integrity.

The dream was simple enough: Harper had had so many dreams about the theatres back in the Smoke, picturing them filled with bright lights and song, only to have them dashed each time she awoke and saw them sitting empty and abandoned. She wrote about this in as much detail as she could on a piece of paper, and stored it in her backpack.

The biggest problem, however, continued to be the water from a tempestuous source. Without an ocean or a waterfall nearby, Harper had started to worry that they'd never get hold of any. Luckily, as January rolled into February and the Wondria began making its way back through the Free Winds district, an opportunity presented itself.

They were travelling south and were due to pass back by Richton-on-the-Water, the riverside city that they'd arrived at after All Spooks' Eve. Surely, in a city formed of canals and streams, they'd be able to find a tempestuous water source – a small bottleneck of rapids? A slightly aggressive babbling brook? Harper was desperate to complete the ingredients list as soon as they could. They hadn't had an attack so far this year, but that didn't reassure Harper: rather, it gave her a horrible feeling that Misfortune was gearing up, getting ready to unleash something worse than ever…

The Wondria settled to the south of Richton-on-the-Water, alongside the cheerful front doors and overflowing window boxes of the canal boats. That afternoon, they had a Theatrics session with Lahiri, which involved attempting to change their appearances to suit different characters, like the actors they'd seen on opening night. Trick was very good: almost as soon as he'd started speaking (playing Old Man Grumble from the play *A Merrimas Haunting*), he'd managed to sprout a long grey beard and an impressive set of bushy eyebrows.

Harper was still struggling to channel Star-Stuff properly – her extract required her to look like a glamorous starlet, but by the end of the session all she'd managed to do was turn her hair a shade of platinum blonde that did *not* suit her at all.

At the end of the session, Lahiri made an announcement. "I will be leading a visit to Richton-on-the-Water's famous floating market this evening. Anyone who wishes to join, we will be converging in the lobby at six sharp."

Harper exchanged an excited glance with Trick. This could be their opportunity to search for the water from a tempestuous source.

At six o'clock, Harper and Trick joined the crowd jostling outside the front doors. When they were all assembled, Lahiri led the way along the canal, across a rickety wooden bridge and onto a series of boats that were all interconnected by gangplanks and rope bridges.

"All right," Lahiri said. "I have to visit the glassblower for more Star-Stuff jars. I want all of you to meet me at the Café Boat in two hours. No exceptions."

They all nodded eagerly, and as soon as Lahiri gave the word, they scattered. Rosie headed straight for a boat stuffed with rails of vintage dresses, dragging Anvi with her. Harper and Trick politely declined their invitation to join them, and waited until they were safely out of sight.

"Okay. Where do we start?" Harper looked around.

"Um…this way." Trick led Harper across a rickety gangplank and onto a boat hosting an outdoor bakery. The scent of fresh bread and pastries hit them all at once, and Harper's mouth began to water. One vendor was icing a twelve-tier Victoria sponge, while another was stretching out lengths of warm dough like putty. Harper motioned to Trick before they could both get distracted by their stomachs, and they quickly wobbled their way across a plank onto a boat that was covered in a domed glass roof. Here, the stalls were crammed with plants of all shapes and sizes. Two men were paddleboarding on a pair of flat banana leaves, while a vendor in full protective gear was wrangling a giant, sabre-toothed sunflower.

"She's really very friendly!" the vendor called desperately to an alarmed-looking couple. "Very good with children and dogs – special price if you buy today!"

Harper shook her head at Trick, and they crossed the boat, ducking to avoid the plant's viciously sharp teeth, which lurched dangerously towards them as they passed.

"Sorry!" the vendor yelled.

They crossed at least a dozen more boats in the next hour, Harper keeping a sharp eye for any slightly turbulent waters. To her dismay, they'd heard a *lot* of talk about the Four Curses. One woman, who was trying on a pair of bat-winged boots at a shoe stand, announced that she was organizing a boycott of *all* theatres until it got sorted out.

As they crossed onto a boat hosting a large Witch trade, Harper suddenly heard a sound that made her blood freeze. A low, sneering voice that was altogether too familiar.

"...I've told you, I have the money. Now give me what I want."

Harper grabbed Trick and pulled him behind a group of Witches who were trying on a series of outlandish hats. Peering through peacock feathers and bunches of wax fruit, Harper was horrified to see Alistair Sharpe, the star-hunter. He was stood at a stall that announced *Spells and charms, mixed on the spot for all your needs!*

"I've already told you," the vendor was saying firmly. "I trade for ingredients. So if you've got any odd socks, old toothbrushes, or anything of the like, I'd gladly sell you the tracking spell. If not, you'll have to take your business elsewhere."

Sharpe began to argue, and Trick nudged Harper. "Let's get out of here."

They edged towards the far side of the boat and dashed over a gangplank. Harper looked back over her shoulder.

"A tracking spell... Isn't that what he was trying to get from Thief?"

Trick nodded. "He must still be hunting the stars."

Harper shuddered slightly. "We need to get away from this part of the market." Harper had no intention of Sharpe recognizing her and adding her to his "people to decapitate" list. She looked around. They were on a boat packed with stalls selling tea leaves in glass jars. Customers reclined on futons with steaming cups, looking very contented.

"Maybe we should double back," she suggested. "The

Goblin Tattooist Display was down a little canal, that might get choppy somewhere…"

"We went that way already, remember?" Trick said. "Into that weird jewellery fair, where that vendor was trying to sell us friendship bracelets that he claimed were definitely not made out of human teeth, but looked very much like they were made out of human teeth."

"Eugh, yeah." Harper shuddered. "All right…so maybe left instead? Towards the Fae Market?"

Trick nodded, and they hurried off. When they reached the Fae Market, they found stalls dripping with crystals, a series of fortune-telling tents and a little stall that had a sign above it that read *Bottled Breezes.*

"Tropical breezes, countryside draughts, all bottled for your pleasure!" The vendor, a Fae man with a glittering black mask, called down to them.

"Why would people want to buy a breeze?" Harper asked.

The vendor seemed affronted. "A breeze is many things, my girl. A breeze is the smell of the place it comes from, the taste, the feel. If you ever wished to carry a piece of home with you wherever you went, a breeze would be the way to do it."

Harper supposed he had a point. She ran her eyes over the bottles for sale. *Breeze from outside a bakery on a winter's morning – bestseller!* read one. *Breeze from the back end of a cow – perfect for enemies!* read another. Harper snorted, then moved her gaze along to the next bottle. This one had an inky-black label which bore the words: *Wind from within a midnight storm*. Inside the bottle were dark wisps of wind, circling about with bits of a storm cloud and a few hailstones.

Suddenly, something clicked in Harper's brain. She grabbed on to Trick.

"Trick, there are bits of a storm cloud in there," she said urgently.

"So?" Trick asked, frowning at her. "Personally, I'd rather have the cow-breeze – imagine Althea's face if we released it into her room…"

"A storm cloud!" Harper repeated impatiently. "Doesn't that sound like *Water from a tempestuous source* to you?"

She didn't wait for Trick to reply before waving to the vendor. "Excuse me, how much for the midnight-storm bottle?"

The Fae man raised an eyebrow. "Storm clouds are a Grade Five listed substance; you have to be eighteen or over to buy them." He looked down at Harper with a smirk. "Are you trying to tell me that you're over eighteen?"

"Well…no, but…"

It was no use: the vendor turned away before she'd even begun to think of an excuse.

"I don't think he's going to sell it to us," Trick said helpfully.

"Yeah, I noticed." Harper looked at the jar. They were too close to turn back now. "I think…we're going to have to steal it."

"*Steal* it?"

"It's the only way!" Harper knew that stealing was wrong, but they *needed* that storm cloud for Thief's spell. Misfortune could turn up any time now – and if it did, everyone at the Wondria could be in danger, and the Board might close the theatre down.

"You distract him," Harper whispered. "I'll go for the jar."

Trick hesitated for a moment, then nodded. "Okay." He walked forwards and leaned against the stall, signalling to the vendor.

"Hello, sir!" he said jauntily. "My name is Nicholas Nightby, I'm a scholar from the Brightwood district. I'm just curious – do you have any other names for what you sell here?"

The vendor looked at the sign, confused. "They're bottled breezes."

"That first bit, though," Trick said, tilting his head. "Would you say 'bottled' is the right word? Don't you think 'imprisoned' might be better? Or 'confined'?"

Harper had no idea what Trick was talking about, but he had the vendor's attention. She ducked behind the stall and made a beeline for the storm jar.

"Are you from the Council or something?" The vendor asked Trick suspiciously. "'Cos I had a permit to catch these breezes."

Harper reached the shelf and stretched her hands upwards,

straining to get them around the jar. It wobbled precariously, then tipped forwards off the shelf. Harper caught it, but couldn't help letting out a small gasp. The vendor looked round, and Harper ducked behind a shelf.

"What about the second part?" Trick asked loudly. "Some of these are stronger than 'breezes', wouldn't you say? That sea air, for example…isn't that more of a gust?"

"Perhaps." The vendor turned to him, sounding very annoyed. "But the stall's called 'Bottled Breezes'. It's been that way since my grandad owned it."

Harper crawled out from behind the shelf and ducked round to the other side of the stall, the jar tucked safely under her arm.

"Yeah. Do you know what – 'Bottled Breezes' is perfect. Have a good day!" Trick said quickly, before turning away and joining Harper.

"Nice work!"

"You too, Nicholas Nightby." Harper grinned. "Why were you asking him so many questions about the name of his stall?"

"I was trying to get him to say that he sold trapped wind," Trick said sadly. "But he didn't go for it."

Harper looked at him incredulously for a moment, then burst out laughing.

"Oi! You two!" The Fae man had stepped out from behind his stall and was pointing at Harper and Trick. "Thieves!"

"Run!" Harper hissed, and the pair of them turned and

sped across the length of the boat. They vaulted over the side, jumping the canal that lay between this boat and the next, and landing rather unfortunately – *slap bang* – in the middle of a fish market. Harper collided with a man clutching an armful of salmon, while Trick fell face first into a display of squid.

"Eugh," Trick said, wiping slime off his face.

The vendor was still shouting after them. Harper grabbed Trick's arm and pulled him across the deck, weaving through the rest of the stalls to reach the other side of the boat.

They ran without knowing where they were going, darting through stalls and displays, bumping into shoppers and yelling apologies behind them as they hurtled on. The stalls and stands gradually grew sparser: they were obviously reaching the outer limits of the market. The sky was beginning to darken; Harper had no idea how much time they had left before they had to meet Lahiri.

Eventually, they skidded to a stop, both of them doubled over and panting.

"Muses!" Trick collapsed to the floor. "I think I'm dying."

Harper clutched a stitch in her side. "I think my lungs are falling out of my face."

It took them both a while to get their breath back. Harper double-checked the bottle, making sure it was still safely tucked in her coat pocket.

"Where are we?" Trick asked once he'd stopped complaining of imminent death.

Harper peered around as well. It was eerily silent, as if this were a part of the city that everyone avoided.

"Harper," Trick said quietly. He pointed to a wooden sign that was stuck into the water, the words faded and smudged, but still legible:

The Old Town Ruins, East End –
Fallen Site
Proceed with caution!

Harper peered beyond the sign. Through the dim light, she could just about make out a half-broken rope bridge which led to an interconnected clump of abandoned, covered rafts.

"This is where one of the stars fell," Harper murmured.

Trick stared at the island of rafts ahead of them. "Do you think that's why Sharpe is here? He's checking to see if it's still in there?"

"Perhaps..." Harper frowned. "But then why would he need the tracking spell?"

"For the others, maybe." Trick shrugged. "There are thirteen out there, after all."

"We should look," Harper said. "If there *is* a star there, we don't want Sharpe to be the one who gets hold of it."

She knew that it was highly unlikely the star would still be there – Lahiri had said that they'd all but disappeared – but she couldn't help feel a thrill of excitement.

"I don't know, Harper," Trick said. "That rope bridge looks *old*. And—"

He was cut off by a strange, thrumming sound, and a churning movement beneath them. The boat they were on pitched sideways, almost throwing them both to the floor again.

"What on Earth was *that*?" Harper asked.

Trick looked over the side of the boat. "I think…" he said slowly, "that's the Mega Mermaid Ukulele Band."

Harper rushed to join him, peering into the water below them. Sure enough, she could just about make out five shadowy figures deep beneath the surface – figures with long, fish-like tails and wild turquoise hair. Harper gaped: reading the word "mermaid" and actually seeing them were two very different things.

The strumming sound came again, and the boat lurched the other way. This time, Harper understood: the strumming was *music*, and it was disturbing the waters around them.

"I think it's about to get choppy in this part of town," Trick said.

"Yep," Harper agreed, her stomach starting to churn. "Let's go."

She and Trick turned and began making their way back the way they'd come. Harper tried not to look back at the Fallen Site longingly. After all, they might not have seen a real-life fallen star, but they had the storm bottle. The ingredients list was complete.

"Let's call on Thief when we get back to the Wondria," Harper said determinedly to Trick as they walked. "We're ending this. Tonight."

CHAPTER SEVENTEEN

The Dreamscape
Transit System

When they called on Thief he agreed to come and do the spell, but said that he wouldn't be able to get to the Wondria for three days. Harper spent those days in a perpetual state of anxiety, convinced that Misfortune would show up before Thief arrived. And what would happen if it did? More accidents, more injuries? *Death?*

On the third day, Harper and Trick managed to slip away early from the apprentice quarters and steal up to the very top floor of the Teaching Wing. The practice rooms there were reserved for Spectaculars whose gifts involved playing the bagpipes, singing opera or performing death metal, and were often unoccupied. Once they were safely inside, Harper took out the egg and threw it against the floor. The lilac cloud appeared, this time forming an entire figure. It grew more and more solid, until suddenly the cloud disappeared, and Thief was standing before them. He stretched out, then looked around.

"Right. Did you bring any snacks?"

"Snacks?" Harper frowned. "That wasn't on the list."

Thief sighed. "I'm just saying, in most Witch circles it's considered polite to provide snacks if someone is doing a spell for you. I'm fond of lemon buns, personally."

"We'll keep that in mind for the future," Harper said. "Here are the ingredients, though!" She held them out, eager to get started.

Thief got to work on creating the spell, bundling all the ingredients together in a hessian bag. Harper wasn't sure just *how* a sock, a jar of peaches and the several other random objects could be turned into a spell, but she was keen to see it. Thief's gingery curls fell into his eyes again as he worked, and he blew them out of the way impatiently. He tied the bag with a length of cord, and it began to shine gently. After a few moments Thief opened the bag again and shook out a glowing, translucent blob that almost seemed...

"Sorry – is that *alive*?" Harper asked incredulously.

"Of course. All spells are alive," Thief said, as though he was announcing that all grass was green. "When you put ingredients together, you create the life of a spell. In return, the spell does something for you."

Harper could hardly believe her eyes. The little blob was dancing around on the floor, wobbling this way and that like a jellyfish. When Thief looked at it, it seemed to straighten up, like it was standing to attention.

"This spell will summon your creature from wherever it is, and trap it in a protective circle within three feet of where the spell sits," Thief said.

"Okay." Fear and anticipation warred inside Harper – fear about having to face Misfortune again, and anticipation about finally being able to be rid of the creature that had brought so much destruction and chaos.

"Right. Stay very still. Witch magic is very precise – a lot more so than your showy Spectacular magic, if you don't mind me saying."

"I do a bit, actually," Trick muttered.

Thief lifted his free hand. For a moment, nothing happened. Then suddenly a wind whipped up around them, flinging Harper's hair across her face so she could barely see. It whirled around them like a tornado, reaching up to the ceiling.

"It's working!" Harper cried.

The wind continued to shriek, making the edges of their clothes flap around like caged birds. As Harper pushed her hair out of her face, she suddenly locked eyes with Trick across the circle. He looked rattled, somehow – almost scared. Harper blinked. She didn't think she'd ever seen something rattle Trick. Was he really *that* suspicious of Witch magic?

Then, as quickly as it had come, the wind stopped.

Blinking away the moisture in her eyes, Harper studied the room.

There was nothing there.

"Did it work?" Trick frowned, wiping an arm across his eyes.

"I – I don't understand," Thief said, staring down at the spell, which was swaying wearily. "The spell was in motion! What happened?" Thief looked around, as though a giant silver cat might be hiding in the corner.

Harper's previous relief was quickly fading as she observed the empty room. "So…it *didn't* summon Misfortune?"

Thief sighed. "Apparently not."

Harper sat down heavily. It was as though the weight of all her worries had suddenly come crashing down on top of her. She'd been depending on the spell to finally end this business with Misfortune. Now it had failed, and Harper was out of ideas about what to do. She dropped her head into her hands. For the first time ever, she felt a tiny surge of longing for her old life in the Smoke. It might have been boring and stifling, but at least there her biggest problems had been detentions and the Carver twins – and if things got too much, she always had her mum to hand, ready with some good advice and a bowl of apple crumble. She felt a pang thinking of her mum and wondered what she'd say if she was here.

"Um – are you all right?" Thief asked hesitantly.

Harper didn't trust herself to talk, so she said nothing.

"I'm sorry," Thief said, sounding genuinely upset.

"It's not your fault," Harper said, raising her head. "I'd just really hoped that would work." Tears stung at her eyes, and she bit her lip hard. Trick took a step closer and put a comforting hand on her shoulder.

"Is there anything else we can do? Anything that would help?" Thief asked.

"I want my mum."

It slipped out before Harper could stop it, and she immediately flushed at how pathetic she sounded. But it was true – her mum *always* had a solution to things, always knew the right thing to say. Letters were fine, but it wasn't the same as talking in real time.

There was a beat of silence, then Trick looked up at Thief.

"What about your eggs?" he asked. "Couldn't Harper borrow one of them?"

"Teleportation devices can only operate within the Hidden Peaks – Magical Transportation Code, Amendment One."

"Oh, yeah." Trick's shoulders slumped.

Thief looked at Harper for a long moment.

"I do have something else…but it might not be exactly what you have in mind."

Harper looked at him sharply. "What is it?"

Thief shifted. "Well…I could help you access the Dreamscape Transit System…"

Harper blinked. "The what now?" She glanced at Trick, but he looked just as baffled.

"It's a Witch invention – a method of communication that can only be accessed through dreams. Dreams are, obviously, difficult things – very hard to move through with any sort of purpose. That's what the Dreamscape Transit System is for – it allows you to exercise control over your dreams, to visit a certain place and converse with certain people."

Beneath the fear and misery, hope flared in Harper's chest. "So – I could talk to my mum? In a dream?"

"Yep."

"How do I access it?"

Thief reached into his pocket and held out an object. There was a beat of silence.

"It's a fishing hook," Harper said, looking up at Thief.

"Yes," he replied simply. "The lines of the Dreamscape Transit System run above everyone as they sleep, but you can't hook onto it unless you have a – well, a hook. Hang it above your bed just before you go to sleep, and it'll give you access."

"Okay…" Harper nodded, digesting this. "So how will my mum get in?"

"Only one person needs the token to access the Dreamscape. Once your mum falls asleep, she'll receive a request to join you in your dream."

"*Amazing,*" Harper whispered, taking the fishing hook with a sudden rush of excitement. "Thanks, Thief."

Thief shrugged. "It's no bother. I hope you get the answers you need."

Harper turned to Trick. "Are you okay? You looked a bit – weird, during that."

"I just – I thought I saw something at one point," said Trick. "But I must have been mistaken."

"Perhaps it was a dud." Harper shrugged. The spell seemed to hang its head, looking so dejected that Harper felt bad and gave it a pat.

"What happens to a spell after you've used it?" Harper asked curiously.

"You can only use a spell once. Afterwards, you're supposed to let them out into the wild, but some people keep them as pets – which isn't sensible, because they're very hard to house-train." Thief stooped to picked up the spell and the egg, blowing his hair out of his face as he did so. "Well – I still owe you one. So if there's anything else I can do, send a message."

"Wait." Harper stepped forwards and reached into her pocket "Here – I have something for you too."

Thief looked down at the object she was holding out with upmost suspicion.

"I – what? What is it?"

"It's a scrunchy," Harper replied. "It'll keep your hair out of your face."

Thief peered down at it, surveying it from every angle. "It's...*yellow*."

"Yep. It'll clash terrifically with your hair," Harper said cheerfully.

Thief took the scrunchy very carefully. "Thank you," he said. "I – no one's given me a present in years."

He gave them a hesitant smile, then smashed the egg against the floor. Harper stood and watched as he gradually dissolved back into coloured smoke and disappeared.

Harper kept the hook hidden in her pocket until she was safely shut in her bedroom that night. She changed into her pyjamas and climbed into bed before taking the fishing hook out of her pocket and examining it. Thief had said *hang it above your bed*. Did that mean...?

Feeling slightly foolish, Harper reached upwards with the fishing hook. For a moment nothing happened, then suddenly, Harper felt a snag, as though the hook had just caught on a piece of fabric. She gave a gentle tug, and the hook resisted: it was hitched on something.

Slowly, Harper unfurled her hand from around the hook. It remained where it was, hanging in mid-air.

Harper stared at it for a moment before lying down in her bed. She shut her eyes and tried to quiet her mind enough to fall asleep. It took a long time – the anxieties of the day were still churning in her head – but eventually, she felt herself slipping slowly into sleep.

When Harper opened her eyes, she knew instantly that she was in a dream. She was standing on some sort of dais – a circular stone platform with a series of cable cars trundling about overhead. They were criss-crossing in all directions, against a backdrop of a starry sky. A sign at the edge of the dais read *The Dreamscape Transit System.*

Harper looked around her. There only seemed to be one way to travel – and indeed, as soon as she took a step towards the edge of the dais, one of the cable cars swooped down to meet her. The door swung open, and Harper stepped inside. It was small and cosy, with panelled windows on all sides. The door swung shut again, and the cable car started to move.

As they rattled along, Harper noticed that each of the cable cars terminated at a different dais. Many seemed to be hosting meetings between people: on one, a couple sat on a pair of cheerful, striped deckchairs, drinking lime cocktails. On another, a family all swam together in a sunken swimming pool, laughing and splashing.

Harper's cable car slowed to a stop, and the doors swung open. Harper stepped out onto a dais that contained a little café with white tables and mismatching lamps. It looked familiar to Harper, somehow.

Gulliver's, she realized, smiling – it looked just like the café next to the Fix-It shop.

Harper noticed other things as she looked around: a wall papered entirely in pages from books, a string of brightly-coloured bunting stretching from one arch to another, a tap that appeared to be flowing with hot chocolate. Harper felt her heart leap: this dais must be *her* dream, made up of all the things that she loved the most.

Harper perched on one of the chairs. Had her mother received the request? Would she be brought here, to Harper's dream, or to a dais of her own?

She didn't have to wait long to get her answer. Out of the darkness, another cable car came rolling in her direction. It halted at the edge of the dais, and the door opened to reveal...

"Mum!" Harper ran forwards with a huge grin and threw her arms around her mother.

"Harper?" Flora was wearing a pair of strawberry-printed pyjamas and looking very confused. "Where am I?"

"We're in a dream. My dream!"

"It was the strangest thing – I'd just dropped off, and suddenly there was this voice telling me that someone from the Hidden Peaks was trying to contact me and asking whether I accepted it. I did, of course, and suddenly I was in a cable car..." Harper's mum hugged her tightly, then looked around. "What is this? I don't remember the Spectaculars having a way to communicate through dreams."

"They don't," Harper admitted. "I got the token from a Witch friend."

"A Witch?" Flora raised her eyebrows. "Well. That's – nice of them, I suppose."

They took a seat at one of the tables. As soon as they sat down, a couple of menus appeared on the table. Harper grabbed one and scanned the listed items eagerly.

"Do you think we have to order from somebody?" Flora looked around the café.

"It's a dream," Harper said slowly. "So I think we just…"

She focused on an item labelled "Hot Chocolate with Absolutely Everything (no, really)"; and a moment later a giant mug appeared on the table in front of her. The name was certainly appropriate: the hot chocolate was topped not only with marshmallows and cream but flowers, seashells and a pair of dice; inexplicably, two knitting needles were also sticking out of the top. It came with a pot of flavoured sugar cubes (*caramel, pineapple, bonfire toffee*). Her mother ordered something called a "Bedtime Surprise", which turned out to be a mug of deep-blue liquid that read out a line of a bedtime story each time you sipped it.

"Once upon a time a wizard wandered down the deserted beach…"

"So…" Harper's mother set down the mug on the table, frowning slightly at the soothing voice that had just issued from it. "This dais that we're on – this is your dream, yes? It's made up of things that are inside your mind?"

"Must be." Harper nodded.

"So, then – what's *that*?" Her mother nodded towards the edge of the dais. Harper looked around, and her blood ran cold.

At the very edge of the dais, Misfortune was prowling up and down. Harper knew it was only a dream manifestation – he was blurry and translucent, and kept flickering out – but it still made her shudder.

"Yeah…that's what I wanted to talk to you about."

Harper took a deep breath, and it all came tumbling out: the Four Curses panic, Misfortune's attacks, Harper's conviction that it was *her* who'd started it all on opening night. She played down her fall in the Costume Department slightly – she didn't want to cause her mother *too* much worry. Her mother listened seriously, nodding her head encouragingly whenever Harper got stuck for words. When she finally ran out of steam, Flora lifted her mug to her lips and took a long sip of her drink.

"The wizard came across a tower, where a princess waved from a high window..."

"Oh, shut up," Flora said to the mug. "Okay. To start with, I'm with your friends on this one – I don't believe that this is your fault. I know the Spectaculars are a superstitious bunch, but your father said and did the wrong things *all the time* in theatres, and he never summoned any Curses."

Harper looked down at the table. She was glad to hear that her dad didn't set much store by superstitions – but she'd seen Misfortune for herself, seen what it was capable of, and it all seemed to lead back to her.

"But whatever this creature is, you can't go around putting yourself in danger, trying to save everyone. You're a first-year apprentice – you don't have the kind of knowledge that Fletcher and the Council have. Let *them* worry about catching this thing."

Harper bit her lip, not meeting her mother's eye.

"Harper," her mother said seriously. "Whatever this is,

it's dangerous, and I won't have you putting yourself in harm's way. Do you want me to write to Fletcher about this?"

"No." Harper shook her head quickly. "He's already working on it."

"Good." Flora looked perturbed. "It's strange that no one's noticed it getting in. You say that Fletcher has security on the doors, and there's no sign of forced entry anywhere else? Are there any secret passageways or tunnels that lead to the Wondria?"

"I don't think so." This sparked something in Harper's mind, though. "Maybe I could look! There might be somewhere that's been missed or overlooked...then at least we could guard against any future attacks."

"I don't mind you exploring the Wondria," Flora said. "But if you find anything, go straight to Fletcher, all right? I don't want you getting hurt."

"I won't," Harper assured her. "I'll be careful, I promise." She felt a new burst of hope at this prospect: they might have failed to trap Misfortune, but she could at least comb every inch of the Wondria and see if she could discover any hidden entrances the creature might be using.

Her mother asked more about life at the Wondria and Harper's friends, and Harper filled her in as they finished their drinks. Flora had just taken the last sip of her Bedtime Surprise – "*the wizard married the princess and they all lived happily ever after*" the story concluded, making Harper snort

– when the hook in Harper's pocket began to glow. Harper glanced down at it.

"I guess that means our time's up," she said, her heart sinking.

Flora stepped forwards, arms open. Harper hugged her mother hard, breathing in her perfume-and-engine-oil smell. Then she turned and stepped into her cable car and watched her mother do the same, before they were taken their separate ways through a world of dreams.

CHAPTER EIGHTEEN

Lunas Bay

The arrival of spring usually indicated a renewal – the world emerging from hibernation, coming to life again. At the Wondria, however, it felt like the opposite was happening. Despite the fact they hadn't faced another attack – *yet* – stories of the Wondria's "ill luck" had become notorious. They hadn't had a sold-out show in weeks. Patrons who were still willing to brave the theatres did so cautiously, keeping their eyes trained on the exits in case Misfortune appeared. Many of them wore talismans or draped wreaths of old vegetables around themselves, to "ward off" evil forces.

"As though a string of mouldy onions is going to repel anything other than their friends," Rosie said scornfully.

The Spectacular Board of Theatrics were still doing their twice-monthly inspections, hanging around the Wondria for days at a time. Harper made sure to save a special glare for Wallace Reed whenever she walked past him – which seemed to be frequently, now she was spending so much of her time searching the Wondria for hidden entrances. Since her conversation with her mother, Harper had set aside at least an hour every day to walk the corridors of the Wondria, investigating any door, staircase and wall that might be concealing a passageway or tunnel. She began to fall behind on homework, prompting a stern talking-to from Lahiri, but she reasoned that there wouldn't *be* any homework if Wallace Reed closed the Wondria. Sometimes Trick joined her, always oddly quiet as they walked together; sometimes it was just Harper, haunting the corridors of the Wondria like a ghost.

They were on track to arrive at the city of Lunas Bay in mid-March. The capital of the Hidden Peaks was surrounded on all sides by the Midnight Jungle – a dense, sprawling wilderness that gleamed with all the colours of night-time. The Wondria, travelling in its tram form by day for once, had to approach on tracks several feet up in the air in order not to get tangled in the thick roots. Harper hung out of the window, watching the jungle speed past. The trunks of the trees were as black as charcoal, covered in gleaming indigo leaves and plum-purple vines studded with silver leaves.

As they slowed to a stop outside a toll booth on the edge of the city, a man – a Witch, Harper guessed, from his bare feet – called up to them.

"What business do you have in Lunas Bay?"

Fletcher waved back at him. "We're Spectaculars with the Grand Wondria Music Hall and Theatre. We're booked for a spring run in the city."

The man's demeanour changed instantly. "The Wondria?" He looked wary – suspicious, even. "Who did you make this arrangement with?"

"The Mayor," Fletcher replied. Harper could sense the tension in his voice. "I have all of our correspondence, if you'd like to see it."

"No, no – if the Mayor's booked you, it's not my place to complain," the man muttered. "Well, your tram is too big for street level, you'll have to go to the top storey."

"Right-ho." Fletcher nodded to the man. "Many thanks for your *warm* welcome."

Trick nudged Harper. "You're going to want to hold onto something."

Harper frowned, but copied Trick, Rosie and Anvi as they all leaned forward and grabbed hold of the seats in front of them – just in time. The whole tram tilted upwards, sending several unprepared apprentices sliding backwards. Harper peered out of the window to see that it wasn't just the tram: the tracks themselves were tilting upwards, climbing vertically parallel to the city walls. Then, with a splutter, the Wondria surged into motion, coursing up the tracks and then levelling out as they chugged into the city.

They rumbled alongside the tops of buildings, passing spires and weathervanes so closely that Harper could have reached out and touched them. The sheer amount of colour and movement below them was breathtaking. There was a bustling town square, cobbled streets lined with elegant cafés and dance halls, and a glittering outdoor lido complete with a giant water slide. Street hawkers marched up and down, selling their wares and advertising experiences to tourists.

"*The Spinning Octopus: seafood imported all the way from the Veiled Seas!*"

"*Two-for-one tickets for the Lunas Bay Gallery's performance art exhibition!*"

"*Guided tours to the Winter Playhouse! See the site for yourself... if you dare...*"

Harper's stomach dropped. "The Winter Playhouse?"

"Where the Four Curses were awoken!" Anvi whispered, glancing uneasily at the tour guide, who was now preying on an old couple sporting jaunty *I LOVE LUNAS BAY* hats. "And where Misfortune showed up for the first time! It's somewhere in the Midnight Jungle."

"Trust the city to run *tours* to it, like it's some sort of amusement park," Rosie scoffed.

Harper glanced around uneasily. The Winter Playhouse – the place where a body had been found, where Misfortune had killed for the first time. It felt like a bad omen that the Wondria had returned here – as though the scenes at the Winter Gala were destined to repeat themselves.

When the Wondria trundled to a stop, a sizeable crowd had already gathered. Some looked excited, and hurried forwards to ask Fletcher about the show. Others looked fearful of what the Wondria might have brought into their city.

What you might have brought in, said a voice in Harper's mind.

For the next week, the shows were slightly busier than they had been – even the threat of a curse couldn't quite deter the city folk from a new, exciting attraction. Their Saturday matinee was half-full, putting everyone in good spirits. Harper had arranged to meet her friends to go to the evening show – Lahiri had set them an assignment to observe the Spectacular actors, to help with their own face-shifting sessions – but, with the proximity of the Winter Playhouse hanging over her, she wanted to comb the Wondria for any possible secret entrances again first.

Harper climbed to the very top of the Teaching Wing, to the row of practice rooms where they'd attempted the spell. (It wasn't as empty this time: a pair of long-haired Spectaculars were thrashing on guitars, screaming along to a song which, as far as Harper could tell, was just the words "DEATH!" over and over again.) She walked up and down the corridor, but, despite tapping on every wall, and searching every crevice, she couldn't see any further staircases or convenient hidden panels. Harper was about to give up and go back downstairs when Lori Montgomery emerged from one of the practice rooms adjacent to the screaming singers.

"Oh. Hello." He blinked, looking surprised. "What are you doing up here?"

"I…" Harper hesitated, wondering whether she should admit the truth. "I was looking for passageways. I've been searching the Wondria for any secret ways in or out – ways that Misfortune could be getting in."

"I see," Lori said thoughtfully. "Well, as far as I'm aware, there aren't any hidden passageways or entrances into the Wondria. Certainly not all the way up *here*. This is the highest floor, so above us there's only the Sky Vaults – and the entrance to them is sealed," he added, seeing a flash of hope cross Harper's face. "The creature couldn't be getting in from up there."

Harper sighed, dejected. "I just want to *help*," she admitted. "I need to do something."

"I know," Lori replied. "But Fletcher's security seems to be working so far – we haven't had an attack since he hired those trolls after your fall. Here, why don't I take you back down to the lobby? The show will be starting soon."

With a final glance around the corridor, Harper nodded. She walked with Lori all the way back down to the ground floor, where he peeled off to go and help backstage. Harper's search had taken longer than she'd expected, and she hurried back round to the front of house to meet Trick in the Gilded Bar. She found him sat at a table with a giant mug of tea, people-watching as the residents of Lunas Bay turned up. He shoved a cup of hot chocolate towards Harper and immediately started filling her in on all the people around them.

"Ivy Winterheart." Trick nodded to a Fae woman in the corner, her face hidden behind an ostrich-feather fan. "Inventor of the city's cable car system – it runs on the complaints of commuters, very energy-efficient."

Harper snorted. "I don't doubt it."

"That's the Teller," Trick continued, nodding over to a man dressed all in black with a balaclava pulled over his face. "Famous graffiti artist. Apparently, his identity is supposed to be some big secret, but everyone knows his name is Tim and he works at the bakery."

In the corner, the Teller pulled up his jacket collar in a way that was presumably supposed to look cool – but Harper thought she could see traces of powdered sugar on his boots. Hiding a smirk behind her mug, she looked around.

"What about her?" Harper tilted her head towards a woman in a long trench coat, who was tapping scarlet-painted nails against a table.

"Ace Malone, host of *The Spectacular Daily Show*."

Harper pursed her lips. She wasn't overly fond of the way the show had been reporting on the Four Curses. Their last special had been called "The Four Curses: Why It's All *Even Worse* Than You Think!"

Fletcher entered the bar to announce the half-hour call, and the patrons began to move towards the Auditorium. Out of the corner of her eye, Harper saw Ace Malone slip a small metal device out of her pocket. She stood and shouted loudly above the chatter: "So, Fletcher – do you have any comment to make about the safety of your institution?"

The crowd fell quiet as Fletcher turned with a frown. Harper saw his eyes narrow as he clocked Ace Malone, but he smiled pleasantly.

"No comment."

"It's just…" Ace Malone thrust the metal device forwards, which Harper assumed must be some sort of voice recorder. "Isn't yours the only theatre to have had *repeated* attacks from Misfortune?"

"We are confident in our security measures. We have no reason to fear any more unwelcome visitors." Fletcher looked steadily at Ace Malone. "It's perfectly safe."

"Do you think your patrons feel the same?" Ace glanced meaningfully around the bar.

"If they don't, they're free to leave," Fletcher said evenly. "I'm not forcing anyone to be here. Ah, Helja – I see you've come to escort our guest out."

Helja had appeared behind Ace Malone in the form of an extremely threatening garden hoe. Ace took one look at her and seemed to back down – but as she left, Harper heard her saying loudly, "This whole place should be shut down! Shut down, I say!"

Several people followed after her, throwing dirty looks at Fletcher. The ones who stayed muttered among themselves, looking around in suspicion.

Harper stared gloomily down at her hot chocolate, Ace Malone's words echoing in her head. *"This whole place should be shut down…"* She took a deep breath and finally voiced the question that had been haunting her for the last few months, but she'd been too afraid to ask.

"Trick…if they close the Wondria, what'll happen to us?"

There was a pause before Trick answered. "They'd have to send us all to whichever apprentice programmes still have space. I mean, we'd still be trained. But…"

"…we wouldn't be together," Harper finished for him.

Trick shook his head. "Probably not," he said, his voice grim.

Harper tried to imagine doing her apprenticeship at another theatre: without Fletcher and Lahiri and Roper, without Rosie and Anvi. Without Trick. It was inconceivable to her. *This* was where she belonged – she didn't want to go anywhere else.

They followed the crowd into the Auditorium and stood at the back. The Spectaculars tried to put on the best show they could, but Ace Malone's outburst had done its job. The audience seemed uneasy, constantly shifting about and looking over their shoulders. Luckily, the final act was Lahiri, who recited a sonnet about the memories of summer. As she spoke, the air gradually filled with the scent of honeysuckle, and a feeling of peace and calm spread through the audience. When she finished, the patrons applauded, before they began filing out of the Auditorium, all sporting beatific smiles and swaying slightly.

"Shall we?" Trick asked, stifling a yawn.

"Hmm?" Harper was preoccupied trying to swat away a bee which she was sure she could hear buzzing around her. "Oh – yeah, let's go."

They followed the crowd out into the lobby, listening to them cheerfully reminiscing about garden parties and punting trips. The security trolls glared as they opened the front doors to let the audience spill out into the warm evening air.

And chaos erupted.

"Help! Help me! Somebody – anybody, please!"

Screams and yells began erupting from the crowd, the people still inside the theatre running for the doors, others turning and pushing back *into* the Wondria. Harper looked around wildly.

"Who is that? What's happened?"

Fletcher was fighting his way through the chaos, Helja and the security trolls on his heels. Trick grabbed Harper's arm and pulled her through the crowd, out onto the cobbled street outside.

"*Muses…*" Trick muttered.

Ace Malone was lying in the street, groaning and whimpering. Her trench coat was torn, and her face and hair were covered in…

"Is that blood?" Harper whispered, feeling sick.

"It can't be." Trick shook his head. "It – it can't be…"

A few patrons had already reached Ace, crouching down beside her.

"Ace? Are you all right?"

"What happened?"

At this question, Ace Malone sat bolt upright. Blood trickled down her face, and her eyes looked wild.

"Misfortune," she gasped. "It was here. It attacked me!"

A wave of gasps and stifled screams ran through the crowd.

"I was just sitting here," Ace Malone continued hoarsely. "Just going over some notes, and it came stalking round the corner… Huge it was, with these giant claws…"

Harper's stomach tightened; she was all too familiar with the description.

"I tried to run, but it viciously attacked me," Ace moaned. "I only escaped 'cos I jabbed it in the eye with my pen…"

"Where did it go?" a man from the crowd yelled.

"I don't know." Ace shook her head. "I couldn't see through all the blood…"

"Excuse me…" Fletcher had finally made it through the crowd and stopped dead as he saw Ace Malone bleeding in the street outside his theatre. One of the men surrounding Ace looked up at Fletcher grimly.

"What was that you were saying about your theatre being perfectly safe?"

CHAPTER NINETEEN

The Winter Playhouse

The news of Ace Malone's attack spread through Lunas Bay like an unpleasant oil slick. By the next morning, the box office staff were getting hundreds of toast post messages, cancelling tickets and demanding refunds. Several queued up outside, wanting to complain to Fletcher themselves – who, as Harper saw at lunchtime, was somewhat preoccupied in trying to fend off a group of bearded men in long robes who'd turned up with handfuls of sage, claiming that they could "cleanse" the Wondria of Misfortune.

"Four attacks," Anvi said, watching with wide eyes as Fletcher none-too-gently shut the doors. "That's four attacks now. And they're getting worse each time."

Harper winced. Anvi was right – this attack had resulted in a far more grievous injury than the others. She couldn't get the image of Ace out of her head, lying on the cobbled street, covered in blood. It horribly brought to mind the article about the Winter Gala – a trail of blood, a body lying outside in the cold.

"I don't believe that Mis— that that creature attacked her," Trick said, watching his uncle lean against the door. "It doesn't make sense!"

Harper frowned. "Why wouldn't it make sense?" She supposed that the other attacks had all been at night, rather than the evening – but surely all that meant was that Misfortune was getting more confident. "Besides, Ace saw it, remember? She saw it before it attacked her."

"Maybe she was mistaken," Trick said mulishly.

The couple of weeks after Ace Malone's attack were the least fun that Harper had experienced since coming to the Wondria. The citizens of Lunas Bay gave the theatre the widest of berths no matter how many enticing posters, free popcorn buckets or dancing balloon animals Fletcher sent out to try to reel them in. The audiences grew even sparser, while several of their own performers took extended periods of absence. (Lady Roberta Helix, claiming "delicate health", had flown out to a five-star spa resort along the Goldhill Coast and hadn't been heard from since.) The mood among the Spectaculars grew bleaker and bleaker, culminating in one particularly horrible day when Rosie turned up to breakfast in a furious mood, claiming that her parents were thinking of pulling her out of the Wondria altogether.

"Apparently, Wallace Reed has already filed the motion to close us down," Rosie told them. "My mum wants me to transfer to a teaching-theatre near where she works."

Harper's heart plummeted. This is what she'd been fearing all week. "What happens now?" she asked, her voice tight.

"They've scheduled an official hearing," Rosie replied, stabbing at a sausage with unnecessary force. "They'll give Fletcher some time to prepare a defence, and then he'll have to go and debate them at the Council Chambers. If he loses, the Wondria will be closed."

Harper looked up and down the table. It was a grim sight: nearly all the apprentices were conversing in low voices, looking morose. Althea, Khyla and Bernie were glaring at Harper from across the room. A second-year boy whom Harper had never even seen before accidentally-on-purpose bumped against Harper as he passed, causing Harper to drop her hot chocolate all over the table.

"Oi!"

"Watch it!"

Rosie and Trick both shouted after the boy. Harper didn't; she just reached for a napkin and started mopping up the table. She could hardly blame the boy – if the Council voted to close the Wondria, they all knew whose fault it would be.

Anvi helped Harper clean up the hot chocolate. "Apparently, now the Board have officially filed the motion, they're going to be here observing every day until the hearing," she muttered. "And they've put strict rules in place. That's why people are angry."

They were given the proof of Anvi's words later that very morning, when Wallace Reed and two other Board members turned up at the apprentice quarters to personally escort them to their Theatrics lesson. They filed silently into the Teaching Wing and up to Practice Room One, where the Board members took up residence along the back wall.

When Lahiri swept in, she pointedly ignored the figures lurking at the back of her classroom. Instead, she turned straight to the apprentices.

"We're going to be looking at a new skill today," Lahiri informed them. "However, it requires darkness, so..."

Lahiri clapped her hands, and the starlight-lamps in the room flickered off. Harper blinked as darkness enveloped them. She heard several apprentices collide in the gloom.

Suddenly, a single light flared into life on the wall. Harper squinted and could just about make out Lahiri crouched in front of the wall, a starlight-torch perched in front of her, throwing out white light. She held her hands up in front of it, forming them into the shape of a small bird. As they watched, the point of light created by the torch morphed to replicate the form of the bird, shining against the dark wall. It was like the opposite of shadow-puppetry: instead of throwing a shadow, the light itself bent to mimic Lahiri's hand-shapes.

Lahiri, looking focused, moved her hands forwards. The light-bird flickered – then popped off the wall completely, becoming fully three-dimensional as it fluttered backwards and forwards in mid-air.

"*Cool,*" Harper heard Trick huff out in awe.

Lahiri pulled her hands apart, and the light-bird disappeared.

"Cool indeed," Lahiri agreed. "This is the Theatrical art of starlight-puppetry. Instead of throwing a shadow, the shape you make with your hands affects the light, which will form itself into a copy. Now, this can be tricky, so don't worry about three-dimensional projection just yet – start by focusing on forming the shapes on the wall."

Lahiri split them into pairs. Harper was with Anvi, and they hurried forwards to grab a torch. As Harper passed the Board members, she heard Wallace Reed mutter, "Seems silly for them to be starting new skills given their situation…"

Harper clenched her fists. The Board were talking as though the hearing had already happened, and their fate was decided. But they still had a chance – didn't they? Fletcher would stop the Wondria from being shut down. He *had* to.

She collected one of the starlight-torches for her and Anvi, and they settled in a corner.

"You go first," Harper said, feeling nervous suddenly.

Anvi switched the torch on and placed it on her knee. She shaped her fingers into the shape of a swan, then closed her eyes. Harper could hear her humming in concentration under her breath, focusing on the Star-Stuff around them.

The light on the wall gave a shimmy, then re-formed itself into a perfect imitation of a swan.

"How are you *doing* that?" Harper asked, half impressed, half envious.

"It's easy, really!" Anvi said eagerly. "Star-Stuff *wants* to help you! Here –" she thrust the torch at Harper – "as long as you can provide a clear channel for it, it'll do whatever you want!"

It was hard not to feel slightly emboldened by Anvi's enthusiasm. Harper considered what she'd said, about providing a clear channel for Star-Stuff. She knew she probably wasn't doing a great job there – with all the thoughts and worries that were usually bouncing around her head, it'd be a bumpy ride to say the least.

Harper drew her knees up, mirroring Anvi's stance, and placed the torch on them. Forming her fingers into a basic shape – a pointy-eared cat – she took a deep breath and focused on the air around her. Her head immediately began chattering, saying that she couldn't do it, that she'd never get the hang of it. Harper let them talk, let them fill her mind with their dismal predictions – and after a few moments, the voices seemed to wear themselves down. They retreated to mutter in a corner of her mind, and Harper was able to properly feel the crackling energy of the Star-Stuff around her.

Right… Harper thought. *Let's try this…*

She moved her hand forwards and imagined the light mirroring it. She felt a movement in the air around her, like a sharp breeze.

"Harper!"

At Anvi's exclamation, Harper snapped her head towards the wall – just in time to see the light finish shaping itself into a cat with pointy ears.

"I did it!" Harper whispered, gaping at the wall.

"I told you!" Anvi lifted her hand for a high five, which turned into a high ten, and then an enthusiastic hug. On the wall, the light-cat lifted its head and sniffed the air, its ears twitching. Harper beamed at it; apparently not all cats were demons in disguise like Truffles.

"Nice, you two!" Lahiri said approvingly as she passed.

Harper could have jumped up and down in triumph. It was a tiny win, but given all the terrible things that had happened recently, Harper was glad for it.

"*And after all,*" a horrible voice in her mind whispered. "*Who knows how many lessons you have left here…*"

At the end of the session, Lahiri held up a hand to get their attention.

"As some of you know, in light of recent events, students will no longer be allowed to leave the Wondria without at least three chaperones." She threw a half-glance behind her at the Board members. "Myself, Yosef and Roper will be running a trip to Lunas Bay this evening, so if anyone has any shopping to do or wants to see any sights, meet us in the lobby at seven o'clock."

Harper did have some shopping to do; her mum's birthday was coming up, and she was determined to find the perfect present. She needed something small enough to send by bottle-messenger, but more exciting than a "nice pen" (Anvi's idea) and more practical than a "small, hardy puppy" (Trick's idea).

She joined Lahiri, Yosef and Roper in the lobby at seven o'clock, and followed them through the winding streets of Lunas Bay. They stopped at the shopping arcade, and Lahiri gave them twenty minutes to look for what they needed. Harper knew exactly where she was heading – an old bric-a-brac shop, which she'd passed several times before. She ummed and ahh-ed over the contents of the shop, going back and forth over packs of Fae fortune-cards, fairy lights shaped like mushrooms and notebooks sealed with small bronze keys, before finally deciding on a hair clip shaped like a fox, which she knew her mother would love.

As she walked back to the main entrance she passed an indoor stone fountain, upon which several street hawkers were sprawled, clearly taking a break. They were sharing tea from a tin mug, and their signs were perched alongside the wall below them: *Ride the Hidden Peaks' fastest rollercoaster, five bob a turn! The Lunas Bay Arena presents: Jousting on Rollerskates, every Friday night! Tours of the Winter Playhouse, every hour on the hour!*

Harper stopped by this last one. "Um – excuse me?" she asked hesitantly.

"Yeah?" The street hawker jumped up so quickly he slopped half the mug over his shoes, prompting a wave of discontented muttering from his colleagues.

"How far away is the Winter Playhouse? From here, I mean," Harper asked.

"A couple of miles into the jungle," replied the hawker. "About an hour on foot, or half an hour if you take one of our special floating carriages. Why – do you want to book in?" He leaned forwards eagerly. "It's only twenty bob, including a free drink in the carriage, or for twenty-five we'll see if we can persuade the Caretaker to pose for a photo…"

"The who?"

"The Caretaker of the Winter Playhouse! Never left, did he? Still lives at the site, looking after whatever was left after the attack. He's a weird bloke – bit of a hermit. But sometimes he'll come out if you throw things at his window. So – you got a mum or dad who can pay?"

Harper was spared from making an excuse by the appearance of Lahiri, who was gesturing to Harper. Apparently, their time was up. Muttering a quick "goodbye", Harper hurried back to where Lahiri, Yosef and Roper were waiting. She clutched her paper bag in her hand all the way back to the Wondria, an idea starting to form in her mind. When she entered the apprentice quarters, Trick, Rosie and Anvi were sitting together on beanbags. Trick was idly sketching in an old programme (probably giving all the performers moustaches and devil horns), while Rosie was plaiting Anvi's long hair.

"Did you get something for your mum?" Anvi asked, beaming up at Harper.

"Um – yeah." Harper put the bag down on a chair. "Trick, can I talk to you?"

Once they were installed in a corner away from the others, Harper took a deep breath.

"I've had an idea – about Misfortune."

Trick looked wary. "Yeah?"

"I think…" Harper hesitated slightly before ploughing on. "I think we should go to the Winter Playhouse."

Trick's eyebrows shot upwards. "What? Why?"

"Because that's where it all started!" Harper replied. "Where the Four Curses were awoken for the first time. Where Misfortune *killed* that person. Surely if anyone has any information about where it came from, it's the people who were there?"

"What makes you think there'd be anyone there?"

"Apparently the old Caretaker is still living there – he never left after the disaster," Harper told him. "He must have seen everything – the Gala, Misfortune showing up, the attack… Maybe he saw what awoke Misfortune in the first place! And then we can try to figure out how to…un-awake it." Harper felt her throat tightening. "Trick, this is our last shot. If we don't do something, the Wondria's done for.

Someone else could be hurt – or worse. And it'll be all my fault."

"It wouldn't be your fault," Trick said fiercely.

"You, Rosie and Anvi are the only ones who think that."

Trick looked like he was about to argue, but something in Harper's face pulled him up short. He chewed on his lip. "But...when would we even go? We'd never be able to sneak out of the Wondria after training – they're watching us too closely."

Harper chewed her lip. "In the morning, then. Before training."

Trick blanched. "*Before* training?"

"Yep."

"Right." Trick paused. "You know, I think I feel the beginnings of a stomach ache coming on..."

"No, you don't," Harper retorted. "Tomorrow morning, six a.m. We're going to the Winter Playhouse."

CHAPTER TWENTY

Sylurjax

Trick was *not* happy to be awake so early.

"You know, I heard once that it's actually *bad* for you to get up too early. Your body goes into shock, and it can shut down…"

"I don't care about shutting down, but can you shut *up*?" Harper whispered. "You're going to get us caught!" Her heart was thudding in her ears. They were creeping down the staircase towards the lobby. If they got caught now, they were done for.

"I haven't even had a cup of tea yet," Trick muttered. "This is *barbaric*."

Luckily, they made it to the front doors without incident – only Helja was up at this hour, and Harper could hear her grumbling to herself in the Auditorium. Harper edged the doors open, and she and Trick darted out into the early-morning chill.

They got lost several times trying to find the edge of the city. After doubling back through several streets, they ended up down an alleyway lined with gambling houses and a grungy-looking pub with a knife stuck into the door. Trick pulled a face as he looked up and down.

"If we die here, I'm haunting you for ever."

"How are you going to haunt me if I'm also dead?" Harper retorted.

"I'll find a way," Trick said grimly.

Eventually, the streets and buildings gave way to the creeping Midnight Jungle. Both of them grew silent as they approached the wall of dark trees.

"So," Trick said after a moment, "where exactly did this street hawker say the Winter Playhouse was?"

"A couple of miles in," Harper replied.

"Right." Trick nodded. "Sure. Did he happen to say anything else – for example, where you should start, whether it was to the north or south, or basically anything that might be of help to us now?"

"No," Harper said stubbornly. "But it's a theatre – it can't be that hard to find. If we just keep going straight, I reckon we'll be fine." Without another word, she pulled back a tangle of vines and stepped into the trees. Trick groaned and followed.

They trod carefully on the uneven ground, afraid to make

too much noise and disturb whatever else might be hiding in the jungle. Harper couldn't help staring around at the canopy of shining blue leaves that stretched over their heads, the deep purple vines coiled around trees like great snakes.

"Oi, watch that branch."

"Ouch – that was my foot!"

They made their way in this clumsy fashion for several more minutes, until they came to a gap in the trees where a shallow stream flowed through, letting some of the weak morning light trickle down to where Harper and Trick stood.

"What now?" Harper asked, peering at the water. "It doesn't look deep, but…"

"Harper." Trick's voice was suddenly deadly serious. "Don't move."

Harper looked up. Trick was staring directly over her shoulder, his eyes wide.

"Oh, really," Harper snorted. "Do you think I'm going to fall for that?"

"I'm serious," Trick stuttered. "There's…there's a…"

Harper rolled her eyes. "Fine! I get it. You, Trick Torres, are the greatest actor the Wondria has ever seen…"

Before Trick could reply, Harper felt something on the back of her neck: something that felt unmistakably like warm breath. With a sickening feeling, Harper slowly turned around, only to find herself faced with an enormous, porcelain-white wolf.

Harper felt frozen to the spot. Trick sounded like he'd forgotten how to breathe.

The wolf opened its enormous mouth.

"What are you doing in these woods?" he growled.

This startled Harper into finding her voice. "Wait – you can *talk*?" she squeaked.

The wolf tilted his head. "Will that be important if I kill you?"

"No, no, don't kill us!" Trick hurried forwards to stand next to Harper. "We wouldn't be worth eating, honest. We're probably far too grubby. I myself have not had a bath in four days." He said this last bit rather proudly.

"We're sorry," Harper breathed. "We're just looking for the Winter Playhouse, we didn't…" She trailed off, her voice giving way to shock and disbelief.

The wolf regarded them both suspiciously. "Why are you searching for the Fallen Site?"

"I – what?" Harper frowned.

The wolf bared his teeth slightly. "I've seen others like you. Skulking around Fallen Sites, hunting for stars. What do you want with them?"

"We don't!" Harper found her voice. "We're not hunting for the stars. There's been some misunderstanding. We're not even looking for the Fallen Site. We're looking for the Winter Playhouse…"

"The Winter Playhouse *is* the Fallen Site," the wolf replied coolly.

Harper stared at the wolf, shocked at this revelation. The Winter Playhouse was the place where Misfortune had awoken, *and* a Fallen Site? That seemed like too much of a coincidence. Were the events connected? Had the impact from the fallen stars awoken Misfortune?

"We didn't know that it's a Fallen Site," Harper said eventually. "We're going there because our home is being attacked by a Curse – a Curse that we think was awoken on the night of the Winter Gala. We thought there might be clues at the playhouse, about where it came from, or how to get rid of it." She forced herself to look the wolf in the eye. "We're not hunting the stars, I promise. But if we don't get rid of this Curse, our theatre is going to be shut down. We're just trying to save our home."

The wolf regarded her for a long moment, then nodded. "You don't seem like the others. I don't see greed in you."

"Oh." Harper gulped. "Um – thanks."

"Who are the others?" Trick asked.

"The star-hunters," the wolf growled. "People who come here searching, hungry for what they think a star could do for them. I saw one just last night – a giant man with a strange, painted head."

Harper shivered slightly, the image all too familiar. "Alistair Sharpe," she muttered, glancing at Trick. "We've met him," she said, turning back to the wolf. "He's been hunting the stars for a long time. Are you...?" She hesitated. "I mean, you seem very concerned for the stars. Are you some sort of…guardian or something? Could you make sure he doesn't find them?"

The wolf huffed, and suddenly Harper got the feeling that he was amused. "Oh, there are no fewer than four stars in this jungle," the wolf said. "But they know to be on their guard from hunters."

"There – what – *four* stars?" Harper gasped. She looked around wildly, half-expecting to be suddenly ambushed by glowing lights. "Where…"

Harper trailed off as she looked – *really* looked – at the wolf. His fur was stark white, the kind of white she'd only seen captured in glass jars at the Wondria. It seemed to shimmer, as though it were coated in a fine, shimmering dust.

Stardust.

She remembered Roper's words from the Muse of Stars Ceremony: "*If you look closely enough, every star has a true form at its centre…*"

"Are you…" Harper could hardly give voice to the thought. "Are *you* a star?"

The wolf looked surprised. He observed Harper, his eyes fixed on hers.

"Well done," he said eventually. "Most of your kind do not recognize us for what we are. They cannot comprehend the truth even if we're standing right in front of them. But if you look beyond the layers of dust and light, every star has an animal form at its heart."

For a moment, all Harper could do was stare, frozen in

a tableau of shock. She looked quickly at Trick, who was staring at the wolf with his eyes blown wide. "Right. But – why *are* you standing right in front of us? Shouldn't you be, you know – in the sky?"

"I assure you, that's exactly where I'd prefer to be, but I was pulled out of the sky several years ago."

"The fallen stars," Harper said faintly. She could hardly believe what she was hearing. Whenever people had spoken about the fallen stars, she'd always pictured vague, translucent shapes floating around like ghosts. Nothing like this huge, heavy and very *solid*-looking wolf in front of her.

"D-do you have a name?" she managed to stutter eventually.

"Sylvrjax." The wolf nodded.

"Sylvrjax," Harper repeated. "I'm Harper, and this is Trick."

The wolf inclined his head at each of them in turn. "So – you two are seeking the Winter Playhouse because you believe that it will hold answers regarding this Curse?"

"Maybe," replied Harper. "It's the best chance we've got."

Sylvrjax looked at them both. "Well, my pack and I are going to the Fallen Site tonight, in the early evening. If you wish to see the Playhouse, we could take you there."

Harper inhaled sharply. "Really?"

Sylvrjax nodded. "We'll be at the eastern edge of the jungle at six o'clock. If you're there, we'll take you with us to the site."

"We'll be there," Harper said eagerly.

With a last nod of his head, Sylvrjax began slinking back towards the trees. At the perimeter, he turned back.

"We will help you – but in return, you must make me a promise. You must promise that for as long as we stars are on the Earth, you will not reveal our true natures to anyone."

"Why not?" Harper asked.

"As long as we walk this land, we are in danger," Sylvrjax replied gravely. "We have only eluded capture so far because so few know of our true forms. If others were to find out, it would only increase the number of hunters on our tail. I won't put my fellow stars in danger."

Harper wanted to tell him that many humans would rather help them than hunt them, but she couldn't fault his logic. "Of course," she promised. "We won't tell a soul."

"You must promise," said Sylvrjax. "And know this – a promise to a star is binding. It cannot be broken without the express permission of the star to whom it was made."

Harper met the wolf's eye. "We promise."

As soon as she said the words, Harper felt the weight of the promise – it settled on her heart like a ball of lead. She shivered slightly – Sylvrjax hadn't been exaggerating.

Trick repeated the promise, then tugged lightly on Harper's arm. They watched Sylvrjax disappear completely, his pale fur flashing through the jungle like lightning against a storm cloud. Then, with one last look into the trees, they turned their sights to the Wondria once more.

CHAPTER TWENTY-ONE

The Parting of Skies

Training that day went painfully slowly. Harper couldn't help but wish for the day to be over so they could go and meet Sylvrjax. As soon as the last session finished, Harper and Trick raced straight to the apprentice quarters, where Harper set about smuggling some bread, four apples and a few sausages from the dinner table into her backpack.

"You don't reckon they're vegetarians, do you?" Trick mused.

Harper stared at him. "They're *wolves*."

"Stars, technically. But we didn't ask."

"Well, sorry if my first thought when faced with a giant wolf-star wandering around the jungle wasn't to ask him whether or not he was a *vegetarian*."

It was harder to sneak out of the Wondria in the evening

– the Board were prowling, the security trolls were on high alert, and Helja had somehow found time among her other duties to patrol the corridors as a mop, chasing down any suspicious-looking apprentices she came across. With a bit of ducking and diving (not to mention a well-timed diversion from Trick involving a Blood Pill and a handful of feathers), they managed to sneak out of the front doors at half past five. They ran through the city, making it to the eastern edge of the jungle with seconds to spare. Sylvrjax was waiting among the trees, another three wolves stood alongside him. Harper's breath caught in her throat.

"Excellent. Sylvrjax, I see you've brought us a snack," one of them said, fixing a pair of amber eyes on Harper.

"Sorry?" Harper squeaked.

"Well." The wolf inclined her head towards the bag of food. "I assume that's for us?"

"Oh – yeah, of course!" Harper quickly shrugged the bag off her shoulder and held it out. Sylvrjax rolled his eyes.

"Ignore Sareni – she likes a joke," he told Harper.

"Well, someone has to," Sareni muttered in reply. "You lot certainly weren't having much fun when I found you moping around the Raven Falls Swamps."

Sylvrjax looked at her. "We were not *moping*."

"You were wallowing. Positively *brooding*."

Sylvrjax huffed. "These are the other two of our number – Harlemunn and Dianita," Sylvrjax told Harper, nodding to the two other wolves.

The wolves gathered around the bag to eat (going straight for the sausages, Harper noticed, shooting a pointed look in Trick's direction). Harper studied each of them in turn. Sareni's fur was creamier than Sylvrjax's stark white. Harlemunn was the smallest – the youngest, perhaps, Harper thought – while Dianita was stocky and silvery.

"So – how are we getting to the Winter Playhouse?" Harper asked.

To Harper's surprise and delight, Sylvrjax lowered himself to the ground and gestured for them to climb on. Harper and Trick both clambered up onto his back. His fur was smooth and silky like sealskin, and as bright as a mirror ball.

"Hold on tight," Sylvrjax growled, and then they were off, loping through the jungle, Sylvrjax covering ground with ease with his long strides.

"What will you do when we get there?" Harper asked.

"We will search the perimeter, make sure that one of our kind is not there. We regularly visit each Fallen Site in turn, searching for the other fallen stars. We fear that some of them may have been captured by these star-hunters, and if they are trapped or incapacitated in any way, they may miss their chance to return home at the Parting of Skies."

"What's the Parting of Skies?"

"It's the most important event across the Celestial cities. It only occurs every half-dozen years or so, usually under a full moon. On the night of the Parting, the stars all gather together for a grand ball in the Sky Ballroom. The last one was hosted by the bear-stars—"

"A dreadful affair," Sareni interrupted. "Bear-stars are *so* easily offended, and they have terrible taste in canapés."

"Anyway," Sylvrjax said firmly. "The point of the ball is for us stars to gather together and say goodbye to the elderly among us. You see, during the Parting of Skies, the Celestial Highway appears, and stars are able to traverse this road down to the Earth. It is the only time that a star can travel between the Earth and the sky. When this happens, some of the oldest among us make the decision to leave the sky and make a new home on the ground."

"But – why?" Harper frowned.

"Stars live for many lifetimes in the sky," replied Sylvrjax. "When they have reached a great age, many decide they are ready to pass on. They travel down the Celestial Highway during the Parting and become regular animals, to live out one final lifetime on the ground. Many animals that you see here on the Earth were once stars."

Harper glanced around at Trick, her eyes widening at this revelation. "So – is that what you did?"

"That depends." Sareni fixed her eyes on Harper. "Do we look elderly to you?"

"I – um – well…" Harper swallowed.

"Sareni," Sylvrjax said warningly.

"Oh, you're no fun."

"Something went wrong at the last Parting of Skies," said

Sylvrjax. "In the midst of the celebrations, there was an immense force that suddenly pulled some of us out of the sky. There were thirteen of us, I believe – thirteen young stars who had no intention of leaving the sky on that night."

"Some of us were badly injured during the Falling," Sareni chimed in. "Sylvrjax, for example, lost his entire sense of humour." She sighed. "Tragic."

"Can you get it back again?" Trick asked.

"We cannot return to the sky until the next Parting of Skies occurs, and the Celestial Highway appears once more," Sylvrjax said in a dignified manner. "It was due to happen this year, but until recently, we didn't think that it would. We were sure that the Muse of Stars wouldn't risk another Parting after what happened last time. But in the autumn just gone, we received a strange message – one that informed us that the Parting will happen again this year."

Harper heard Trick's sharp intake of breath. She looked at him, but he was staring at Sylvrjax. "Who sent you the message?"

"We do not know."

Harper frowned. "And you said it usually happens under a full moon…" Four full moons had already passed this year, including the Ember moon at the beginning of April. "So… the Parting of Skies could be as soon as next month? At the Silver moon?" she asked.

"Indeed." Sylvrjax nodded gravely. "Which is why we are revisiting the Fallen Sites now. I first found Harlemunn at his Fallen Site in the north, which he'd revisited several times looking for answers. If the other stars have heard the rumours about the upcoming Parting of Skies, they may return to their own Sites, looking for clues. If we cannot find them, I fear that we're too late, and they've all been captured."

Sylvrjax had slowed as they talked. Now, he rounded a corner and stepped out into a large clearing circled with indigo trees. Harper heard her own gasp echo into the space as Sylvrjax stopped, allowing Harper and Trick to slide off his back and gaze around.

The Winter Playhouse had clearly once been quite something to behold. It was smaller than the Wondria, but well-formed, and entirely domed. It looked like it had been built from snow and enchanted somehow to never melt. An arch of frozen roses surrounded the doorway, and a pair of marble polar bears guarded the entrance. Around it, the wreckage of the Gala was still apparent even all these years later: skeletal remains of stages, carriages and audience stands littered the clearing. Grass had grown up long around the theatre itself, and vines had begun to creep, spider-like, over the doors.

Sylvrjax nodded to Harper. "Go. We will see if any more of our kind are here. If not, we will do what we can to help you."

Before Harper could even say "thank you", the wolves had bounded off in separate directions, disappearing quickly amid the debris. She saw Trick staring after them for a moment, before turning to Harper.

"So – I suppose we should start there, then," he said, gesturing to the Playhouse.

Harper nodded and they began to pick their way towards the doors. Harper gave a half-glance up at the sky as they walked – the sun was just beginning to set. She figured they only had another hour or so before they'd be missed at the Wondria. Feeling a wave of fresh determination, she brushed some of the weeds from the door frame – sending several mice scurrying out of the way – and knocked on the door.

There was a short silence. Harper just had time to wonder if they'd done the right thing – it suddenly seemed unseemly, somehow, to turn up on a stranger's doorstep and demand information about a potentially traumatizing event from years ago – before the door swung open.

The man who stood in the doorway cut a grand figure. He wore a ruby tailcoat and knee-length, polished leather boots. He had salt-and-pepper hair, sandy-toned skin and a beard that stuck out so much it looked like it was making a bid for freedom from his face.

"Who are you?" he asked in a gruff voice, looking them up and down.

"Um – I'm Harper, and this is Trick," Harper replied, using her best "aren't-I-just-a-delightfully-polite-child" voice. "We had some questions we wanted to ask, if you don't mind. About the night of the Winter Gala."

The man glanced between them suspiciously. "School project, is it?" he asked.

"Yes…" Harper nodded. "We're conducting interviews about what happened that night…with Misfortune…"

"Misfortune," the man snorted. "Right. Well, I suppose you'd better come in…"

He held the door open for them, and they detangled themselves from the weeds below their feet to step into the lobby. Inside, Harper was surprised to see that despite the weeds and vines that had begun to claim the exterior of the theatre, the interior was spotless – the pearl-coloured carpet as flawless as a fresh snowfall, the ivory bannisters of the staircase shining as if they'd been freshly polished that morning.

"This way," said the man. He took them along a dim corridor, before opening a door which revealed a small dressing room. Looking around, Harper noticed a mahogany drinks trolley stacked with bottles, a clothing rail with a selection of silk tailcoats, and a mirror surrounded by circular lights.

"I'm Solomon, by the way," the man said, inviting them to sit down with a sweep of his hand. Harper perched on a wooden stool, while Trick plonked himself down on a pouffe.

"So – you were the Caretaker of the Winter Playhouse?" Harper prompted gently.

Solomon drew himself up proudly. "That I was. The very first Spectacular theatre ever to have graced the Hidden Peaks," he added pointedly. "Beat the Wondria by six hours and three minutes."

Harper could almost feel Trick supressing the urge to roll his eyes.

"We were small, grant you, but we had the best company you'd ever seen. The night of the Winter Gala we had three stages around the clearing, and we rotated our performers on and off all evening. It was supposed to be a celebration – a celebration of one year in the Hidden Peaks, a year since we escaped the Smoke and started a new life here."

"And then Misfortune showed up." Harper prodded gently.

"Exactly," Solomon said grimly. "I assume you know what happened next – people running, screaming, general pandemonium. That *creature* running about, causing havoc. Took out two of our stages; most of the performers fled in terror…"

"And it killed someone," Harper said quietly.

Trick shifted next to her. Harper glanced at him, but his eyes were fixed on Solomon.

Solomon bowed his head. "So I heard. I didn't see that happen, though – I saw it slink off into the woods, and later on people started saying that a body was found. Horrible, it was. Just horrible."

"Did you see where it came from?" Harper asked urgently. "Was there anything that awoke it? Anything that could be reversed?"

"It came from the woods, and it returned to the woods." Solomon sighed. "And we were left with the mess."

"What happened afterwards?" Trick asked, leaning

forwards. "Did you manage to fix the mess that – that the creature made?"

Solomon nodded. "We started to. We knew some people might be scared to come back, but we thought if we did something special – a big musical premiere, or an exclusive celebrity concert – it might draw people in. And who knows? It might even have worked, if the Council hadn't come poking around."

"The Council?" Harper frowned.

"They hadn't classified all the Fallen Sites then," Solomon informed her. "It took them the best part of two years to classify all thirteen of them. A few weeks after the Gala disaster they turned up, stuck their noses in, then declared this whole clearing a Fallen Site." He sighed. "That was it for us. If people were superstitious about Misfortune, they were most certainly superstitious about Fallen Sites. Once we knew we were sitting on top of one, there was no recovering."

"So why did you stay?" Trick piped up. "I mean – you're a caretaker, but there's not really anything to – um – caretake."

Solomon drew himself up. "What kind of caretaker would I be if I abandoned my post as soon as things got difficult? Besides, I wanted to make sure that it survived, just in case anyone ever came back."

Harper was suddenly struck with a terrible sadness at the thought of Solomon sitting alone in this theatre, with nothing left to take care of but a couple of carved polar bears and a family of mice.

"Of course, it's given me plenty of time to think about that night," Solomon muttered quietly. "Plenty of time to figure out what really happened."

"What did really happen?" Harper leaned forwards. "With Misfortune?"

Solomon looked at her. "Everyone calls it that," he said quietly. "But that thing isn't what everyone thinks it is."

Harper frowned. "What do you—"

She was cut off by a sound that made her blood run cold – a commotion outside in the clearing, followed by a series of howls.

"What the Muses…" Solomon muttered as Harper and Trick leaped up in unison. Harper ran to the window and peered out, but it was too dark to see much.

"We have to go," she said, already heading for the door. "Sorry."

"Wait!" Solomon cried after them. "I haven't told you about—"

A loud clanging sound joined the howls outside, followed by a low, harsh voice. Harper flung the door open and sped out of the dressing room, Trick firmly on her heels. They raced back along the corridor and across the lobby to the main doors. Harper threw them open and crashed into the clearing, panting.

The sight that greeted her was like a punch to the stomach. The wolf-stars were all struggling against the weight of giant steel nets, which had been thrown over each of them.

Three of them were trussed on top of a large wagon, and a figure was winching up the last bundle – a figure with a chequered suit and a painted head.

"Sharpe," Harper whispered to Trick.

Sharpe shoved at the net, shunting Sylvrjax onto the wagon with the others. The wolf snapped at Sharpe, but his teeth simply clashed against the steel.

"What do we do?" Harper hissed in a panic. "We can't let him take them!"

Sharpe jumped off the wagon and headed round to the front. It was now or never.

"Come on!" Harper whispered, nudging Trick and darting towards the wagon. She grabbed on to the side of it and hoisted herself up, crawling forwards until she was face to face with the wolves.

"Harper, what are you doing?" Sylvrjax said. "You two need to leave!"

"We can't just let them take you! Hang on, we'll get you free somehow…" Harper started searching the wagon for some sort of weapon, anything sharp enough to cut through the nets. Trick bent down and began yanking at the knots.

"Harper!"

With a roar, the wagon suddenly shuddered into life, juddering under their feet and almost pitching Harper to the ground.

"No, no, no…" In desperation, Harper tugged at the nets with her hands, cutting red welts into her fingers as she pulled. Trick was hacking at the knots with a stone, but they were thick and unyielding.

"You two have to get off the wagon!" Sylvrjax growled.

"We can't just leave you!" Harper cried.

"If he finds you on here, he might kill you. Go!"

Harper knew that Sylvrjax was right, but it still took everything she had to jump down off the wagon as it started to roll forwards.

"Listen," Sylvrjax said urgently. "I fear that the hunter may have already captured all the other stars. But if you see any others out there, warn them that they're being hunted!"

"We will!" Harper whispered, jogging forwards to keep up with the wagon. "What do they look like?"

"There were four of us wolf-stars," Sylvrjax said. "The other stars that fell were two ravens, a peacock, a stag, a couple of squirrels, a bear, a rabbit and some kind of large cat – a panther, I think."

Harper felt all the breath leave her body as the truth slammed into her like a high-speed tram.

A *panther*.

She turned to Trick, her mouth dropping open in utter shock.

"Trick...*Misfortune*."

The return journey was a blur. They'd fled the scene as soon as the wagon had trundled away, forgetting to even say goodbye to Solomon in their need to get away from Sharpe. Trick had pulled Harper back through the jungle, almost dragging her at points.

"Trick – ouch! Watch it!"

"It's late," Trick had said. "We need to get back!"

Harper understood his urgency – if they were caught sneaking back in, they'd be in serious trouble given the Board's new rules. But all her thoughts were centred around Sylvrjax's words.

A panther.

The creature wasn't Misfortune – it had never been Misfortune. It was one of the *fallen stars*. Harper's mind was racing – what about the other Curses? Sylvrjax had mentioned birds, squirrels, a stag…creatures that came *"on wings"* or scurried *"on tiny claws"* or had *"cloven hooves"*, just like the song described. Had *all* the alleged sightings of the Four Curses really been sightings of stars?

They got back to the Wondria just as the scarce few patrons still willing to brave their theatre were beginning to trickle out from the show. Trick pulled Harper round the corner, waiting for a large group to come through the doors so they could sneak in under their cover. Concealing themselves among swishy skirts and long coats, they ducked into the lobby.

Unfortunately, someone was waiting for them.

"So," said Lahiri, folding her arms, "where exactly do you think you've been?"

CHAPTER TWENTY-TWO

A Warning

Harper and Trick stood before Lahiri in her office. Her face had the expression of rolling storm clouds, hanging heavy in the sky before the first crash of thunder.

"The rules about not leaving the Wondria without chaperones were put in place for your safety," Lahiri said quietly. Too quietly. "Would you care to explain why you consider yourself above them?"

"We don't," Harper replied quickly. She wanted to explain, to tell Lahiri that they'd been trying to help – but they were bound by their promise to Sylvrjax not to reveal what they knew about the stars.

"Do you have any idea how it would have looked if the Board had seen you?" Lahiri snapped. "Do you think that they wouldn't have used it against us in the hearing if we can't even ensure that our own apprentices follow the rules?"

Harper looked down. She hadn't considered that.

Lahiri's eyes flashed between them. "From now on, neither of you will be allowed to leave the Wondria. You will not be permitted to attend any extracurricular sessions, or the evening shows, or any other activities. You will return to the apprentice quarters at the end of the day, and you will remain there for the remainder of the evening."

"For how long?" Harper cried.

"For however long I deem necessary, Miss Woolfe. Now, you will return to the apprentice quarters immediately."

Her tone left no room for argument. Harper glanced at Trick, and together they turned and trailed out of the room. As they walked back to the Living Wing, Trick glanced at Harper. "Are you all right?"

"I don't know," Harper said. The revelation about the stars had been tempered somewhat by the unpleasantness of getting caught by Lahiri, but now it all came flooding back.

"It's not Misfortune," she said slowly. "It never was. That's what Solomon was trying to tell us, what he'd figured out – it was a star, all along! That's why the sightings only started a few years ago – after the stars fell – even though the rhyme has been around for eons. And it's not just Misfortune. Think of the other creatures in the rhyme! Death *'comes on wings'*, Malady *'scurries on tiny claws'*… Most of the sightings of the Four Curses have probably been sightings of the stars!"

"It definitely makes sense." Trick nodded.

"The Winter Playhouse was on top of a Fallen Site," she continued. "The night of the Gala, the panther-star must have been returning to it, like Sylvrjax and his pack did." Harper took a breath as the full implications of their discovery set in. "And this means...it's not my fault. If the Four Curses aren't real – if that creature isn't Misfortune – then I didn't summon it here. I didn't bring ill luck down on us!"

"I've been telling you that from the start," Trick pointed out.

After months of carrying the weight of guilt and fear, Harper felt practically light-headed at the realization that this really *wasn't* her fault. Something unlocked in her chest, something that had been sitting there since All Spooks' Eve – maybe even since opening night. But – if she hadn't summoned Misfortune, then why *did* the creature keep turning up at the Wondria? And why would a star be attacking people?

"Do you think it was the Falling?" Harper asked. "Do you think something happened to the star to make it – I dunno, go bad or something?"

Trick was staring at the floor. She poked him in the ribs. "Oi, I'm talking to you."

"I don't know," Trick said, frowning.

Harper thought about what Sylvrjax had told them. The Parting of Skies was looming. If they could ensure that all the stars crossed the Celestial Highway back to the sky, then surely there'd be no more sightings of the Curses? They'd go back to where they belonged, including the panther-star, and this nightmare would finally be over. But with the stars captured by Sharpe, that was going to be far easier said than done.

When they reached the apprentice quarters, Harper was surprised to see Rosie and Anvi waiting up for them.

"Where have you two been?" Rosie demanded. "It's almost eleven!"

"We – um…" Harper looked at her feet. "We snuck out."

Anvi gasped, her eyes flying wide. Rosie, on the other hand, frowned at them. "Why?"

Harper glanced at Trick.

"We were trying to get to the…um…Lunas Bay Library," Trick improvised. "We thought we might be able to find something that would help Fletcher with the hearing. But Lahiri caught us coming back and has basically put us under house arrest."

"Oh *no*," Anvi groaned sympathetically. "Did you explain it to her? Does she know you were trying to help? Me and Rosie could vouch for you if you want…"

"She seemed pretty set," Harper replied grimly. "Thank you for waiting up for us, though." Even through the fog of shock and confusion, she was touched that their friends had been concerned about them.

"But she'll have to let you out for the concert, surely?" Rosie asked urgently. "She has to!"

"What concert?" Harper frowned.

Rosie's eyes widened. "You didn't hear? It's all over the city! One sec…" She ran over to the mess table and returned with her radio. "I think *The Spectacular Daily Show* are still reporting on it…"

She set the radio down on the table, fiddling with the buttons until she reached the right channel.

"…*Our biggest story of the day was the surprise announcement that Tornio Nocturne, composer of the original Four Curses opera, is coming out of his self-imposed retirement to put on a one-night-only concert! In a statement released by him yesterday, Nocturne stated that he was 'deeply saddened' by the current plight of theatres. In a bid to help the arts recover, he has pledged to perform an exclusive concert at the Lunas Bay Arena…*"

Rosie looked like she was about to expire with excitement. "Can you believe it? Tornio Nocturne is doing a concert! Right here in Lunas Bay!"

"I thought he was a recluse?" Harper frowned.

"He is, normally," Rosie replied. "But he's coming out of exile to do this one concert! Surely Lahiri will have to let you go. I mean – what if he performs *The Octopuses' Lament*? Or *The Seven Untimely Deaths of Horatio the Headless*?"

Harper shared a glance with Trick. "I don't think so."

"She's seriously angry," Trick added.

"Maybe she'll have cooled off in the morning?" Anvi suggested hopefully.

"Maybe," Harper agreed, although she didn't think so.

She didn't have the energy to debate with them – and besides, with everything they'd learned tonight, a concert by a famous Spectacular was far from her top priority. She yawned. "I think I'm going to go to bed."

Trick nodded at that, and they both sloped off towards the ladders. Harper collapsed onto her bed the moment she was in her room, but she found it difficult to sleep. Her mind felt as if it'd been shaken up like a snow globe. Everything she'd thought she'd known and learned over the past few months had been turned on its head.

Eventually, buried deep under her blankets, Harper slipped slowly into sleep – and once she did, something very strange happened.

Harper gradually became aware of the feeling of floating. She felt weightless, as though she had come untethered from the ground. Frowning, she blinked her eyes open to find that her room had melted away around her, and she was surrounded by a flat, black darkness that seemed to stretch on endlessly.

As her eyes focused, Harper found that she *wasn't* floating: she was standing on a large stone dais. It was only then she realized where she was.

"Someone within the Hidden Peaks is trying to contact you via the Dreamscape Transit System," a smooth voice echoed from above. "Do you accept?"

Harper frowned. Who'd be trying to contact her through the Dreamscape? The only person she knew who could access it was Thief. If he was trying to contact her, it might be an emergency…

"I accept," Harper said. A familiar trundling sound came from behind her, and she turned to see a cable car arriving at the dais. After a brief hesitation, she walked over and stepped inside as the door opened.

The Dreamscape was different this time. There were no figures meeting joyfully on daises, no other cable cars trundling gently past. There weren't even any stars in the sky. Harper felt like she was the only living thing there. As she stared around at the unending darkness, a sense of dread began to settle over her.

The cable car dropped her off at another dais. Harper frowned as she looked around. From her experience so far, she'd seen that daises in the Dreamscape represented people's dreams: they held gardens and funfairs, loveseats for intimate chats or lively parties for dancing. This dais, however, was empty. There was nothing to suggest whose dream she'd arrived into.

"You were seen."

A low, cool voice echoed around her. Harper spun around, looking in all directions, but there was nobody there.

"Perhaps you thought you were being sneaky, trying to free the stars from the wagon. But my employee saw you."

Harper froze on the spot. *My employee.* Did that mean…?

"Sharpe. He's…working for you?"

"Clever, aren't you?"

Harper shook her head, confused. Sharpe *wasn't* trying to find the stars for himself?

"If Sharpe had seen us," Harper said slowly, "he'd have killed us."

"Not if I'd expressly told him to capture the stars and leave no trace – a couple of dead bodies is something of a trace, don't you think?"

Harper shivered at the tone of the voice. She looked around again, searching for any hint as to who it was, but the dais remained bare.

"Who are you?" she asked, her voice echoing around the darkness.

"That is no concern of yours. But this is: Alistair Sharpe is working on my orders. And I've noticed that you seem to be rather in his way. Getting him locked up by the Brightwood authorities, trying to interrupt his haul in the jungle." The tone of the voice suddenly got harsher. "Consider this a warning: the next time I hear of you meddling in our hunt, I will step in myself. And trust me, that would be most unpleasant for you."

"You're not going to get your hands on any more stars," Harper said fiercely. "We won't let you."

The voice laughed. "You're too late. Those stars are mine."

Harper's stomach twisted. That made it sound like Sharpe had already captured *all* the stars, just as Sylvrjax had feared. Was that true?

"But…the Parting of Skies…" she muttered.

"The Parting of Skies is immaterial," the voice said. "The stars are caged, and hidden well. I've had my employee stash them in one of the most secure locations in the Hidden Peaks – somewhere rather close to home for you, in fact. They won't be able to cross the Celestial Highway when it appears. They'll be trapped down here, and they'll belong to me."

Harper felt sick. He was taunting her, dancing around the edges of where he'd hidden the stars without actually revealing anything. She thought of Sylvrjax and Sareni and the others, her chest twisting painfully as she pictured them in cages. Through her fear and anger, another horrible thought suddenly struck Harper: if the stars remained on the Earth, their promise to Sylvrjax would prevent them from ever revealing what they knew about the stars and the so-called Curses. If they couldn't explain to the Board and the Council what had really been going on, there was no hope for the Wondria.

"Why are you doing this?" Harper asked furiously.

"I don't think that's any of your business, now, is it?"

Harper narrowed her eyes. "I'm not afraid of you, whoever you are."

"Oh, really?" the voice answered.

The stone underneath Harper's feet suddenly cracked open. She threw herself to the side as the entire dais split in two, the two halves moving rapidly apart from each other. Harper scrabbled against the stone, clutching on to a jagged piece of rock as her legs swung wildly above what was now just a steep drop.

"Stop it!" she yelled furiously.

"I thought you weren't afraid?" the voice said coolly.

Harper could feel her hands slipping, the stone slowly sliding through her grip.

"Stay away from my plans. It can get far worse than this," the voice said, just as Harper lost her grip. She found herself falling, wind roaring in her ears as she plummeted down into nothingness…

She woke with a start, her heart pounding in her chest. The room was dark and still, but she felt like she could still hear a faint echo of the voice whispering in her room.

CHAPTER TWENTY-THREE

Plotting Face

If we don't find a way to free the stars, they'll be trapped down here. The Parting of Skies will happen, but they won't be able to go home – and we'll never be able to save the Wondria!"

Harper and Trick were walking to training, and Harper had just finished recounting her terrifying ordeal in the Dreamscape. Trick had turned pale when she told him about the mysterious "employer" who'd spoken to her, and now he looked downright ill.

"But – how are we supposed to free the stars when we don't even know where he's hidden them? Where's this 'secure location' he's got them in?"

"I don't know," Harper chewed on her lip. "He said something about it being 'close to home' – close to the

Wondria, I guess that means. Do you think it's somewhere in Lunas Bay?"

"Maybe," Trick said thoughtfully. "It *is* the biggest city in the Hidden Peaks, there must be loads of places to hide stuff..."

When they entered Practice Room One, Lahiri flashed them a disapproving look. Harper felt a stab of anxiety – part of her had been hoping that Anvi was right, that Lahiri might have cooled off a bit this morning, but apparently not.

Lahiri turned to the class and placed her hands on her hips.

"End-of-year projects!" she announced. "After your spring break next week, you'll all be heading into your final terms as first-year apprentices. Starting now, and continuing through the final term, you will prepare individual presentations, demonstrating whatever you believe to be the best of your abilities. Your act can be from the strands of Mechanics or Theatrics, and will be presented on the penultimate week of the summer term."

Harper groaned internally. Between the revelations about the stars and the Four Curses – not to mention her little visit from Sharpe's employer – she thought her head might actually explode if she had to think about anything else.

"I don't know why we're bothering," Althea Reed muttered. "This place will be closed by the end of term. And we'll no doubt have another attack before then..." She kicked the back of Harper's chair, and Bernie and Khyla snickered.

"*No, we won't!*" Harper wanted to scream. "*Not if an evil ex-Magician has caught the panther and hidden it away with the others!*"

But she couldn't say that – not without revealing *how* they knew this. The idea of the panther-star being trapped, unable to attack them, wasn't as comforting as Harper had imagined – not if being trapped was going to prevent it from returning to the sky and out of their lives for good.

It was all so *frustrating*. After her conversation with Sharpe's employer, Harper could see exactly what needed to be done – what would get them all out of this mess. If Harper and Trick could free the stars in time for the Parting, then all the stars could cross the Celestial Highway and go home to the sky – including the panther-star. Once that had happened, Harper and Trick could reveal what they knew without breaking their promise to Sylvrjax. They could go straight to Fletcher, to the Board – to the Council themselves – and tell them the truth: that the Four Curses weren't real, that they'd never been real. That all the sightings had really been of fallen stars – stars who by that point would be safely back in the sky, *including* the one that had been attacking the Wondria all year. Once the Council knew that there was no more threat to the Wondria, surely they couldn't vote to shut it down? They could save the Wondria, save everyone – if only they could figure out *where* the stars were being held and set them free.

"This morning, you'll be coming up with initial ideas with

whichever teacher is best suited to your chosen discipline." Lahiri's voice broke through Harper's train of thought. "I will be overseeing any Theatrics projects. Tulsia any workshop projects, Roper any costumes, and so on." She nodded to the door. "You are free to leave now and go and discuss your ideas with them."

There was a scraping of chairs and rustling of bags as several apprentices rose and started heading for the door. Harper shook her head, trying to clear her racing mind of stars and Curses so she could focus on what was in front of her. She had been falling behind in her apprentice work over the past few months – and now Lahiri was upset with her, she had to find a way to get back on track with her training, as *well* as figuring out what to do about the stars.

An end-of-year presentation... Harper wanted to do something Mechanical, that was for certain. But it needed to be something that was *hers*. Something that would set her apart from everyone else...

Abruptly, Harper hit on an idea. Picking up her backpack, she hurried out of Practice Room One and dashed back to the apprentice quarters. She climbed up to her room and opened her wardrobe, rummaging through it until she found her old dressing gown – the one she'd been wearing when Fletcher, Trick and Helja had collected her from the Smoke all those months ago. She retrieved a slip of paper from the pocket and hurried back to the main wing of the Wondria, descending below the stage to the Scenery Workshop. She found Master Tulsia at a workbench, cheerfully ignoring two lurking Board members who were poking gingerly at an immersive forest-scape, which seemed to be winding its way threateningly around them.

"I wondered if I'd be seeing any of you lot down here." He grinned. "So – you want to do something Mechanical for your presentation?"

Harper nodded and presented the sheet of paper she'd collected. "I want to make this," she said.

Tulsia examined the page. It was crumpled from being in her dressing-gown pocket for so long, but the little mechanical dragon that Harper had designed at her school in the Smoke – in what seemed like a different life, a different world – was still visible.

"I've seen mechanical animals used in the shows before," Harper said to Tulsia. "Could I do something similar with this?"

"I don't see why not," Tulsia mused. "We could make it move, fly, even breathe fire if you want."

"Well –" Harper bit her lip – "there is an adjustment I want to make…"

She explained her idea to Tulsia, marking the planned changes on her original diagram. Tulsia's face was suffused with excitement when she finished.

"I think that's certainly doable," he said cheerfully. "We could begin now, if you want."

"Sounds good," Harper replied with a grin. She went to

fetch a pair of protective goggles, then hesitated. She kept thinking back to what Althea had said in Practice Room One, about this all being pointless.

"Do you think there will be an end-of-year presentation?" she blurted at Tulsia. "Or…do you think we'll be closed down by then?"

Master Tulsia was silent for a moment. He pursed his lips, making his moustache wriggle like a caterpillar, before replying.

"I don't know if anyone can answer that," he said honestly. "The Council will either vote yes or no at the hearing – it's a fifty-fifty chance. But if you want my opinion…" He glanced around at the workshops of the Wondria, smiling slightly at the immersive forest, which had wrapped itself entirely around the Board members and was blocking their indignant attempts to break free. "I don't think the old girl's done for quite yet."

Harper half smiled at that. Some people – like Althea Reed – seemed to have decided that the Wondria's closure was a foregone conclusion. It was nice to know that *someone* believed that they still had hope. Still, she wasn't willing to gamble the future of the Wondria on a fifty-fifty chance.

A week into their punishment, Harper grew desperate enough to attempt to sneak out of the apprentice quarters. They were in the middle of their spring break, and the other apprentices had been enjoying (heavily chaperoned) trips to the city and working their way through their hauls from the Chocolate Zombie (a zombie who, so the story went, hid dismembered chocolate heads around homes, some filled with cream, others with cabbage). Harper, on the other hand, had spent the break exhausting her books, searching for mentions of "secure locations" around Lunas Bay. She'd read about secret underground banks, mountaintop bunkers and archives at the bottom of the sea, but she had no idea which, if any of these, Sharpe and his employer might be using to hide the stars. Harper needed more information – and she was fairly sure she knew where to look.

She waited until late at night before attempting to escape. She hesitated at the door, wondering if she should wake Trick, before deciding not to – at least this way, if she got caught, only one of them would get the extra punishment.

Harper crept along the silent corridors of the Wondria, her breath sounding loud and echoey. She climbed up to the Teaching Wing until she found herself outside Fletcher's emerald door. She figured that if anyone had any clues that could help them, it'd be him – especially since he'd been keeping an eye on Sharpe. If she could just find out where Sharpe and his employer were hiding the stars…she'd solve the problem of *how* exactly they were going to get there later.

"…how long for?"

A voice came from within Fletcher's study, and Harper flattened herself against the wall.

"Until the hearing." Lahiri's voice answered the first. "Fletcher said he's going to be coming and going a lot, preparing our defence. He's appointed me as acting Showrunner until the Council makes its decision."

Harper's heart sank. Fletcher must be struggling with his defence if he'd temporarily relinquished his Showrunner responsibilities. Not for the first time, she felt a surge of frustration. If only they could tell Fletcher about the stars! Surely he'd be able to send out search parties around Lunas Bay and find out where Sharpe had hidden the stars. But their promise to Sylvrjax prevented them from doing that. They had to keep their promise, so Harper knew that they needed to figure this out on their own.

"I've sent messages to some of the other theatres that have apprentice programmes," Lahiri continued. "To see if they have any spaces available."

"It's really reached that point?" the other voice – Roper's, Harper realized – asked gently.

"Fletcher hopes not. But we have to be practical." Lahiri sighed. "If the Wondria closes, we have to have a plan in place for the apprentices."

"I'll help in any way I can," Roper offered. "I suppose this is the best place to find you now?"

"Yes – I figured I might as well work from here. Saves me having to lug all those toasters to my own office."

Roper huffed out a laugh. "All right. I'll let Yosef know as well."

"Thank you. Oh, and tell any Spectaculars who might want to start applying for other jobs that they can come to me for references."

There was silence for a moment. "I will," Roper said eventually. "Muses help us."

Harper heard footsteps approaching the door, and quickly scuttled round the corner. A moment later, Roper emerged from the study, yawning. She rubbed her forehead with her hand, before making her way up the corridor in the opposite direction to where Harper was now crouched.

Harper sat for a moment, her heart thudding unevenly. If Lahiri was contacting other theatres to take the apprentices in, she couldn't have much faith in Fletcher's bid to save them. Was she just being cautious? Or did she know that it was hopeless?

With Harper's plan scuppered – there would be no breaking into Fletcher's office tonight – she made her way back along the corridors and down the winding staircases, until she ended up back in the lobby. She looked around at everything that made up the Wondria: the painted ceiling, the golden Auditorium doors, the Gilded Bar stacked with sparkling glasses. She couldn't bear to lose it all now.

As she made her way back to the apprentice quarters, something tickled at the back of her mind. She kept returning to Roper's last words: *Muses help us...*

Too tired to figure out what was bothering her, Harper clambered up to her room and tumbled into bed. The words echoed in her head just before she went to sleep.

Muses help us.

When Harper woke up, she had a plan.

With the morning light streaming in from her window, Harper dressed quickly and slid down the ladder to the apprentice quarters. Looking around, she was surprised to see that it was a hive of activity. Apprentices were jostling by the window, snatching at a cloud of bottle-messengers which were approaching just outside. Harper walked over to them, peering at the scene before her curiously.

"What's going on?"

Rosie, who was in the centre of the crowd, scrambling as hard as anyone, turned her head briefly to grin at Harper.

"Tickets for the Nocturne concert! They're arriving today!"

As the bottle-messengers drew close to the window, Rosie ducked under the arm of a frankly terrified-looking junior apprentice and lunged towards them. She snatched one out of the air and upended its contents into her hand. The scroll of paper that fell out was thick and white, with gilt edging and swirly writing. Harper leaned over Rosie's shoulder to read it.

ADMIT ONE: TORNIO NOCTURNE
LUNAS BAY ARENA
Evening of the Silver moon

Tornio Nocturne is a triple Chamber Award-winning composer. His works include The Opera of the Four Curses, *and* The Ballet of the Gosling Prince.
He is joint first on The Spectacular Times' *list of Most Influential People, and winner of* The Brightwood Morning Show's *Silkiest Hair competition.*

Harper peered down at the date. The Silver moon… If the message that Sylvrjax had received was true, the Parting of Skies could well be happening on that same night.

Speaking of the Parting of Skies… Harper glanced around, looking for Trick. She spotted him descending from his ladder and ran over to him. He was yawning, his hair mussed from sleep, and as Harper approached him, he looked at her with suspicion.

"You're wearing your plotting face," he said accusingly. "It's too early for you to be wearing your plotting face."

"I think we need to talk to the Muse of Stars," Harper rushed out.

Trick's eyebrows almost disappeared into his hair. "'Scuse me?"

"Sylvrjax said that the stars haven't been able to reach the Muse of Stars – but perhaps we can!" Harper explained. "If we can get his attention, surely *he'll* be able to figure out a way to find and free the stars!"

Trick cocked his head to one side. "Right…but how do you propose we talk to the Muse of Stars?"

"The orbs!" Harper said triumphantly. "The orbs that we used on the night of the Muse of Stars Ceremony! They were made to get his attention, right? To give thanks? If we can grab a few of those, send them up to the sky, like a signal..."

"Fletcher keeps those orbs locked in his study," Trick informed her. "And I don't know if you remember, but Lahiri's banned us from going anywhere other than training and the apprentice quarters."

"I know." Harper quickly explained about her excursion the night before and what she'd overheard outside Fletcher's study.

Trick frowned as she spoke.

"Fletcher said he'd be going away for a bit to work on his defence, but I didn't know he was leaving Lahiri in charge." He worried his bottom lip with his teeth. "That means we'll be in even worse trouble if we get caught sneaking in!"

Harper paused for a moment, looking over at the crowd around the window. Althea had deliberately elbowed two other apprentices in the face to get to her ticket, and was now proudly showing it off while her victims staunched their bleeding noses in the background.

"My father's arranged a private meet and greet," she announced smugly. "I'll be having high tea with Tornio after the concert..."

Harper sucked in a breath. "That's it – the night of the Tornio Nocturne concert. Everyone will be out, watching the show – including Lahiri! She'll be supervising the trip.

We're grounded anyway, so no one will think anything of us staying behind. We can try and get inside Fletcher's study then."

"But...that's the night of the Silver moon." Trick frowned. "The Parting could be happening that night!"

"Even better," Harper replied. "In fact, the Muse can *ensure* that the Parting happens that night – so that once he helps us free the stars, they can all go home, and *we* can tell everyone what we know in time for the hearing!" It wasn't a perfect plan, but it felt like their last hope.

"All right." Trick nodded. "Let's talk to the Muse of Stars."

Chapter Twenty-Four
One Night Only

*A*s the night of the concert approached, the apprentice quarters were filled with a flurry of activity. For those going to the concert, bottle-messengers began to appear frequently at the windows, lugging parcels of new clothes and Nocturne merchandise that people had ordered. Rosie used an entire bottle of Chameleon Hair Formula to turn her plum bob into a waist-length, ink-black sweep of hair ("Nocturne had hair like this during his goth phase," she explained to Harper). Meanwhile Anvi spent hours in the apprentice quarters rehearsing aloud what she'd say to the composer if she got to meet him ("Should I say that I'm a fan? Or is that too...fan-ish? Would 'admirer' be a better word? But then, perhaps that's too aloof...").

Harper was nervous about the night of the Silver moon

as well, but for wildly different reasons. She had no idea if her plot to talk to the Muse of Stars was going to work. If they failed, then the Wondria was surely doomed – and who knew what would happen to the stars themselves, trapped by the awful Sharpe and his mysterious employer.

On the day of the concert, all the apprentices rushed back from training to start getting ready. Harper arrived later than the rest of them – as hers and Trick's plan could only be put into motion once everyone had left, she'd spent all afternoon in the Workshop, tinkering with her little mechanical dragon. She was so close to finishing it – she just needed to add a little wind-up key to get it to work. She had it stashed away in her backpack and every time she thought about it, she felt a glow of pride. She was determined to knock everyone's socks off in the end-of-year show – if the Wondria made it that far.

Although Harper wasn't going to the concert, Rosie insisted that she "join in" with the getting-ready proceedings. Harper selected her brightest outfit (postbox-red dungarees with a blue shirt and gold boots), and Rosie painted her nails midnight-black.

"Are you excited about tonight?" Harper asked.

"Yes…" Rosie replied, frowning as a blob of nail varnish smudged slightly. "Although, I'm worried that Nocturne's only going to play his more well-known stuff. Personally,

I think some of his best work is from before he was famous – in his early days as a composer he wrote a seven-minute-long piece called 'Ode to a Cheese Scone'. It's very moving."

"Oh." Harper personally disagreed with this – no one needed to sit through seven minutes of music dedicated to savoury baked goods.

Once their friends were ready, Harper and Trick went down to the front doors with them to wave them off. Almost everyone in the Wondria was going to the concert – only Harper and Trick were remaining, with Lori Montgomery stationed to make sure they didn't get up to any mischief. Harper tried to look suitably sad about not being allowed to go to the concert, but in truth she was practically bouncing with anticipation – they didn't have much time to put their plan in action. She waved to Rosie and Anvi as they joined the bustling crowd that was funnelling towards the Lunas Bay tram station, then cried out indignantly as a red-headed woman barged right into her, sending her spinning around.

"Hey—" Harper started to protest, but her words died on her lips. Beyond the heaving crowd, a figure was stealing towards the Wondria. Harper squinted, trying to peer through the closely packed bodies. For a terrifying moment, she thought she saw the flash of a painted head, the swing of a side door – but as the crowd filtered away, there was no one there.

Trick nudged Harper. "What's wrong?"

"I...I thought I saw Sharpe," Harper said hesitantly.

"But maybe I was wrong…" After all, why would Sharpe be at the Wondria? He'd be with the stars, surely. She must have been mistaken – her worries making her see things that weren't there.

"Come on," she said to Trick. "Let's get those orbs."

They ran back into the Wondria, their footsteps echoing around the lobby. Lori was perched in the Gilded Bar, and Harper made sure that he saw them heading for the apprentice quarters, before doubling back on themselves when he looked away. Moving as silently as they could, they took the doors to the Teaching Wing and started climbing up towards the fifth floor, where Fletcher's study stood.

"He has a chest where he keeps a lot of important things," Trick told her on the way. "The Wondria keys, old photographs, my baby teeth…"

"Your *teeth*?" Harper repeated.

"Yeah, he's a weirdo." Trick shrugged. "Anyway, we should check there first."

Harper flung out an arm to stop Trick as heavy footsteps suddenly rang out from the corridor adjacent to theirs. They shared an uncertain glance. Surely Lori couldn't have followed them up without them noticing? Taking a breath, Harper inched forwards and peered around the corner.

A tall figure in a chequered suit was marching down the corridor towards them. His attention was focused on a small hessian bag in his hands – *a spell?* Harper wondered fleetingly – but there was no mistaking him.

"It's Sharpe!" she hissed. "It *was* him that I saw!"

"But…why is Sharpe in the Wondria?" Trick asked.

"I don't know," Harper whispered. "But he's about to come round that corner and catch us." She looked down the corridor. It was long, and there were no rooms to hide in. Even if they ran, Sharpe would round the corner and see them long before they got to the end.

"I'll distract him," Trick said. "You get to Fletcher's study and find the orbs."

"What?" Harper hissed. "No way!"

"If he finds both of us, we're done for! At least this'll buy you some time!"

"But—"

"Besides." Trick actually grinned. "We both know I'm the greatest actor the Wondria has ever seen."

Before Harper could argue, he'd bounded around the corner.

"Evening, my good man! Are you here to escort me to the concert?"

Harper risked a glance at them. Sharpe was staring at Trick, clearly at an absolute loss for what to do.

"You – what?"

"My name is Prince Egbert, of the Veiled Seas. My father said that he was sending a security escort for my personal protection. Now, I must warn you – my family have *many* enemies. It all started when my great-great-grandfather invaded the kingdom of Foxhall…"

Harper knew she had to move: Trick was giving her an opportunity, and she couldn't waste it. Turning on her heel, she ran the length of the corridor away from Trick and Sharpe. She raced up three flights of stairs, ignoring the stitch thudding painfully in her side, until she reached the fifth floor. Finally, there it was – the emerald-green door of Fletcher's study. The orbs were so close…she was just a few feet from it when a voice suddenly rang out from a nearby room.

"Is that you, Sharpe?"

Harper froze. "Um…yes," she said, trying to make her voice low and sneery.

"I trust we're on track?"

The voice sounded familiar, somehow – low and melodical.

"Yes," Harper grunted.

"Good. I want that star captured and this whole place deadlocked before that useless lot find out that there is no concert."

Harper gasped as she realized where she knew the voice from. It was the same one she'd heard in the Dreamscape – the one that had warned her off the stars. Sharpe's employer.

She inched forwards until she was peering around the doorway of the room the voice had come from.

She was faced with a large, disused dressing room with circular windows and a thick carpet. A huge dressing table and mirror stood in one corner, and the walls were adorned with portraits of famous Spectaculars who had performed at the Wondria.

However, none of this was what caught Harper's attention. Her eyes were instead firmly fixed on the face staring at her out of the mirror: the reflection of a man with thick dark hair and smooth, pale skin. A face Harper recognized from newspapers, articles, and Rosie's seventeen posters.

It was Tornio Nocturne.

He turned around slowly until he was facing Harper, a nasty smile playing across his face.

"Oh, dear. You're not Sharpe, are you?"

CHAPTER TWENTY-FIVE

The Recluse

Harper stared at Tornio Nocturne. His face was smooth and unlined, his hair neatly combed. He was wearing a sharply cut tailcoat and a pair of polished boots, and was sprawled in the chair like that cat that had not only got the cream, but devoured it from a silver bowl and ordered seconds. He was wearing some sort of scent that smelled overpoweringly of violets, invading Harper's nostrils and making her feel sick.

"I don't understand," Harper said at last.

"Oh. How sad for you," Nocturne replied mildly.

Harper shivered as the voice echoed in her mind. She remembered it laughing gleefully in the Dreamscape as the floor had disappeared from underneath her feet.

"You – Sharpe is working for *you*? But – why? What use

are the fallen stars to *you*?" Harper couldn't make sense of it. Tornio Nocturne was already rich, famous and powerful – what did he need the stars for?

"If I hadn't any use for them, I'd have hardly gone to all the trouble of pulling them out of the sky in the first place, would I?" Nocturne stretched lazily.

Harper's mouth fell open. "*You* pulled them out of the sky?"

"Indeed." Nocturne sat up a bit straighter, looking proud of himself. "An impressive bit of magic, but I pulled it off rather neatly."

"Neatly?" Harper snorted. "They scattered all over the place as they fell – was *that* part of your plan?"

A flash of resentment flashed across Nocturne's face. "Obviously, I intended to draw them directly to me, but stars are slippery things."

"And it's taken you six years to find them all?" Harper taunted. She knew it was risky to antagonize him, but if he lost his temper then perhaps he'd reveal something about where he'd hidden the stars. "Doesn't sound that impressive to me."

"I am a public figure," Nocturne snapped. "I have to be extremely careful about what I am seen to be doing. My employee, too, cannot simply waltz around unnoticed. And until recently we thought we had the luxury of time. We were sure that that dratted Muse of Stars wouldn't risk holding another Parting, after what I'd done at the last one. But last autumn, Sharpe discovered a message that had been sent to the stars – a message stating that the Parting would be happening this year." Nocturne sighed. "That put a bit of pressure on my search. I needed to make sure I'd captured and trapped all of the stars before the Parting happened, in case that dratted Muse took them all back again."

"Although it wasn't really you, was it?" Harper needled. "Sharpe was the one doing all the work."

Nocturne's eyes flashed. "I might have had someone else doing the heavy work, but *I* was the one keeping everyone nice and distracted, so that no one would notice what we were doing."

Harper followed his eyes to a poster of the *Four Curses*. "You...it was you! You started the rumours about the Four Curses!"

"As an anonymous source, obviously." Nocturne smirked. "Just after we discovered that message in the autumn, I started spreading a few stories here and there about recent sightings. Spectaculars are such a superstitious bunch – so willing to believe in fairy tales and legends. It was the same story at the Winter Gala – something turned up that they didn't understand, and they were all too willing to pin it onto an absurd superstition. So, while your Spectaculars have been scaring themselves silly over pigeons and stray tabbies, my associate and I have spent the last few months hunting without interruption." Nocturne grinned at Harper. "It's working very well, I must say. All I need is the panther-star and my collection will be complete."

Harper sucked in a breath. So Nocturne *didn't* have all the stars yet – one was still free, even if it was the one who'd been terrorizing the Wondria.

"What do you mean 'collection'?" A horrible image of glass cases and blank, soulless eyes flashed into Harper's mind. "What are you going to do with the stars?"

"Oh, I don't think you need to know that, do you?" Nocturne said. "Don't worry – I'll be off as soon as I have that final star."

"Well, you're in the wrong place," Harper spat. "The panther-star isn't here."

"You're wrong about that," Nocturne said airily. "That star has been at the Wondria *every single night.*"

Harper gaped at him. "That's not possible."

"But it is. That star eluded me for a long time – every time I tried to track it, I could have sworn it kept disappearing off the face of the Earth for hours at a time, before turning up in unexpected places. I had no idea what was happening. This year, I managed to fine-tune a Witch's tracking spell, and I discovered the places weren't random – they coincided perfectly with the route of a certain Grand Wondria Music Hall and Theatre. And when I looked closer, I saw that the star was often *inside* the Wondria – that it might go out into the surrounding areas, but it always started from within the Wondria, and returned here at the end of the night."

Harper couldn't get her head around this. How could

they possibly have missed a giant panther-star being here every single night?

"Of course, that made it slightly more difficult," Nocturne said. "Capturing wolf-stars out in the woods is one thing, but quite another to conduct a search in a very well-known and well-guarded theatre – even if my Four Curses rumours did work rather well in driving audiences away from your theatre. Still, I knew that I couldn't just walk in here on an ordinary evening – I had to devise a reason for it to be as empty as possible."

"So you planned the concert," Harper finished for him. "You knew that everyone would attend, so you could come and look for the star without being interrupted."

"Precisely."

"Well. Unfortunately for you, it isn't empty. I'm here." Harper folded her arms, trying to look braver than she felt.

Nocturne laughed. "Well. You've got guts, I'll give you that. But you've got in my way for the last time…"

At that moment, a bottle-messenger came whizzing into the room. Nocturne caught it and shook out the message inside. He scanned the words, his eyes widening before his face settled into a deep scowl.

"Would this have anything to do with you?" he asked Harper, raising the slip of paper. "A certain blue-haired flea making trouble for my employee?"

Harper's breath caught, but she tried not to let her emotions show.

"Mmm. Well, I'm afraid he's got himself rather...caught up in my plans." Nocturne had a strange expression on his face. "He's going to have to come with us."

Harper couldn't hide her feelings this time. "No!" she yelled, trying to dodge past Nocturne to the door.

The composer moved quickly. He slid something out of his sleeve, catching it in his hand. It was a long, slim stick, roughly cut and a strange, off-white colour. He flicked it, and Harper suddenly felt herself being propelled backwards across the floor. Another flick, and a cupboard door burst open behind her. Harper was forced into it, toppling backwards as she did. She pushed herself up immediately, but Nocturne had already slammed the door in her face. Harper heard a lock click on the other side.

"Where are you taking Trick?" she hollered, hammering on the door.

She heard Nocturne chuckle on the other side of the door. "That's right – for all your interfering, you never did find out where my secure location was, did you? Well, your little friend can tell you when I return him – if there's anything left of him, that is."

Harper heard his footsteps getting quieter and quieter. She threw her full bodyweight against the door and shoved with all her might, but it was too late.

Nocturne was gone.

It was easy to lose track of time locked in the cupboard. Harper tried everything she could to get out: pounding against the door, feeling around the walls for any holes or weak spots, poking at the ceiling for a trapdoor. Nothing worked. She wondered how long it'd be before someone came looking for her. Was Lori still downstairs? Would he notice they weren't in the apprentice quarters?

Another ten minutes trickled on. Harper was attempting to kick down the door when suddenly she heard footsteps coming along the corridor.

"Hello?" a voice said from outside. "What's all this noise about?"

A rush of relief ran through Harper: she knew that voice. "Lori!" she screamed. "Help me!"

"What the…!" She heard footsteps hurry into the room. "Harper? Is that you?"

"Yes! I'm in the cupboard!"

Lori rattled on the door handle. "Harper, I'm going to break down the door – stand back!"

Harper stood against the far wall of the cupboard. Lori kicked the door once, twice – then it flew open. Harper blinked, the light hurting her eyes after so long in the cupboard. Lori stared down at her.

"What happened?"

"I – he –" Harper didn't even know where to begin. "We need to get hold of someone – Fletcher, Lahiri, anyone!"

"Fletcher's with the Council." Lori frowned. "And

Lahiri's chaperoning the concert trip. Harper, what's going on?"

"Trick's gone." Harper's voice faltered. "He – they've got Trick."

Saying it out loud somehow made it more real, and Harper felt a choking panic descend upon her.

Lori's face turned from confusion to concern. "Who's got Trick? Where is he?"

"Nocturne!" Harper cried. "I don't know where they've gone, I…"

"Nocturne?" Lori looked bewildered. "*Tornio* Nocturne?"

Harper couldn't answer. She felt her throat tighten up.

"All right." Lori placed a hand on Harper's shoulder. "Listen – I'll go to the Arena. I can skin-sing and then fly there – it'll take ten minutes, tops. I'll tell Lahiri what's happened and bring her back here, then we can figure out what we're going to do. Come on – come and wait in the apprentice quarters."

He placed a hand on Harper's shoulders and steered her out of the dressing room. Harper tried to protest, but she could hardly think through the haze of dread. Lori marched her down the stairs, across the empty lobby, and back up to the apprentice quarters.

"Wait in your room," Lori said urgently. "Lock the door and don't answer it to anyone."

Harper began climbing the ladder to her room. She heard Lori start to sing in a low, melodical voice, and quickly looked over her shoulder. In the blink of an eye, a hawk had appeared on the balcony – and in another second, Lori had disappeared, and the hawk was soaring off into the darkening sky. Harper's breath hitched – it was the first time she'd ever actually *seen* someone skin-sing, and it was quite something to behold.

Once Lori was gone, Harper stumbled into her room and slumped to the floor, a feeling of hopelessness creeping over her. What if something happened to Lori on the way to the concert? How would they catch up to Nocturne and Sharpe? How would they find out where Nocturne had hidden the stars and taken Trick?

Suddenly, through the haze of panic, a thought struck Harper. The Spectaculars were all at the concert, but there was someone else she could call on. She stumbled over to her wardrobe and took out the now-very-fragile-looking egg. She smashed it against the floor.

The lilac cloud formed immediately into Thief's face. "Harper?"

"I need your help," Harper said. "It's Sharpe – he's got Trick."

Thief's eyes widened. The smoke-face winked out, and a second later Thief was standing in her room, fully formed. "What?"

Harper explained the events of the evening as quickly as she could. "…and the other Spectaculars are across town at the concert, and I don't know what to do…"

"Okay – Harper, stop talking." Thief held up his hand. "Sorry. But let's think about this for a second. Do you have any idea where Nocturne might have taken Trick?"

Harper forced herself to calm down and *think*. "He was taking Trick to the location where he's been keeping the stars. But I don't know where that is! I've been trying to figure it out, and I've not got anywhere—"

She was cut off by a strange shudder that swept through the air. Harper felt it move through her physically, as if she'd been hit by a giant tidal wave. At the same time, a screeching, clanking noise echoed around them – the sound of metal on metal, loud and terrifyingly final.

When it passed, Harper looked up at Thief. "What was that?" she gasped.

"A deadlock spell." Thief looked perturbed. "It'll seal all the entrances – no one will be able to get in from the outside."

Harper frowned, Nocturne's words from earlier floating into her head: *"I want that star captured and this whole place deadlocked..."* But Nocturne and Sharpe were gone – weren't they? Why would they still be here, casting a deadlock spell around the Wondria?

Unless...

"They're still here." Harper's voice came out hoarse. "*Trick's* still here. They're locking down the Wondria so no one can get inside. Because..." The realization knocked all the breath out of her. "The stars are *here*! This was his 'secure location'! He put the stars in the Wondria!"

Harper felt like she was on the verge of laughing, or crying, or quite possibly screaming into a pillow for the rest of eternity. How many sleepless nights had she had since Sylvrjax and the other wolf-stars had been kidnapped? How often had she combed the same books, desperately searching for clues? And all the while the stars had been right under her nose, hidden somewhere within the Wondria. "Close to home" – just like Nocturne had told her in the Dreamscape.

"It makes sense." Thief nodded. "Who would bother to look in a regular old theatre? Especially one that's always moving. But where in the Wondria would be big enough to hide thirteen fully-grown stars without anyone noticing?"

Harper ran through a list of locations in her head. The Auditorium, the Gilded Bar, the Scenery Workshop…all of them were too public, too frequently used. There was no way that Sharpe could have been sneaking in and out, stashing stars in a corner without anyone noticing them. It had to be somewhere empty, somewhere no one ever went…

"The Sky Vaults," she said slowly.

"The what?"

"They're old storage facilities, inside the domes of the roof," Harper explained quickly. "Where they keep old bits of costume, set, that kind of thing. Apparently, it's so overrun with junk, no one ever goes in there. Which means…"

"…it'd be the perfect place for Nocturne to hide the stars," Thief finished. "Okay. How do we get there?"

Harper chewed on her lip, remembering her conversation

with Lori. "The entrance is sealed. I didn't see any locked doors or stairs leading up from the top floor…"

"Perhaps it's in the ceiling," Thief suggested. "Like a trapdoor. Let's go and look."

Harper hesitated for a moment. Lori had told her to stay here, to wait until he and Lahiri got back: but if Nocturne had deadlocked the place, they wouldn't be able to get in, and Trick was in danger *now*.

"Okay," she said. "Let's go."

They scaled the ladder down to the apprentice quarters and exited into the corridor. As they jogged down the stairs, Harper noticed a little blue blob – she didn't know how else to describe it – peering out of Thief's pocket, looking this way and that.

"Hey," she said, pointing. "Isn't that the summoning spell? The one that didn't work?"

Trick looked a little guilty. "Ah – yes. Well, I know I said it wasn't sensible to keep spells as pets, but…" He looked at Harper earnestly. "It's *cute*."

The spell tilted its head at Harper. She looked at it sternly.

"You're doing that on purpose," she said, resolving to not find it cute in any way.

They crossed the lobby into the Teaching Wing and climbed up, up, up, until they reached the topmost floor of the Wondria, where Harper had been only weeks before, searching for hidden entrances to the Wondria.

Not that it mattered, she thought to herself mulishly. *The star was here all along.*

"Do you see anything?" Thief asked, peering upwards.

Harper scanned the ceiling. It was an off-white colour, with an ugly, swirling pattern, but there was nothing to suggest that it might be concealing a secret trapdoor. She walked up and down the length of the corridor, her hands balling anxiously into fists at her sides. She was starting to panic that her instinct had been wrong when Thief suddenly stopped and pointed.

"Hey – what's that?"

Harper craned her neck up. There, on the ceiling, was a tiny silver button – small enough that you'd miss it completely, unless you were looking very carefully. Harper was no expert, but a button in the ceiling seemed like something that might logically lead to the revealing of a secret door...

"How are we going to reach it?" Harper glanced around for a handily placed chair or box, anything that could get her high enough to reach the ceiling. "Perhaps I could – *argh*..."

The end of her sentence descended into an undignified squawk as Thief bent down and hoisted Harper onto his shoulders. When he straightened up, Harper wobbled, almost falling backwards. She yelled and grabbed on to his head for dear life.

"Ouch – watch my hair!"

"I wouldn't have to watch your hair if you'd given me a

bit of *warning*," Harper complained. Despite her irritation, she couldn't help but grin slightly as she glanced down and noticed that Thief's orange curls had been twisted into a vague topknot at the back of his head with the scrunchy she'd given him. She'd been right – they *did* clash horribly.

"Can you reach it?" Thief asked.

Harper extended an arm up towards the ceiling, keeping the other wrapped tightly around his head for balance.

"Almost…" Harper stretched as far as she could, wobbling precariously on Thief's shoulders. "Just a little further… There!" Harper jabbed the silver button, and at once, the ceiling began to move. The ugly swirls began to unfurl, bending back on themselves like leaves in a strong wind. Thief hopped out of the way, with Harper still clinging on to his shoulders, as a hole appeared in the ceiling. A delicate silver staircase began to spiral down from the hole, coming to rest exactly at their feet.

"Right." Thief deposited Harper none-too-delicately back on the floor. "You ready?"

Harper looked up at the staircase that led to nothing. She had no idea what they'd find in the Sky Vaults – all she knew was that she had to save her best friend and the stars. "Ready as I'll ever be."

Chapter Twenty-Six
The Sky Vaults

The silver staircase led to a cavernous, dusty room, so dim that Harper could barely see. The roof arched high over Harper and Thief's heads, criss-crossed with beams and rafters. Harper reached into her backpack, rummaging around for a moment before coming up with a silver starlight-torch. She switched it on and shone it around, allowing the light to illuminate their surroundings.

Harper could see immediately why no one came up here. "Messy" was a *vast* understatement. It was more like a mess had come alive, moved in and made its own mess, which in turn had come alive and made even *more* mess. Piles of old sheet music and librettos were stacked precariously to the ceiling in a line of wonky columns. An entire corner was taken up by a pop-up puppet theatre, complete with a set of dusty marionettes depicting milkmaids and goats. A giant oak chest held an array of rusted broadswords, plus a shield that had been graffitied with the words, *McCubbins is a numpty.*

"Oof," Thief huffed as he too emerged into the room. "This place is like a Witch's paradise."

Harper nodded in agreement. Even the most industrious of Witches would have a hard time scavenging every piece of leftover junk in here.

"Come on," she whispered, taking a determined step forwards. They had no time to waste. There was a door at the far side of the room, so Harper immediately made for that. It creaked loudly as she opened it, and Harper held her breath, waiting for a shout or running footsteps. When none came, she gestured to Thief and peered into the next room.

For a split second, Harper's heart stopped. The room appeared to be filled with figures, lining the perimeter, poised and ready to attack. Harper stumbled backwards into Thief, flinging her hands up in self-defence, before she realized that none of the figures were moving. She brought up her torch and squinted at the figures, moving the beam of light from one to the other. She could see that they were all sporting half-finished, obviously abandoned costumes: tulle gowns with concealed weapons, suits made from a patchwork of foil sweet wrappers, and elaborate cloaks edged with beads or playing cards or tiny, embroidered faces.

"They're costume dummies," she breathed.

A quick glance around the room told Harper that Trick wasn't in here, however, and she and Thief hurried through the centre towards the next door. This one was solid iron. It took both of them hauling with all their might to prise open a big enough gap for them to slip through.

They found a narrow wooden corridor on the other side that weaved drunkenly from side to side before coming to a low arch. Harper stepped through it, her breath hitching as she saw what lay on the other side.

Like the others, this room had a domed ceiling and a dank, musty smell. Lanterns had been lit around the perimeter, casting a strange, flickering light across the floor and walls. The wall nearest to them was hung with chains, while the wall opposite was piled with iron cages. Through their thick bars, Harper could see various animal forms, including...

"Sylvrjax!" Harper ran over and reached a hand in, Thief just behind her.

"Harper?" Sylvrjax rumbled. "Is that you?"

Harper felt a wave of pure rage wash over her. She looked up and noticed that each cage had a roughly made sign on top of it: *Wolf-star. Bear-star. Raven-star.* She saw Sareni, Harlemunn and Dianita shivering in equally small cages.

"*What* is going on here?" Thief asked, looking at the caged stars in horror.

"It's the composer," Sylvrjax told them. "Harper – his plan is to kill us. All of us, at the same time."

"*What?* Why?" Harper was aghast.

"Killing a star releases a huge amount of celestial energy," Sylvrjax said. "He must want to harness this energy into something. And now he has all thirteen of us…"

"All thirteen?" Harper felt sick. "He has the panther-star?" Had Nocturne managed to capture it while she'd been locked in the cupboard?

"Technically, yes," Sylvrjax replied. "But—"

"Harper," Thief's voice rang out from her right. He was standing in front of a cage, staring inside. Harper glanced up at the sign on top of it, and read the words:

Panther-star.

Harper swallowed as she approached the cage. She'd very much hoped never again to have to face the creature she'd once believed to be Misfortune, even though she now knew the truth of what it was. But Thief had such an odd expression on his face… Harper jogged closer.

She blinked once, then twice. The figure inside the cage wasn't a star at all.

It was Trick.

Harper ran forwards. "Trick?" She grabbed the bars of the cage. "What's going on? Why did they put you in a cage?"

Thief pulled a piece of metal out of his pocket and started picking the lock. In a matter of seconds, the cage door swung open – but Trick didn't step out straight away. Instead, he looked up with a strange expression on his face – a sort of expectation, mixed with fear and dread.

"I don't understand…" Harper found herself staring at the sign again, at the two simple words etched into it.

Panther-star

She suddenly felt as though she'd been frozen to the spot. Images filled her mind all at once. Trick's reluctance to be out too late… Leaving the party early on Merrimas… Practically dragging her back towards the Wondria after Sharpe had captured the stars… His hesitation towards the summoning-spell, and the look on his face as it had been activated… Trick's steadfast insistence that it *wasn't* Harper's fault that the creature had turned up. And the way the creature had looked at her when she'd first encountered it – like it *recognized* her.

When Harper's vision cleared, she looked at Trick, shivering. She could tell that he knew from her face what she'd figured out. And she knew from his face that it was true.

"It's you," she said, her voice hoarse from the shock. "*You're* the thirteenth star."

CHAPTER TWENTY-SEVEN

Stylisclaw

Harper stared at Trick. "How?" She closed her eyes, trying to clear her thoughts. "How…? What…?"

"I can explain," Trick said quickly.

"You…the star…" A horrible thought struck Harper, and she stumbled backwards from the cage. "You attacked us. You *killed* someone."

"No." Trick stepped out of the cage towards them. "None of this is what you think it is. Please, just let me explain."

There was silence for a few moments as Harper looked at her friend. She knew the horrors that the star had unleashed. She'd seen it with her own eyes. But how could it all have been *Trick*?

"Start from the beginning," Harper choked out eventually. "*What* is going on?"

Trick took a deep breath. "It all started the night we crossed over to the Hidden Peaks – the night that the stars fell. That first night, we camped out on the southern side of the Midnight Jungle. I was upset about the accident. I snuck out, thinking I could go to the gateway and see if you'd found it yet. But then I heard this weird singing in my ears…and it led me to him."

"To the panther-star?" Thief asked. He was staring at Trick, his face a mask of shock.

Trick nodded. "When I saw what he was and how badly he was hurt, I wanted to help him. So…" He looked up at Harper. "I tried to skin-sing."

Harper's mouth dropped open. "*You* can skin-sing?"

"It manifests young," Trick reminded her. "I'd started to get these weird dizzy spells – I had one just before the crossing, remember? But I wasn't sure what it was, until the singing led me to him. I thought if I could sing myself into his skin, it might give him some extra strength to heal. But it went wrong." He hung his head. "When you skin-sing, you're supposed to be able to sing your way out again whenever you want. But when I tried it, we both transformed back into my form. Maybe because my ability hadn't manifested properly, or maybe because he was a star rather than an animal…but he got stuck. Ever since then…" Trick swallowed. "Most of the time, I'm in my own skin, with him inside me. But I feel sorry for him – being stuck there. So at night, I sing us into his skin, so he can stretch his legs."

Harper closed her eyes briefly as Nocturne's words came back to her. "The star has been in the Wondria *every single night*."

"What about the attacks?" she whispered. "The Winter Gala…"

"He didn't mean to attack," Trick said. "The Winter Gala was on the anniversary of the Falling. He was restless, and he wanted to return to the Fallen Site, to look for clues – just like Sylvrjax said the others had! I tried to tell him it was a bad idea, but he's really stubborn."

He's talking about the star, Harper thought faintly. *The star that…lives inside him.*

"I sang us into his skin, and then we went into the clearing. As soon as he showed up, people panicked," Trick explained. "He didn't mean to cause any damage, but there were crowds screaming and stampeding…he was just trying to get away."

"What about the body in the snow?" Harper demanded.

"That 'body' was *me*," Trick replied. "We got lost in the woods after the Gala. He tried to find his way back to the Wondria, but then morning came. I just about managed to sing back into my own form, but I was freezing and exhausted, and collapsed in the snow. I could've died, but he used his warmth to keep me alive. As for the 'hikers' that found us, they were completely sozzled. They found a body that wasn't moving and assumed it was dead. They went for help, but I was gone by the time they came back. That should have been a clue that I *wasn't dead,* but I suppose it made for a good story, so it stuck."

Harper thought about the words that had haunted her since Merrimas: *one dead…a body lying in the snow.* Except it wasn't a body after all – it was Trick.

"We agreed to stay more low-key after that," Trick said. "To stay close to the Wondria when I transformed us – usually around midnight. We had it under control, until this year."

"What happened this year?" asked Thief.

"I started training," Trick said simply. "Once I was an apprentice, I was allowed in parts of the Wondria I'd never been to before, I could see the shows as much as I wanted… I got overexcited, stayed out too late. After opening night, we had a little accident with the lanterns…" He looked at Harper.

Harper pictured the smashed lanterns, the precarious metal pole. "All Spooks' Eve?" she asked.

"There was so much to see – I couldn't help staying out," Trick admitted. "He woke up just before midnight, and he was in a right grump – yowling and hissing inside my head. Eventually, I found an abandoned corridor and sang us into his skin, just to quieten him down. Everyone was in the Auditorium or backstage, so I thought he'd be able to get to my room without being seen, but he got lost and we ended up in the Auditorium instead. He didn't mean to make the chandelier fall, he was just panicking and trying to get out. It was the same thing the night of the tribute band – I'd managed to sneak away from the concert, and I thought the Costume Department was empty. He was getting impatient, so I transformed us... I had no idea *you* were in there!"

"But he chased me!" Harper protested.

"No, he *recognized* you," Trick replied. "From my memories. He was trying to get you to help him – but then you fell down the stairs." He looked down. "He felt awful about that. We both did."

Thief gasped suddenly, his hand going to his head. "The spell! That's why it didn't work – because you were already in the room! There was nothing to summon, because the star was already there, inside of you! I *knew* it wasn't a dud spell."

The spell in his pocket peeked out and blew a raspberry at Harper.

"What about Ace Malone?" Harper said suddenly. "She was attacked!"

"No, she wasn't," Trick said grimly. "I knew it couldn't have been 'Misfortune', obviously – I was watching the show with you, and I could feel the star snoring in my head the whole time. So I checked the Costume Department the next day, and sure enough, a bunch of the Blood Pills were missing. Remember – the things that Roper was using on All Spooks' Eve, to make it look like people were bleeding?"

"What – you're saying she *faked* it?" Harper said incredulously.

"Ace Malone is a talk-show host." Trick shrugged. "She wanted the best story."

Harper rankled at this. Ace Malone's attack had led to the motion to close the Wondria. They were on the verge of being shuttered for ever, all for the sake of a *story?*

"Why didn't you tell anyone?"

"I knew some missing Blood Pills weren't enough evidence," Trick replied. "And I could hardly tell them the other reason why I knew it wasn't Misfortune."

"But why didn't you tell *me?*" Harper finally exploded. "Why wasn't this the very first conversation we had? 'Oh hi, I'm Trick, I'm eleven years old and by the way, *I transform myself into a giant panther-star every night!*'" All the fear and frustration that had been building for months was suddenly unleashed. "I've been walking around since All Spooks' Eve believing that a Curse was attacking us, and that it was *all my fault!*"

"I tried to tell you that it wasn't your fault!" Trick protested. "I told you those old superstitions weren't true!"

"But you knew it wasn't a threat!" Harper shot back. "How could you keep that from me?"

"I promised him," Trick said quietly. "After the Winter Gala, and the way people reacted to him, he asked me to promise to not reveal his identity to anyone." He looked at Harper steadily. "Remember what Sylvrjax told us? How a promise to a star *can't* be broken without their permission?"

"But – you've told us now," Thief pointed out.

"Yeah, well – we had a little chat recently about how reasonable 'never tell anyone ever about my true identity' was," Trick said. "He agreed that I could tell people in *absolutely necessary* circumstances. Which –" Trick looked around at the cages – "I reckon this is."

There was a small silence. Harper took a few breaths, trying to get her feelings under control.

"I'm not saying I'm not still hurt," she said eventually. It was all too raw, too close. "But…I understand. I understand why you couldn't tell me. But from now on, you have to promise that you'll be honest with me. About everything."

Trick's eyes widened hopefully. "I promise!"

"No more secrets."

"No more secrets *at all*." Trick's face took on a familiar mischievous look. "Would you also like to hear about how I once tried to keep a Fireslug as a pet, and it crawled into Fletcher's boots and burned his foot? Or how I once had noodles from a Fae market and spent the whole night…"

"All right, *some* secrets are fine," Harper grumbled.

She glanced up at the words written across the top of the cage. *Panther-star*… Underneath the shock and hurt, Harper couldn't help but feel a tiny bit of wonder. It wasn't every day that you found out your best friend could transform into a *star*.

"So…do Nocturne and Sharpe know about this?" Thief asked.

"Yep," Trick said glumly. "The tracking spell went haywire as soon as I stepped around the corner. Sharpe caught me and sent a message to Nocturne, and *he* figured it out."

"Speaking of Nocturne," Thief chimed in. "We need to figure out a way to get you all free before he appears."

"He went off with Sharpe," said Trick. "I think he was giving him instructions on what to do while Nocturne was, um – *dealing with* the stars."

Harper thought fast. "Okay. Thief – pick the rest of the locks and get the stars out of their cages. I'll distract Nocturne while you get away. Then we can worry about how to contact the Muse of Stars."

"No."

"Absolutely not!" Trick and Thief spoke at the same time.

"Nocturne wants to *kill the stars*," Harper told them. "If he finds you escaping, we've got no chance of stopping him!"

"Then I'll come with you," Trick said. "No, listen – he can't hurt me, not really, 'cos he knows that if he hurts me, he hurts Stylisclaw, and he won't risk that." He blinked at Harper's confused face. "Oh – that's his name. I call him Styl for short. He hates it."

"I suppose it's better than Misfortune," Harper replied. "Right. So, we'll go and distract Nocturne while Thief frees the stars."

Thief still didn't look happy about this, but he relented. "Fine. But as soon as they're free, I'm coming back to help you."

Harper steeled herself. "Where did Nocturne go?"

Trick nodded towards another door. "That way."

With a last look at Thief and the stars, Harper turned and

made for the door. She swung it open carefully and stepped through with Trick hot on her heels. They climbed a rickety set of stairs and emerged into a room that was barely a room at all – in fact, as Harper looked around, she realized they were in the rafters of the roof, right at the apex of the dome. The floor beneath their feet was little more than a lattice of beams, with a narrow walkway winding across them and a *very* sheer drop below. With a glance at Trick, Harper began to edge along the walkway, holding on to the rafters for balance.

"I can't believe Nocturne wants to kill the stars," Harper whispered as they made their precarious way across the narrow path. "He's already one of the most famous Spectaculars of all time. What more does he want?"

"Quite a bit, as it happens," drawled a voice from behind them.

CHAPTER TWENTY-EIGHT

The Muse of Stars

Harper whipped around, her heart in her mouth. Tornio Nocturne was leaning against one of the beams, arms folded, a small smile on his face. The scent of violets stole towards them, and Harper stepped backwards to avoid the cloying sweetness, almost putting her foot straight through a rotten beam below her. She grabbed on to Trick for balance as Nocturne held up the long, white stick Harper had seen him use at the Wondria.

"Do you like it?" he asked smugly. "I bet you can't guess what it is."

Harper didn't wait around to play guessing games. "Run!" she yelled, spinning on her heel. She fled through the rafters as fast as she dared, trying very hard not to look at the drop below them. Glancing backwards, she saw Nocturne make a slashing motion with the stick – what *was* that thing? – and the piece of walkway directly in front of them crumbled away, crashing down into the room below. Harper skidded to a halt, but Trick grabbed her hand and jumped across the opening, pulling her with him. They landed heavily on the other side, and Trick swayed, almost falling backwards, before Harper grabbed him and yanked him forwards.

"This way!" Trick gestured to a narrow spiral staircase at the far end of the rafters. They leaped for it, half running, half falling down it. As they reached the room below, Harper looked up: she could see Nocturne striding across the latticed beams above them, moving quickly towards the staircase.

"We don't have long," Harper whispered, her heart thudding. "We need to get hold of that weird stick thing – that's where his power is coming from."

"Yeah, but how?" Trick panted back.

Harper looked around the room they were in. It was dark and littered with old backdrops. Peering through the gloom, Harper could see that some featured faded pictures of castles, enchanted forests and rolling fields, while others had been covered over with grey dust sheets. Harper pulled the starlight-torch back out of her pocket and shone it at the sheets. The seed of an idea sprung to life in her head.

"Come on," she hissed, pulling Trick over to the backdrops and taking hold of the corner of a dust sheet. Thrusting the other side at Trick, she tied her corner hurriedly to one of the backdrops, and motioned for him to do the same, so that the sheet was stretched out taut like the sail of a ship. With a jolt of terror, she heard Nocturne's steps on the staircase. Harper crouched behind another backdrop and focused the torch on the dust sheet.

"When you get a shot, go for the stick," she whispered to Trick.

"When will I—"

"Just hide!" Harper hissed. Trick dived behind her, and barely a second later, Nocturne emerged from the spiral staircase. He stood at the bottom, his sharp eyes scanning the room.

Taking a deep, silent breath, Harper thrust her hands in front of the starlight-torch, making the same cat-shape she'd made in the Theatrics class. She cleared her mind and felt the cold, crackling energy of the Star-Stuff in the air around her. Breathing deeply, she focused on the torch and felt the Star-Stuff rush through her, transforming the beam of light into a perfect replica of a cat, shining against the grey sheet. Harper saw Nocturne glance towards it, then towards the source of the light. He smirked and took a step in her direction.

Harper focused all her attention on the light and pulled her hand forwards as she'd seen Lahiri do. Her light-cat strained, then loomed forwards off the sheet altogether, diving towards where Nocturne stood. He stopped in his tracks, then was forced to duck with a snarl as the light-cat swiped a paw at him. He stumbled, but the stick remained clutched in his hand.

Harper moved her hands, opening the cat's mouth. In the air, the light-cat snapped at Nocturne, and he stumbled, backing away from where Harper was crouched.

"You think a few light-tricks are going to beat me?" he shouted into the darkness.

Nope, Harper thought, grimly satisfied as she saw a blur of movement to her right. *Just distract you.*

As Nocturne whipped around once more, trying to wave away Harper's light-cat, Trick pelted out across the floor. Turning too late to stop him, Nocturne seemed to freeze as Trick leaped for his hand, grasping for the stick. For a moment, Trick hung, suspended in the air. Then he gave a yell of triumph and landed on the ground – with the stick clutched in his hand. He threw it down immediately and stamped on it, hard.

"No!" Nocturne lurched towards Trick. Harper's heart felt like it was about to burst out of her chest. Had they done it?

Nocturne shoved Trick aside, plucking the stick off the floor. Harper saw with a lurch of dread that it was cracked, all the way up, but not broken.

"You," the composer snarled, rounding on Trick.

Harper threw herself out from behind the backdrop and hurled herself at Nocturne, but not before he'd got his arm around Trick, pinning him in place in front of him. Nocturne lifted the cracked stick and pointed it at her.

"Stay where you are."

Harper froze in her tracks.

"Not as breakable as it might look, is it?" Nocturne said, flicking the stick. "Wood or glass might splinter beneath a foot, but bone – bone is made of stronger stuff."

Harper felt sick. "That's – that's made of bone?"

"Star bone. I thought I might as well do some experiments before I kill them – borrow a rib or two, nothing they'd miss too much. When you work with star bone or teeth or blood, there are no need for channels, like with light and dust. No need to sing or play or dance around like performing monkeys in order to get Star-Stuff to do your bidding. You just command, and it obeys."

Harper shook her head; she didn't want to imagine anything like it. "Let him go," she demanded.

"You know, this reminds me of a conductor baton," Nocturne said idly, holding the stick up to the light. "When I'm conducting an orchestra, I'm in complete control. The musicians move when I tell them to move, they play what I tell them to play. As it turns out, when you have the power of star bones, you can turn that control to other things as well."

Harper glanced helplessly around the room. There was no other door that she could see, and no windows – they were inside the Wondria's roof, for Muses' sake! How were they going to get out?

Nocturne noticed her glance and grinned. "Yes – it's a little confined in here, isn't it? Shall we get some fresh air?"

"No—" Harper suddenly found herself soaring through

the air, straight towards the inner arch of the roof. She threw her arms over her head, expecting to splat against the roof like an insect, but at the last moment the inside of the dome simply melted away, and Harper was flung out into the night air. She landed on the main dome of the Wondria and began to slide down, clutching desperately at the smooth roof. Her fall was only broken by the lower tier of the dome, which brought her to a stop just before she sailed clean off the edge. Harper looked at the city of Lunas Bay sprawled out before her, lit up against the night sky, and thought about screaming for help. But would they even be seen from up here, let alone heard?

"Do you know what a cadenza is? I've always been fond of the phrase." Nocturne's voice came from above her. Harper looked across the roof to see him standing at the edge of the hole he'd made, Trick pinned beside him. "A cadenza is the moment in a piece of music when the orchestra as a whole rests, while a soloist plays. One single voice, rising above the rest."

Trick struggled against Nocturne. Despite his slim build, Nocturne seemed to have no trouble keeping hold of him, and the composer's appearance seemed as perfect as ever. It had to be magic of some sort, Harper thought – magic maintaining his looks, his sharp clothes, the overwhelming sweet violet scent that leached from his skin.

"And I suppose that's you, is it?" Harper said, struggling to her feet. "One voice, rising above the rest?"

"I'd say so." Nocturne nodded. "I'm the one who wants to push us further. If we wanted to, Spectaculars could be more powerful than Witches and Fae-Folk and all the rest. More powerful than Muses!"

"Why would you want to be more powerful than a Muse?" Trick yelled. "Just to make yourself feel superior?"

"I am superior!" Nocturne practically stamped one of his polished boots. "Do you want a demonstration? Hm…how about we make your friend here take a walk off the edge of the roof?"

Harper barely had time to register Trick's horrified face before she felt herself being yanked up and turned around, so she was facing the edge of the smaller dome. An invisible force started pushing her from behind – first one foot, then the other was forced forwards as if a gale-force wind was blowing at her back.

"Stop it!" Trick was wriggling madly, but the composer had a tight grip on him.

Harper clenched her fists and tensed her muscles, trying to resist the force behind her, but it was no use. She took another step forwards.

From below them, there was a sudden blur of movement. A stream of figures flowed out of the Wondria – four wolves, two ravens, a stag, a bear, a peacock, two squirrels and a rabbit. Sharpe was running for his life just ahead of them, fleeing across the square and into the alleys beyond. Thief ran out after the stars, chasing Sharpe. Even through her fear,

Harper felt a powerful surge of relief. They'd done it – the stars were free.

Distantly, she heard a bell from one of the far-off towers in Lunas Bay chime midnight. She looked up at the sky, even as her feet forced her another step forwards, dangerously close to the edge of the roof. The Silver moon was at its apex, hanging fat and round like a pearl against the throat of the sky.

"No! NO!"

Harper felt the force from behind her suddenly drop away as she heard Nocturne yell. She blinked, realizing that she could control her limbs again, and jumped away from the edge of the roof. Spinning around, she saw a strange tableau: Trick with his foot in the air, which had clearly just connected with Nocturne's hand – a hand which was open and empty. The star-bone baton was spinning through the air, arching up, up, up, then plummeting beyond the edge of the roof.

"Yes!" Harper gasped, at the same time Nocturne roared, "No!"

His face was twisted in pure rage as he surged forwards, reaching his hand out desperately towards the baton. He seemed to have forgotten that Trick was in front of him, and as he stretched, his weight pushed against Trick. Trick wobbled, swaying horribly like a tightrope walker, before toppling over the edge.

Harper screamed as Trick fell forwards, plummeting

straight down towards the ground. There were no smaller domes to break his fall – just endless, empty space between him and the street below. Harper threw herself forwards, her hand stretching out desperately even though she was far too far away to catch him. As he fell, Harper saw Trick move his lips, saw him chant something, before suddenly a silver light engulfed his body. Harper watched, breathless, as the light shifted, grew, reshaped, until…

…an enormous silver panther shot out a huge paw, its claws digging into the roof tiles, halting the momentum of the fall. Harper watched in awe as it hauled its huge body up the side of the roof, claws grappling onto the tiles as easily as she might push her hands into freshly fallen snow.

"Stylisclaw," Harper breathed.

The panther turned its face to her. His silver fur glowed in the moonlight, and his eyes were black and bright. He nodded once to her, then turned his attention to Nocturne. Stylisclaw pounced, knocking the composer off his feet and pinning him to the ground. Nocturne gave a shriek of rage, but it was no use: without his baton, he was no match for a large, very solid panther-star.

Harper looked up to the sky. The clouds were shifting, and a low, rumbling sound was slowly filling the air. It was happening: the sky was parting. She scanned the expanse above them. Did the Muse of Stars know where they were? Would he be able to find them?

"He doesn't know they're here," Nocturne howled. "He

can't send the Celestial Highway to them if he doesn't know where they are!"

Harper looked out across the sky, her thoughts turning over. They needed a beacon – something bright and brilliant, something that would let the Muse of Stars know where they were, show him that they needed his help.

She was reaching for her backpack almost before she'd thought of a full plan. She pulled it open and shoved her hand inside, her fingers closing around metal. She lifted out the mechanical dragon, the one she'd designed all those months ago in the Smoke, the one she'd been working on just today in the Workshop. If she could get it charged up, then the extra features that she'd given it would be the perfect beacon – but she hadn't added the wind-up key yet. All the Star-Stuff she'd filled it with sat dormant inside, waiting for a burst of energy that she couldn't provide.

Or...could she? Finished Mechanical objects were created with Star-Stuff to give them their powers. But there was another way to work with Star-Stuff – to channel it directly through song or dance or speech, the way that Theatrics did. If she provided the channel, could she funnel all that energy into the dragon? Could she kick-start it herself?

Harper knew she had to try. She focused all her attention onto the dragon and cleared her mind. It'd been getting easier and easier to do since her breakthrough in the light-puppetry lesson. She sensed the Star-Stuff almost at once:

felt the bright, cold blast of it as it turned its attention towards this possible channel. She remembered what Lahiri had said on their first day – that you had to be clear about what you wanted, or you'd just confuse the Star-Stuff. Harper closed her eyes and began to hum.

At first, she wasn't even sure what she was humming – then she realized with a smile that it was an old song that her mum used to dance around their kitchen to. It was a song about love, about dreams, about things that could lift you off the ground. As she sang, Harper allowed her mind to fill with images of things that lifted *her* up – she pictured her mum hugging her tight, and her dad playing his trumpet with the silver bow tie around his neck. She pictured Trick giving her the sketchbook full of memories, and Lahiri telling her she'd done a good job, and Rosie and Anvi waiting up for them after they'd snuck out. She held the mechanical dragon tightly in her hands and focused all those thoughts into it.

Harper shivered as she felt the Star-Stuff funnel down her arms, bringing her out in goosebumps. It rushed forwards to where she was directing it, like a laser beam shooting directly into the heart of the dragon in her hands.

The dragon began to glow, faintly at first, then brighter as more and more Star-Stuff flowed into it. The metal grew colder in Harper's hands, until she could hardly stand to hold the dragon. Dipping her hand slightly, Harper pitched her creation into the air.

The dragon clicked into life in the air, copper wings unfurling, tail twitching this way and that as it hovered in front of her. Its brilliant onyx eyes blinked awake, and with a flap of its gleaming wings it turned in mid-air and looked Harper straight in the eye.

"Light it up," Harper said.

For a moment, she almost thought she saw the dragon smile, before it shot straight upwards into the air. It flew until it was no more than a tiny, glinting dot against the pitch-black sky...then opened its mouth, and the sky exploded.

When she'd first hit upon the idea of building her dragon, she'd asked Master Tulsia if it was possible to make the dragon breathe light instead of fire – colourful, burning lights, like the ones that sometimes lit up the skies in the Hidden Peaks. The dragon was a creation she'd conceived of in the Smoke, so she'd wanted to add something to represent her life as a Spectacular as well – something bright and brilliant.

The light blazed fiercely against the night sky. It was tinged with pale blue and silver, violet and soft pink. It danced above their heads, luminous and burning and *very* difficult to ignore.

The stars below her seemed to catch on to what she was doing. Sylvrjax tossed back his head and howled, the other three wolf-stars quickly joining in. The bear-star roared to the sky, the ravens screeched and cawed, and even the little rabbit-star let out a brave squeak.

"What are you *doing*?" Nocturne's face was twisted in rage. "Stop!"

Harper felt the wind whip up behind her. She spun on her heels, her mouth dropping open as she looked towards the sky. She couldn't quite find the words to describe what was coming towards them. It was like a hurricane – a mass of pure energy. Wisps of blue and grey swirled around each other at top speed. Harper squinted as it came closer, and thought she could just about make out a shape in the centre of the mass: a human-shape, riding on the back of a giant bird.

"No!" Nocturne screamed at the sky.

The Muse of Stars soared over Harper's head and halted above Nocturne. The wind grew louder and angrier, and Harper had to hold her hair back from her face to see what was happening.

A funnel of energy extended down to the ground like a tornado, engulfing Nocturne in wisps of black and blue. It whirled around him, almost completely obscuring him from view. Then, with a final crash of wind, the tornado seemed to implode in on itself. A force rushed out from it with a shrieking noise, hitting Harper and sending her reeling backwards.

When she looked back, Nocturne was gone. The tornado retreated into the whirling mass above them, which lingered but moved slightly higher, so that the violent wind around Harper dropped and she could see properly again.

For a moment, Harper simply gaped at the place where the

composer had been standing just a split second before. Before she knew what was happening, Stylisclaw was vaulting over to the dome where she was perched, landing heavily in front of her. He ducked his head and tossed her up onto his shoulders, then leaped back upwards, his claws digging into the side of the dome as he climbed towards the hole in the roof. Once they were safely back inside, he deposited Harper on the floor.

"Are you all right? Did he hurt you?" she asked, looking the giant panther over for injuries. He huffed once, then shook his head, sitting back on his haunches.

Harper reached out a hand hesitantly. "Can I?"

Stylisclaw inclined his head, and Harper reached out to touch his back. His fur was soft and silky. She ran a hand along his head, and he huffed again, flicking his tail.

Harper looked at him curiously. "Not much of a talker? Muses, it must be a *nightmare* for you being in Trick's head all the time."

Stylisclaw didn't reply, but he tipped his head in a way that made Harper think that he agreed.

"Harper!"

Suddenly, Thief was running across the room towards them. "What happened? Where's Nocturne?" he asked.

"I'm not sure," Harper admitted. "Once the Muse of Stars arrived he sort of…funnelled all this wind and energy around Nocturne, and the next thing I knew he was gone."

Harper looked over Thief's shoulder. Sylvrjax and the rest of the stars were bounding up the stairs too, crossing the room and crowding around the hole in the dome. Harper threw her arms around the wolf's neck, hugging him hard.

"So, what happens now?" she asked as she pulled back, looking up at the sky. The whirling blue mass still hung above them, but Harper fancied that it had taken on a much friendlier air.

"Now," Sylvrjax replied. "We go home."

Harper nodded. She was sad to say goodbye to the wolves, but it was where they belonged. She looked at Stylisclaw. "What about you?"

Stylisclaw shook his head, his eyes looking mournfully up at the sky.

"I guess as long as he's stuck inside Trick, he can't return," Thief said.

"Can't we separate them somehow?" Harper looked at Sylvrjax.

"Skin-singing is a human gift – a rare one, at that. It is not the domain of stars or Muses," Sylvrjax replied. "If there is a way to separate them, they must find out what it is."

Stylisclaw looked at Sylvrjax for a long moment, then nodded once. He turned away from the sky, settling onto the floor, his giant head resting on his paws.

Harper rested her hand on his neck. She felt relieved that Stylisclaw wasn't going to go back to the sky and take Trick with him, but also intensely sad for the star who was stuck down here, where he didn't belong.

A sudden burst of light came from the sky. The clouds

above them parted completely, and suddenly, Harper could see it: a shining road made from pure light extending from the sky directly down to where they stood.

"The Celestial Highway," Harper whispered.

The two squirrel-stars were the first to move: they bounded towards the hole in the roof then leaped off into the air. Harper drew in a sharp breath, scared for a moment that they were about to plummet downwards, but they landed neatly on the shining road and took off towards the sky.

There was a flurry of movement as the rest of the stars followed suit. The raven-stars took flight, soaring upwards. The bear-star ambled through the hole, falling several feet and making Harper shout, before it was yanked, upside-down, towards the highway. Sylvrjax pressed his nose to Harper's face and started to lead his pack towards it.

"Wait!" Harper called. Sylvrjax looked round. "Sylvrjax – we need to tell people about you – about what's really been happening this year. If we can't, they'll still close the Wondria down. Once you're safely back in the sky, can we tell them the truth?"

"Of course." Sylvrjax nodded his head, before turning and leaping into the air.

Harper felt a sudden lightness as Sylvrjax and his pack landed on the Celestial Highway and turned towards the sky. Once all the stars had crossed over, there was a small implosion and the stars, Celestial Highway, and the Muse himself, vanished.

There was silence in their wake. The dragon returned to Harper's shoulder and perched there. Stylisclaw let out a heavy sigh, and on impulse, Harper dropped a quick kiss against his giant head. She took a last look at the sky, then turned to Thief.

"So – what now?"

Thief smiled slightly. "Now – I think they might want an explanation." He nodded downwards.

Harper peered down into the city. In the time it had taken the Parting to occur and the stars to return, a crowd had formed in the square. People were peering up at them, their mouths wide open, frozen in absolute shock. At their centre were Lahiri, Lori and – Harper noticed with a leap of joy – Fletcher.

"What were those?" a voice called from the crowd.

"Curses!" another yelled.

"No – they were ghosts!"

"They were minions of the Apocalypse! We're all doomed!" someone shrieked, falling to their knees and covering their head.

"They weren't any of those things!" Harper shouted down, before the crowd could descend into chaos. She glanced across at Stylisclaw, who had retreated into the room where no one could see him. He seemed to read Harper's question in her face, and he nodded his large head once. Harper turned back to the crowd and took a deep breath.

"They were stars."

CHAPTER TWENTY-NINE

Starlight

The truth of the stars caused quite the stir in the Hidden Peaks. While there had always been stories about stars having "hidden forms", the revelation that they were, in fact, animals, sent a lot of people into a frenzy. The Scholars and Masters of the Brightwood district went into overdrive, announcing the all-night openings of their libraries and observatories, publishing dozens of academic papers detailing what this new information meant for Spectaculars, and hosting talks with so-called "experts" who claimed that they'd known the truth about the stars all along. Reports stated that the Council were considering making the night of the Silver moon an annual holiday, to celebrate this important discovery. Multiple journalists and reporters turned up at the Wondria, wanting to interview "that kid who was on the roof", but Fletcher cheerfully evicted them all, which suited Harper just fine.

It'd been one of the strangest weeks of her life: all leading on from the revelation she'd shared on a rooftop with a crowd of shell-shocked strangers.

Once the stars had returned to the sky and she'd revealed their true natures to the crowd, there'd been uproar: gasps and yells, questions and demands. Fletcher had managed to appease the crowd with a mixture of charm and free drinks, convincing them to stay outside for their own safety while he went to investigate what had happened. As Fletcher had walked towards the Wondria – the deadlock lifted now that Nocturne was gone – Thief had turned to Harper.

"Well – time for me to go, I'd say."

"What?" Harper had been dismayed. "But you helped us! You freed the stars! Don't you want everyone to know?"

"Not particularly," Thief replied. "I'm still something of a fugitive, remember. And anyway, I've never done so well in front of crowds." He fidgeted, clearly keen to be gone before Fletcher arrived.

Harper glanced at Stylisclaw, who was also watching Thief, apparently listening to every word he was saying.

"So – what are you going to do now?" she asked Thief.

He shrugged. "I've got a few things of my own that I need to sort out. I'll head north, probably. And I'll try my hardest not to get my head chopped off along the way."

Harper snorted. "That'd be good."

She looked at the spell, which was sleeping in his pocket. "Are you going to release that into the wild on the way?"

Thief shook his head ruefully. "I don't think I can. I've named it now, I'm attached."

"You named the spell?"

"Yep. Meet Euripides Barnebus Zebedee, the First." He grinned at Harper's face. "I'm kidding! I named him Squidge."

Harper didn't think that was much better, but she decided that arguing over the silliness of a name for a pet spell was probably a losing battle.

"Here, take one of these." Thief reached into his pocket and brought out a golden egg. "This is an infinite egg – it'll allow you to send messages through it as many times as you want, and it'll always re-form. If you need me, just crack it and I'll come."

"Thanks," Harper said, pocketing the egg carefully. "For everything."

Stylisclaw padded over, looked at Thief very seriously, then licked his face from his chin to his hair. Thief spluttered, and Harper laughed at his shocked expression.

With a last grin at them, Thief smashed an egg against the ground and disappeared in a cloud of lilac dust.

"Miss Woolfe?" Fletcher appeared in the room, his eyes widening as he was faced with the giant panther that had been terrorizing his theatre. "What is going on?"

Harper looked at Stylisclaw, who gave a shrug of his giant shoulders.

"I think we've got some explaining to do," she said.

Now, a week later, Harper was standing in front of Fletcher's emerald study door, having been summoned by bottle-messenger. It felt a world away from the last time she'd been here, when she'd overheard Lahiri talking about closing down the Wondria. Harper knocked, and Fletcher's voice called for her to come in.

When Harper opened the door, she found Fletcher at his desk, his hand resting on his chin. He smiled at Harper, looking a little weary, but not angry.

"Ah, Miss Woolfe. Thank you for coming."

"It's, um – fine." Harper flushed slightly. "What did you want to see me about?"

"Well, firstly, I just wanted to give you an update. You'll be pleased to hear that the Spectacular Board of Theatrics are dropping the motion to close the Wondria."

Harper's heart leaped. "They are?"

"Indeed. Now they know that the so-called 'Curses' are, in fact, stars – and a whole crowd of people attested to the fact that those stars are now safely back in the sky – the threat level has been significantly diminished. They might hang around for a few days to tie up some loose ends, but the Wondria will remain open."

Harper felt a surge of joy and relief. She had felt sure that the Board would drop the case when they heard the truth, but it was still good to hear Fletcher say it officially.

"What about Nocturne? And Sharpe?"

Fletcher sighed. "Sharpe has disappeared. And as for Nocturne…"

Harper didn't like the tone of his voice. "What about him?"

"Well, I've told the authorities your story, of course. I pointed out those hideous cages – not to mention the giant hole blown in my roof – but they don't seem convinced that that's evidence for *him* specifically being involved. They've suggested that, perhaps with all the excitement of what was going on, you and Trick may have – ah – imagined some things. It's almost," he mused grimly, "as though being famous and having lots of money makes people less inclined to investigate your wrongdoings."

Harper felt a prickle of anger. *Imagined* it? "So, after everything he did, he's just going to get away with it? Just because he's rich and famous?"

"I wouldn't say 'get away with it'. After all, we can't be sure that he's even still *alive* after what happened on the roof. Who knows what the Muse of Stars might have done with him. But no – the authorities won't be investigating him." Fletcher met her eyes. "But rest assured, Miss Woolfe, should Tornio Nocturne ever rear his head again, we will stop him."

Harper nodded. It still bothered her, but she knew that Fletcher would keep his word.

"What about the rest of the public?" she asked. "They

know that the Wondria isn't dangerous any more, right?"

Fletcher smiled. "I believe so. The relief of knowing that the Four Curses are *not* among us has made a lot of people willing to look at the past few months in a much more forgiving light. Indeed, many people are already coming forwards and – *ahem* – 're-evaluating' their sightings. Putting them down to coincidence or accidents, or simple, human panic. Oh –" Fletcher added mildly – "it's also about to be leaked that the attack on Ace Malone was entirely fabricated. That should help dispel any lingering fear."

"She confessed?" Harper was incredulous.

"Oh no. But the story somehow found its way to *The Spectacular Daily Show*, and several of her now-ex-colleagues seemed more than happy to expose her."

"Good," Harper said firmly.

"The second thing," Fletcher said, "is that, as far as the general public are concerned, all thirteen stars returned to the sky. No one else knows that one of them is still very much on the ground, and indeed, trapped within my nephew. Trick wants to keep this information to himself for now – I trust that it's safe with you?"

"Of course it is!" Harper said, surprised. "If Trick doesn't want to tell anyone, then no one's going to hear it from me."

"Good." Fletcher smiled.

"Do you think you'll be able to separate them?" Harper asked quietly.

Fletcher rubbed his face. "This isn't something I've ever heard of before. It'll require a lot of research." A glimmer of his old expression came back onto his face. "Luckily, I'm *extremely* clever."

Harper nodded. "I'll help, in whatever way I can."

Fletcher looked at her. "I'm glad he has you. I always think that keeping secrets about oneself must be a lonely business. I'm glad there's at least one person in it with him."

Harper wasn't sure what to say to this, but a warm feeling bubbled up inside her, and she smiled.

"Now, I'd return to the apprentice quarters if I were you," said Fletcher. "I know that Helja has been stuffing you full of healthy, hearty meals this week to help with the shock – and I believe that cabbage, liver and spinach is on the menu tonight," he chuckled, meeting Harper's eye. "Trick is going to be *thrilled*."

Harper could hardly believe how quickly things went back to normal – or at least, as normal as things ever were at the Wondria. Although Fletcher had persuaded Lahiri to lift their punishment, their end-of-year performances were still coming up, which meant Harper spent most of her time scurrying between the Workshop and the apprentice quarters. After seeing her creation work so well on the night of the Silver moon, Harper could hardly wait to showcase it at their performance.

Aside from their presentations, the main topic of discussion among the apprentices was the Tornio Nocturne concert – or lack of. Apparently, the story was that Nocturne had been "taken ill" and been unable to attend last-minute. Instead, everyone had been treated to a "special concert" from the Lunas Bay Primary School's amateur orchestra. Rosie's eye twitched whenever she spoke about it.

Harper's peers didn't know about Nocturne's involvement with the stars – after the authorities had dismissed Harper and Trick's claims, they'd quashed the story very effectively, and Harper didn't want her friends thinking she was making things up as well. Still, it was hard for her and Trick to look at the posters on Rosie's wall, and to hear her friends' hopes that he'd do another concert again someday.

On the evening of the end-of-year show, the Auditorium was packed with Spectaculars. Harper stood backstage, watching her fellow apprentices make last-minute adjustments to their projects, warming up their voices and stretching their limbs in ways that made Harper's muscles ache just looking at them. The attitudes of the other junior apprentices had warmed considerably since the revelation about the stars – now it had finally been proven that Harper was not responsible for bringing ill luck down upon them. Some had said "hi" and chatted to her a bit, and Khyla Griffin, Althea's right-hand girl, had even given Harper something that *might* have been a smile (or might simply have been indigestion). Something, however, was still troubling

Harper. Trick's explanation had made sense of almost everything that had happened over the last year – the opening-night accident, All Spooks' Eve, the Costume Department attack – but they still hadn't been able to work out why the stage had exploded at their first presentation.

After the revelation about Ace Malone's "attack", Harper had an inkling of an idea, and she was determined to see if she was right or not. Placing her mechanical dragon carefully on a shelf in the wings, she crept over to the other side of the stage where Althea was standing, preparing for her presentation.

Harper wasn't sure what Althea's presentation was supposed to be – it seemed to involve her flouncing up and down with a gemstone peacock on her head. Harper made to walk past Althea, pretending to stumble at the last moment and bash into her, hard.

"Agggh!"

Harper tumbled to the ground, grabbing on to Althea's costume and taking her down with her.

"What are you doing?" Althea shrieked. "You *klutz*!"

Harper didn't care what Althea called her. She swooped down and grabbed a couple of items that had just rolled out onto the floor.

"*I knew it!*" she said, holding the objects up in front of Althea's face. Clutched in her hand were two tiny vials of starlight.

"*This* is why the stage exploded at our last demonstration, isn't it?" Harper demanded. "It was you! You set off two types of Star-Stuff that you knew would react badly together!"

Althea glared at her. "You can't prove it."

"*Why* would you want to sabotage me?" Harper asked. "I mean – you had to sabotage yourself as well, and your friends! Surely it wasn't worth it?"

Althea picked herself up off the floor and dusted down her costume primly. "Look – just because you've managed to worm your way out of all this, doesn't mean that I wasn't right about you. You don't belong here. You never will." With that, she swept away.

Harper watched her go. Once, those words would have cut her to the bone. Now…she found that she didn't care too much what Althea said about her. After everything that'd happened recently, she knew that she'd more than proven her worth among the Spectaculars. And if anyone else was still in doubt, they wouldn't be after her presentation.

The house lights went down, and the first-year apprentices took to the stage one by one. Anvi sang and conjured a series of clouds, ranging from candyfloss-pink to deep, stormy purple, filling the stage with rain and snow and the occasional flash of lightning. Rosie painted her hands with twining leaves and vines that moved across her skin, coiling up her arms and across her shoulders, blooming with vibrant flowers. Trick performed a very long and dramatic death speech from a great Spectacular tragedy, stringing out his convulsions for a full ten minutes before finally falling upon the stage in a swirl of red ribbons.

Finally, it was Harper's turn. She took a deep breath and

straightened the bow tie that was back around her neck.

"May you be cursed with the stings of a thousand bees!" Trick grinned at her as he jogged off the stage.

"And may your toes be chewed off by wolves," Harper replied, before stepping out onto the stage.

The Auditorium was plunged into darkness, just as she'd asked. Harper walked carefully across the stage until she reached the centre. She reached into her pocket, her fingers closing around metal, and drew out her dragon.

"Light it up," she whispered, and threw her hands up.

The Auditorium blazed in a burst of light. Blinking against the sudden flare, the audience were lit up in white, lilac, blue and rose. The dragon swooped low over their heads, spreading its luminous colours all over the Auditorium. The lights jumped around like flames, reaching higher and higher until they were flickering up around the chandelier.

"Just like the *Aurora Montina*!" a woman in the front row gasped to the man beside her. "Remember, we saw them on our honeymoon!"

The dragon let out another breath of light: but this time, instead of crashing like a wave over the Auditorium, the light separated into a mass of glowing balls, like the orbs they'd released at the Muse of Stars Ceremony. They bobbed over the audience's heads before spiralling up towards the ceiling and winking out like candles. The dragon returned to Harper's shoulder as she stood, illuminated by the light that it had created – that *she'd* created.

The audience burst into applause. From her position, Harper could see Fletcher beaming and Lahiri nodding in approval. Roper and Yosef were on their feet clapping for all they were worth. And best of all, sparing a glance into the wings, she could see Trick, Rosie, Anvi and the other apprentices jumping up and down, cheering for her.

Harper grinned, and in that moment, she felt like she could have lit up a hundred Auditoriums with no bother at all.

On their final day of term, Lahiri gave them all their presentation results. They'd all passed with good marks – even Althea, which Harper tried not to feel *too* grudging about. Both she and Trick had been awarded a gold standard grade – her for "impressive feats of Mechanics", and him for "impressively elongated and gruesome death acting" (Trick grinned and immediately announced his intention to have it framed and hung above his bed).

As an end-of-year treat Lahiri brought in a giant chocolate cake, baked by her wife, and they all sat around Practice Room One happily eating slices.

"So, is this it?" Harper said, licking icing off her fingers. "We've got the *whole* summer off?"

"Yeah," Trick replied. "But don't get too excited – we won't be sunbathing on beaches for weeks on end. Summer is the Wondria's busiest season, so Fletcher always finds things for the apprentices to do – darning costume shirts, or helping to rig lights, or running round after Lady Roberta Helix, fetching her sparkling water at the *exact* right temperature."

Hearing this, Harper was secretly pleased. After spending so long worrying that she was going to lose all of this, she wasn't about to complain about spending some of her summer helping out with sewing and rigging. Sunbathing on the beach sounded boring, anyway.

That evening, most of the apprentices decided to go into the city. Apparently, the Observatory had opened its doors for a stargazing sleepover, inviting people to come and use their most powerful telescopes to see if they could spot the forms of the stars. Trick had obviously had to decline – he was determined to do a better job of keeping Stylisclaw's secret, and had resolved to be inside at least an hour before midnight every night. Harper elected to stay back with him, and they spent the evening toasting crumpets while Harper started a new letter to her mum – she had a *lot* to catch her up on.

For a while they sat in companionable silence, the only sound the scratching of Harper's pen. When Harper finished her letter – with a list of suggested dates for her mother to come and visit her over the summer – she shook out her aching wrist and looked at Trick.

"Does it ever get confusing? Having two sets of memories in one head?"

"Not for Styl, so much," Trick replied. "He reckons that

I've been alive for so little time my memories would hardly fill a thimble. For me – yeah, sometimes. Occasionally I get a glimpse into his memories from the sky. Of being in this limitless space, of having lived for an infinite number of years…" He shuddered slightly. "Honestly, it gives me a headache."

At this, Trick set down his crumpet. "I better get to my room – it's almost midnight."

Harper packed up her books and said goodnight to Trick on the ladders. When she got into her room she changed into a pair of bright, comfortable pyjamas, but she didn't get into bed. Instead, she stood at her window, her hand clutched at her side, looking up at the stars. Ever since they'd returned to the sky, Harper had fancied that she could almost make out their animal shapes: the flash of a wing here, the twitch of a giant, fluffy tail there. As she looked up at them, there was just a tiny twinge of fear at the back of her mind, an anxious voice that wondered if Nocturne really was gone, or whether he'd be back – for the stars, for Stylisclaw, for Harper herself. Harper shook her head, trying to dispel her mind of the notion. They'd beaten him once, hadn't they? If he came back, they'd just have to figure out a way to do it again.

In fact, when Harper thought about everything she'd overcome this year, she could hardly believe it. She'd turned up in the Hidden Peaks in a dressing gown and slippers, knowing nothing of Spectaculars or Star-Stuff, or any of the magic that lay hidden across a border. She could never have imagined how hard this year was going to be – how much darkness she'd be faced with – but there were other things she couldn't have imagined either. How it'd feel to hold starlight in your hands, to stand on a stage and have an audience gasp with wonder at something you'd created, to feel the staunchness of friends that stood by you no matter what.

The clock in the apprentice quarters struck midnight, and a few moments later, Harper heard a scuffling noise from two doors down. From the window of Trick's room, a massive form bounded out into the night. Stylisclaw stretched, his claws scraping against the ground; then he looked up and saw Harper watching.

Harper let her hand unfurl on the windowsill, revealing what had been enclosed in it: her tiny mechanical dragon, its brass scales glinting slightly in the moonlight. Harper pitched it out of the window, and it came to life easily, looking Harper directly in the eye.

Harper nodded towards the star, and the dragon seemed to understand. It whirled around and leaped up into the air, unleashing a tiny stream of colourful light as it went. Harper watched from the window as the panther-star turned and bounded off into the night, her tiny metal dragon circling protectively overhead.

The End

Turn the page for an exclusive
sneak peek at Harper and Trick's
next Spectacular adventure!

The Wild Song Contest

Harper looked down at the object in her hand and sighed. "This isn't how hats work."

Trick rolled his eyes in a way that very clearly said he had no patience at all for how things were supposed to work. "Your point being...?"

"Hats," Harper pressed, "Are for keeping your head warm. Or shielding you from the sun. Or for old ladies trying to out-do each other at weddings."

"And yet," Trick retorted, "Here we are."

Here was outside the Wondria, which was currently perched somewhat precariously on the edge of a rocky ledge. Throughout the warmer months they'd gradually climbed higher into the mountains, visiting small towns and villages that were cut off by the snow in winter. The late summer sun pierced through the clouds, glinting off the grand golden doors and domed roof. Spectaculars and apprentices alike were gathered in a crowd, murmuring excitedly, all of them clutching onto hats of various shapes and sizes.

"Does everyone have a hat? Get your hats here, one per person!"

Fletcher's voice carried across the clearing. He'd clearly raided the Costume Department and was walking around with armfuls of hats swinging off his elbows and wrists like some sort of bizarre salesman: bonnets and bowlers, shiny black top hats and giant, floppy sunhats decorated with dried flowers and ribbons. Spectaculars who were still empty-handed flocked to him, grabbing at the selection and squabbling over the biggest, fanciest hats. Fletcher himself was sporting a deep purple trilby which was decorated with several large cabbages and what might have been a live mouse.

It was the very last week of the long summer holidays that the apprentices had enjoyed. In the absence of daily training, they'd been assigned various jobs to do around the Wondria: helping to mend broken props, polishing spotlights, running errands for the performers during the shows. Harper had spent a solid week as Lady Roberta Helix's personal assistant, fetching drinks for both her and her reflection and sorting through the ridiculous mounds of fan mail and gifts she received after each show (this occasionally had its perks: if Lady Roberta Helix felt like her dressing room was getting "a bit busy" she'd let Harper take some things home with her, meaning that Harper often returned to the Apprentice Quarters at night bearing elaborate flower displays, fruit baskets, and once, a highly realistic bust of Lady Helix's head and shoulders made out of red velvet cake). During the days, many of their teachers had led chaperoned trips into the towns and cities they'd passed through: they'd attended a fashion show in the Baroque city of Perssion, heard a lecture on Witch history in the floating assembly hall of the River Colossus, and had their auras read by a Fae-woman who'd set up a tent outside Brightwood University. This last trip had been highly amusing: the Fae-woman had frowned at Harper and Trick for a while before informing Harper that she had a bright future ahead of her, then telling Trick in a very serious voice that his Aura was deathly allergic to sugar, and he needed to stop eating it at once. Harper had almost cracked a rib laughing at his face, and Trick had fumed all the way home.

"Right then – gather round, everyone!"

Fletcher's voice brought Harper out of her reverie. Apparently satisfied that everyone had received a suitable hat, he strode to a point in the centre of the clearing where a giant red "X" had been somewhat ostentatiously painted on the ground.

"Welcome to the Ceremony for the Muse of Air!" Fletcher announced to a round of applause and cheering. Harper clapped along, feeling both excited and nervous about what was to come. She'd attended a handful of Muse Ceremonies at this point, and they all seemed to be a mixture of enchanting and downright hideous: she hadn't forgotten the Muse of Stars Ceremony last year, when they'd set a stream of beautiful glowing lights bobbing across the lake, then been unceremoniously dumped in the freezing water.

"I know this Ceremony is something of a favourite amongst you all, but please queue in an orderly fashion and wait your turn," Fletcher said. "Anyone seen using excessive force of elbows, knees or other pointed objects to try to skip the line will receive a stern frown and have fifteen minutes deducted from their hat time."

"That means you, McCubbins!" someone in the crowd yelled.

Satisfied that his warning had been taken seriously, Fletcher stepped forwards and positioned himself on the X. He lifted his hat and held it in one hand just above his head, as though he were raising his hat to someone. For a moment he simply stood, frozen like one of the living statues they sometimes saw in the bigger cities. Then, Harper's mouth dropped open in astonishment as Fletcher's feet slowly began to rise off the ground.

"No way," Harper huffed.

Fletcher rose steadily into the air like a hot air balloon, still clutching onto the rim of his trilby hat (the mouse peered over the side, squeaked in fright and promptly dove behind one of the cabbages). Once he was about twenty feet into the air, he waved merrily down to them all before turning a neat loop-the-loop.

"Are you joking?" Harper looked at Trick. "What – how?"

"A gift from the Muse of Air," Trick grinned. "Once a year only! Come on, let's get in the queue."

They joined the jostling line, and Harper watched in increasing excitement as each Spectacular and apprentice before them stepped onto the cross on the ground, lifted their hat to the wind, and were lifted off the ground in a whoosh of air. Soon the sky was filled with figures, spinning and whirling and high fiving each other as they bobbed about like boats on the sea.

When Harper's turn came, she all but ran to the X on the ground. She looked nervously down at the hat in her hand.

She'd selected a floppy crimson affair, trimmed with a silver ribbon. It was jaunty, but it hardly seemed sturdy enough to lift her off the ground.

"Just lift it straight up!" Trick called encouragingly.

Harper took a breath, then lifted the red hat above her head. For a split-second she felt a bit silly, but then she felt a gust of wind billow into her hat and fill it like a helium balloon. The hat tugged upwards, and Harper only just managed to cling onto it as the ground fell away from her feet.

Harper gulped as she looked down, the figures below her seeming to get very small, very quickly. She gave an experimental kick of her legs, an astonished laugh bubbling up inside of her as they swung through the air. She let out a whoop as she climbed higher, joining the other Spectaculars in the air. I'm flying, she thought, slightly hysterically. I'm actually flying!

"Good form, Miss Woolfe!" Fletcher nodded to her as he sailed past. He stayed perfectly upright as he bobbed through the air, as though he were paddle boarding on a placid lake. Harper tried to balance herself in a similar way, but it was hard with absolutely nothing to balance against. She swung this way and that, starting to feel slightly seasick.

"Keep your knees straight!" Trick called, floating up beside her. He was grinning manically, clutching onto a woolly hat with an absurdly large bobble on the top.

Harper tried this method and was relieved to find that it did indeed work. Now that she was upright, she managed to look around and observe the scene around her. She saw Lahiri soaring elegantly around, holding onto the ribbons of a lace-edged bonnet. On the other end of the elegance spectrum was her friend Anvi Patel, who had not one, but four hats clutched in her hands, and was zooming about haphazardly, shrieking with delight.

"Fancy a game of air dodgems?" Trick called, suddenly diving towards her and knocking into her hat with his ridiculous bobble.

"Don't you dare!" Harper just managed to swerve out of the way. "I know where your sweets stash is, and I'm not afraid to sabotage it."

As it turned out, there were plenty of other games to play in the sky. Fletcher led an airborne Conga around the highest dome of the Wondria, while several apprentices began a game of Chicken, zooming at each other from opposite ends of the clearing and seeing who would yank their hat to the side at the last minute (this game was brought to a swift end after Trick and Rosie, both too stubborn to change course, conked heads with an impressive thunk).

Find out what happens next in
The Spectaculars: The Wild Song Contest

Acknowledgements

This book would never have come into being without a truly Spectacular team behind it. HUGE thanks, endless gratitude and mugs of pine tea to:

Chloe Seager, for being a superstar agent, for your amazing work on the manuscript and finding Harper & Trick the perfect home!

Alice Sutherland-Hawes, for your belief and incredible work on the first drafts.

My editors at Usborne, Becky Walker and Alice Moloney – you lifted this book to a level I could never even have imagined, and your enthusiasm for this story from the beginning has been truly incredible – I couldn't be more grateful that *The Spectaculars* found a home with you!

The whole team at Usborne for bringing this book to life – this process has been a total joy thanks to your support and hard work.

Nathan Collins, for creating the STUNNING cover, map and chapter headings, which made me literally jump for joy when I saw them.

Clare Baalham for the copyedits and Nozomi Tolworthy for the sensitivity report – thank you so much for your work!

My amazing, supportive friends & family who always believed in my imagination and waited very patiently (or in some cases, impatiently) for me to finally get round to sending this story out.

My sisters, Amber and Bethany, for always saying "when" rather than "if" I got published, and generally being the best sibship a person could possibly have.

Grandma, for being the backbone of our family.

Mum & Dad, for absolutely everything – literally none of this would have happened without your support and belief.

And last but not least, to theatre workers everywhere: performers, light and sound technicians, stage managers, costume designers, wardrobe staff, playwrights, musicians, prop makers, front of house workers, directors, set designers, and the many, many more people that it takes to make theatre as magical as it is. You are all Spectacular.

About the author

Jodie Garnish is a playwright and performer, usually based in London. She studied Drama at the University of East Anglia before going on to train at Drama Studio London. She has had plays produced at various London theatres and at the Edinburgh Fringe Festival, which were critically acclaimed.

Her career as a performer, including in shows designed for young people, has allowed her to shape the world of *The Spectaculars*, as well as giving her good insight into what young people love. She's thrilled to have combined her passion for performance and children's literature in her debut novel.

 @JodieGarnish

It was midnight, and the
stars were falling...

There are thirteen Fallen Sites hidden
throughout this book, did you find where all
these stars landed?